Pre-Marital Murder

Candy Justice

For William —
Thank you for
being such a great
Helmsman editor!

Candy

DEDICATION

In memory of my parents, Bob and Carol Chisholm, who inspired me by living their lives with courage, integrity, and humor.

CHAPTER ONE

Considering I am an average non-criminal, it's surprising how many times I've had my house surrounded by cops, arson investigators, helicopters, and police dogs. Did I mention the postal inspector who called the bomb squad when a really large package mailed from a country known for terrorism was mailed to me? And when they "disarmed" the package and it turned out to be a quilt mailed to me by my uncle who was on a business trip, all the cops looked at me with annoyance, and the head of the bomb squad said, "Miss Faire, what made you think this was a bomb?"

See what I mean? It's never my fault, but it's a running joke with my friends and neighbors that I'm a catastrophe magnet.

Several of us were having dinner at Wang's and my fortune read, "You will always live in interesting times." After they stopped laughing, everybody had their favorite story to retell.

Jeno likes the one about the massive manhunt that ended up focusing on my house, because my nephew had left the extension ladder leaned up against the house when he wanted to see if he could get in the attic window. The ladder made the cops think the suspect was hiding in my attic. I stood on the porch in my robe while cops searched my house as a helicopter shined a light down and the dog squad arrived to help. Needless to say, the suspect was not in my house.

And that arson "incident" wasn't really an incident. It was just a big misunderstanding and no real harm was done and was absolutely not my fault.

My friend Dan, who is a prosecuting attorney, never lets me hear the end of the red car incident. I wanted to give away an old car that wasn't worth selling, so I put a sign on the car saying, "Free to good home." I had no idea the nice man whom I agreed to give it to was a notorious car thief, who came to my house to get the title while driving a car he had just stolen. The cops ended up conducting a sting operation in my driveway.

And of course, there are the natural disasters and mishaps I always seem to be present for. I was a kid in California on vacation with my family when the Northridge Earthquake hit in 1994, and the last night of my New York vacation was ruined by the Northeast Blackout of 2003 — tickets to *The Producers* down the drain.

I could go on and on, but you get the picture. Exciting things happen around me, but rarely to me. There are those who claim this is because I was a cops and courthouse reporter before settling down as a columnist. But really none of those things happened in connection with my work as a reporter. I think it's just the opposite.

So it really shouldn't have surprised me or anybody else I knew that I got a call one day from the mother of a man who had fallen or jumped from one of the bridges over the Mississippi River at Memphis the night before he was to be married. I didn't know him, I didn't know his mother, and I had no personal connection to the situation. I had read the newspaper story about the incident and saw it on the TV news, but after the guy's death was declared a suicide, I never gave it another thought. Not until Maggie Magee, his mother, called me at my office and asked me to help her solve her son's murder.

I tried to be kind to her and listen to her story, although I got impatient as she told me her son did not commit suicide, but rather was murdered. Not just murdered, but murdered by the FBI and the murder covered up by the local cops. When she told me that her suspicions had been confirmed by a psychic she hired, it was the final straw, and I found an excuse to get off the phone, telling her I was a journalist, not a detective, and wishing her luck in solving the case.

It was an all-too-familiar scenario. Nobody ever wants to believe that someone they love was so hopeless, so distraught that he or she would choose to die. An accident or murder is easier to accept. I felt terribly sorry for Maggie Magee, especially when she talked about how you never get over the death of your child, especially your only child. But there was nothing I could do but sympathize, and even that wasn't easy, given the level of her delusion.

A few days later, Maggie Magee mailed me two home-made DVDs of her son, Logan — one a video of the rehearsal dinner shot a few hours before Logan died and the second a compilation of still photos and video, snippets of his life from birth until his and Caroline's engagement party. It had been originally put together by Logan's best friend as a wedding gift for Caroline, who Logan was to marry on May 25. Instead, it was projected onto a screen at the church where Logan's memorial service was held on June 4. The police told the family that the bodies of jumpers were rarely recovered from the Mississippi River, so after 10 days they went ahead with the memorial service.

At first I resented her sending the videos. I had told her I couldn't help her, so she should have left me alone. Just what I needed — being stalked by a bereaved mother with a bag full of conspiracy theories.

I vowed I would mail the videos back without even watching them, but there was nothing on TV that night and nobody called and I had just finished the novel I was reading. So I watched the videos and then watched the rehearsal dinner again. What I saw I couldn't shake off. Logan Magee was obviously a man in love, a man looking forward to the future. I didn't believe for a minute all that conspiracy stuff Mrs. Magee was clinging to, but neither did I believe that Logan Magee had killed himself.

CHAPTER TWO

The next day at work, I just couldn't seem to get started on my column. I kept staring at the computer screen, my fingers on the keys, as if I expected any minute that my fingers would start mysteriously moving of their own volition. I don't believe in writer's block. You can't believe in it when you work at a daily newspaper. They pay you to write so you do. But news is easier to write than a good column. I haven't missed a deadline yet, but some days it's easier than others.

The paper promotes me as a columnist and blogger, which makes me cringe. I know that someone my age is supposed to worship social media, but I guess I have an old soul because I generally hate social media and what it has done to the job of reporter or editor. I love writing a well-thought-out and well-crafted column for the print and web editions, but I have no interest in blurting out my every half-formed thought and opinion on social media, but the paper forces me to. And don't even get me started on Facebook — I flatly refuse to embrace that adolescent time waster. I don't care about what parties people go to or their children's baby pictures. Although I have found that I kind of enjoy Twitter, but mostly on a personal level – exchanging opinions on sports or movies or books. But don't tell anyone I like Twitter — I might lose my well-earned reputation as a technophobe.

The truth is that I don't hate technology—how did reporters ever do their jobs before laptops, smart phones, and Google? And how did they write a story on a typewriter? And I like being able to read the New York Times and Washington Post online while I'm in my pajamas. But I also like to find my own local paper in a plastic bag in my driveway every morning.

Anyhow, that morning, when my fingers didn't fly across the keys as I had hoped, I went to Plan B — staring out the window. My 10th floor office is tiny but has a great view of downtown, the Mississippi River and the two main bridges between Tennessee and Arkansas. I never get tired of looking at the river.

On days like this, if the river doesn't distract me, I can find something else, anything that will distract me, like the guy standing at the bus stop in front of the paper who kept checking his pulse while he waited. I'm fascinated by odd-ball stuff like that.

Ed, our online editor called to see when I would be turning in my blog, and I asked Ed if he had any idea why somebody would constantly check his pulse at a bus stop, and all Ed said was, "Britt, why are you so damn weird?" He said it, I think, with affection and actually seemed to be waiting for an answer, but I just said goodbye and hung up, also with affection.

Plan C is always lunch. To say I'm not a morning person is an understatement. Some times I write my column from home on my laptop and don't get dressed until mid afternoon. But that's only on days when I know exactly what my column will be about and how I want to approach it.

On a day like this when I'm not sure what I want to write about or just can't seem to get started, I get up by 9 and get to the office by 10 — my theory being that if I'm dressed and sitting at a desk in a real workplace, I am more likely to do real work.

The problem with that is that I really don't feel my day starts until I've had my lunch. I hear people talk about how a big lunch makes them sleepy and lazy, but I do my best work and my fastest work after lunch and after dinner. (Food for thought?)

So I left the newsroom, took the elevator down and walked to my car in the back parking lot, still mulling over a couple of column ideas I had. I drove down Linden and took Front Street past the entrance to the Hernando Desoto Bridge, which is commonly called "the new bridge" or "the I-40 bridge."

The one Logan Magee jumped off was the old bridge, officially called the Memphis-Arkansas Bridge. Both of the bridges take you from Tennessee across the Mighty Mississippi into West Memphis, Arkansas, which is anything but mighty. Truck stops and a dog-racing track are the claim to fame of West Memphis — Memphis, Tennessee's poor cousin.

I almost stopped at Front Street Deli for a sandwich (there was a parking spot available right by the front door) but decided to go on out to Mud Island. I swear it had nothing to do with the fact that the DVDs sent to me by Maggie Magee had a Harbor Town return address.

I eat out there a lot either at Miss Cordelia's, an upscale little grocery store with a small restaurant attached and outdoor tables, or at Tug's when I want a hamburger and to watch a Grizzlies game on TV with a convivial group of strangers.

On this day, I got my favorite sandwich, the Tuscan Sun, at Miss Cordelia's and planned to take it to a bench overlooking the river. Downtown Memphis runs along the river bluff and out in the river just a few hundred yards is Mud Island. Half of Mud Island is a river park and outdoor theater accessible to the public only by monorail, but the north end of the island is reached by a small bridge and is a residential development called Harbor Town.

There are apartments out there, and some charming, but reasonably priced zero-lot-line homes. But the heart of Harbor Town and certainly its showplace are the homes that face the river — grand homes on small lots to maximize the number of homes with breathtaking views of the river and spectacular sunsets. The houses are distinct from each other in architectural style, but they are all two or three stories and all have porches, balconies, large windows and sometimes even a widow's walk on top to give the owners full access to river views.

Before I ate my sandwich, I drove past the address on the video envelope. During our one phone conversation, Mrs. Magee said that since her son's death she had been living in his house.

I thought surely it would be one of the more modest homes on the island, but it knocked my socks off. Logan Magee had lived in one of the river-front homes, a pale blue Victorian style house with white trim and wrap-around porches upstairs and down. How does a 34-year-old bachelor afford such a house? Family money? Something less innocent?

Anyhow, after a slow drive past the Magee house, I parked across the street and ate my chicken, provolone and sun-dried tomato sandwich, while enjoying the early summer sunshine. Several people walking their dogs or themselves passed on the sidewalk beside me. There were a few bicyclists, and an older woman with two little girls passed by.

Then came the common sight nowadays of a young mother in spandex running clothes, galloping along pushing one of those big-wheeled baby strollers with a golden retriever on a leash attached to the stroller.

At first I just smiled at the ever-efficient professional woman using her lunch hour to get exercise for herself and the dog, while simultaneously taking the baby out for some fresh air. She probably had low-fat yogurt for lunch back at the office, and for dinner, one of those services where a home-cooked, gourmet meal is delivered to your house after work.

As I was sitting there enjoying my favorite hobby — making up back-stories for strangers — the baby started to cry and the woman and dog stopped near me to attend to the little one. It was a baby boy, if his tiny Nikes, New York Giants T-shirt and miniature Braves baseball cap did not lie.

The dog did his part by wagging his tail and sniffing the baby, and the mom unfastened the strap holding the baby in the stroller and scooped him up into her arms. She swayed gently from side to side until he was quiet, kissed him all over his face and head, and smiling, she strapped him back in the stroller and took off again.

I couldn't help but wonder — if that baby boy grows up and then is said to have flung himself off the bridge on the eve of his wedding, would that mom just accept the verdict and go on with her life? Would she have trouble accepting her child's suicide? If she got desperate enough to hire a detective or even a psychic, would that make her a crazy lady?

I pulled out my cell phone and called Jack Trent. I could always count on Jack to talk some sense into me or at least to try.

CHAPTER THREE

Jack Trent threw the folder onto the desk in front of me.

"There it is, look for yourself," he said.

"How do you know I'm not doing a big investigative piece on the police department and that you'll get in trouble for showing this to me?"

His laugh was loud and honking, but it was one of the things I liked about him. Most cops don't have a good sense of humor, especially homicide detectives. They would say they do, but I don't call crude jokes and cruel remarks about dead people a good sense of humor. Though Jack has his moments of typical cop insensitivity, he's got a genuinely good sense of humor, too.

"Britt, don't you think I know you by now. You've got that nosy, just-curious look on your face. If you were working, you'd be up front with me about it. Besides, you know I'd do anything for you, as long as it wasn't blatantly illegal. You're a pal."

There was a time when Trent wanted to be more than pals with me, but when he asked me out on numerous occasions, I always told him it was a conflict of interest. I was a cops reporter then and he was a cop, a news source. It was that simple, I said, but of course it wasn't really that simple. He's kind of nice looking and nice and a lot of fun, but I never could get around the fact that he's a homicide cop. It's prejudice, I freely admit. I just can't believe that someone who deals with death and mayhem all day every day could be a kind, gentle boyfriend or husband. It's not fair, but hey, prejudice never is. I've always called him by his last name like the other cops do, which is strange for me, who has never called people by their last names, except in print.

When I started covering courts, instead of the police beat, that excuse not to go out with him wasn't as easy to use, but a lot of homicide cops testify in court, so I could still say it was a no-no for me to date a cop. Now I'm a columnist, and I don't know what excuse I'll use now. Maybe I won't make an excuse next time.

After looking through the file folder on Logan Magee, I asked Trent if he remembered the case.

"I remember it because it was the guy's wedding day when he jumped. You don't get too many wedding-day suicides. Usually someone has to be married for a while before they want to jump off a bridge."

I rolled my eyes at the bad joke. "Are you absolutely sure it was a suicide?"

"Listen, Britt, you know I'm the king of cold cases. I'm a pit bull if I think there's foul play and somebody needs to pay, but I swear there was nothing to indicate homicide."

He *was* the king of cold cases — he was known for taking files home with him on weekends and not giving up. That was another thing I liked about him. He said it was just his job, but I always believed it was a greater sense of justice and perhaps concern for the victims and their families.

"But couldn't it have been an accident? There was no note or signs of depression."

"A guy cleaning his gun can accidentally kill himself, but not a guy standing in the middle of a bridge over the Mississippi River, not even with the new bike/pedestrian thing. It's not the kind of place you take a stroll and accidentally fall over the rail.

"Maybe if he was drunk, he might do something stupid like that," I said, not even convincing myself.

"You've been talking to the mother, haven't you?"

I nodded yes.

"She called me, too," he went on. "In fact, she calls me about once a month when she comes up with another hair-brained theory. I feel for that lady, I swear I do, Britt, but she's a loony tune. A psychic told her he was murdered? Give me a break!"

The other cops I know wouldn't have been able to say all that without profanity. I always wondered if Trent was really squeaky clean or if he just refrained around me. I had never heard him use more than an occasional "hell" or "damn," which are Sunday School words compared to most of the homicide guys' language.

"Mrs. Magee thinks the FBI killed her son and the local cops covered it up."

"Britt, you know that's a load. There's no love lost between us and the feds. If we thought they offed somebody, we'd be the first to pin it on them."

"You've got a good point," I conceded. "Besides, what motive would the FBI have for killing this average Joe the night before his wedding?"

"None, but I guess somebody else could hate him enough to kill him or could want him not to get married for some reason."

"Maybe the bride's father was in the Dixie Mafia and put out a hit on him to keep him from marrying his daughter," I said, half seriously.

"You're sounding as loony as the mother now. No, it wasn't a professional job. The pros don't take time to make it look like suicide. They'd just whack him and disappear, and they wouldn't do it in the middle of a busy bridge."

"I guess not. Did any witnesses ever report seeing a jumper?"

"No, but I'm sure plenty of people saw the car sitting there, but they probably just thought it had broken down. Even BMWs break down sometimes."

"Still, it's odd that nobody saw him jump."

"So, is Britten Faire taking on the case of the mysterious disappearance of Logan Magee?"

"Probably not, but I think I will go out and at least talk to the mother. Maybe I can help her buy into the idea of an accident and get her to let the murder conspiracy go, so she can have some peace. She sent me a video of the rehearsal dinner, and I tell you, Trent, Logan Magee looked and sounded for the world like a very happy, very-much-in-love man."

"You're a hopeless romantic, kid."

"Just the opposite. I've been to plenty of weddings where one or both people didn't seem particularly in love, my own wedding included, but this Logan Magee seemed head over heels."

"Maybe she's the one who changed her mind, and when she told him the wedding was off, he went head-over-heels over the guard-rail."

CHAPTER FOUR

After leaving Jack Trent's office, I went back to the office and wrote my column about the young mom with the baby in the park. I didn't relate it to Logan Magee, of course, and certainly didn't write about the baby growing up and committing suicide.

Instead, I used the incident as the centerpiece for a column about how our mothers, when we're growing up, tell us, "You'll understand when you grow up and have children of your own." My column pondered the idea that some of that stuff you grasp just by growing up, and other things maybe we'll never really understand until we become parents ourselves, like how much parents worry about their children no matter how old the kids get. I'm 32 years old, and my parents still, during every phone conversation, at some point tell me to be careful.

I closed the column with a story about interviewing an older woman of indeterminate age, who talked about how she worries that her son doesn't eat right and that he smokes. "How old is your son?" I asked her. "61," she said. "They're never too old to stop worrying about."

After I finished the column and sent it directly to the city desk for editing, totally ignoring Ed's order to send it to the web desk first, I left the building trying to decide what kind of food I was in the mood for.

I should be the paper's restaurant critic. After all, I'll bet nobody who works there eats out as often as I do. I take that back — there are probably people, single guys mostly, who eat out as often as I do, but I'll bet there's nobody who eats at as many different restaurants as me.

On second thought, I'm probably not snooty enough to be a restaurant critic. I'd probably never give anybody a bad review because I can always find something I like anywhere. That's not to say that I think every restaurant is equally good or that I like everything on every menu. Not by a long shot, but I've cracked the code on eating out.

You'll never go wrong if you just follow a few basic rules. Don't go to a great hamburger place and order fish or a salad. Don't go to a restaurant that specializes in down-home plate lunches and order the one Italian dish they have on the menu, especially if it's preceded with the word, "Italian," as in "Italian Spaghetti." Don't go to a Chinese restaurant run by non-Asians, and if it *is* an authentic Asian restaurant with a buffet, don't try the pizza or French fries.

I know single people who eat cereal for dinner or have pizza delivered when they'd really like to eat at a good restaurant, but they won't go there alone because they feel like a loser saying, "Table for one."

Not me. I know I'm not a loser, so why should I care what somebody holding a stack of menus thinks of me. Same for the other diners. Either they are with other people and are too busy talking and eating to notice me or they're eating alone, too.

I usually eat *at* restaurants because I think food always tastes better fresh from the kitchen, instead of sweating in a Styrofoam take-out container for 20 minutes. But that night I picked up a cheeseburger and bowl of potato soup from Huey's and took it home. Something Jack Trent had said made me anxious to watch the rehearsal dinner video again.

I changed into shorts and a T-shirt and set up my dinner on

the coffee table between the sofa and TV set. When I told Trent that Logan Magee looked like a happy man in love on the video, Trent said maybe the bride was the unhappy one and that maybe she broke off the engagement after the video was shot.

Apparently the video camera was set up on a tripod rather than operated personally by somebody, because the camera never moved and was focused on the whole area — the rooftop of the Peabody Hotel. There were tables and chairs set up around the rooftop with black tablecloths and white napkins with modernistic black and white centerpieces.

A jazz trio was playing in the background, so you couldn't hear anything that was said while the guests mingled and had cocktails before dinner. So I studied Caroline whenever she was in the frame. She had shoulder length blonde hair and had a dazzling smile, which she flashed sporadically, as opposed to constantly beaming.

I knew a girl like that in high school and several at Ole Miss — girls who could look pleasantly cool most of the time and occasionally honor you with a gorgeous smile that would knock your socks off. I could see the looks of gratification on the faces of those who got that smile at the rehearsal dinner, almost as if they had accomplished something important by earning that smile of Caroline's.

Logan and Caroline circulated around the room during the cocktail hour, sometimes together holding hands and sometimes separately. When they were apart, Logan would never give his full attention to who he was talking to. He never went long without glancing Caroline's way. Did I imagine it or did he look at her with a little anxiety sometimes? Was it jealousy or something else?

For Caroline's part, she looked happy when she was beside Logan, but when they were apart, her eyes didn't seem to search out Logan in the crowd. Was she just too cool for that, or did she love him less than he loved her? And there seemed to be much to love. Logan Magee was tall, dark, and handsome, as they say, and I didn't need to hear his voice to see that he was charming everyone he talked to as he worked the room.

How sad that the Logan Magee I was watching, Maggie Magee's baby boy, was just hours away from plunging to his death into the fast-moving, churning waters of the Mississippi River.

I turned off the DVD and dug through my purse for Maggie Magee's phone number. I was relieved that she wasn't at home — I really didn't want to talk to her on the phone again. I simply left her a message saying that I would come over to her house about three the next afternoon unless she called me at the office to say that time wasn't good for her.

CHAPTER FIVE

As I drove across the little bridge to Mud Island the next day and turned right onto Island Drive., I was still thinking about Caroline and Logan and wondering what could cause her to kick him to curb the night before their wedding, if indeed she did break up with him.

I wasn't wondering what Maggie Magee would be like. I had a pretty strong mental picture in place — a rosy cheeked Irish woman in a white apron with tousled hair and a wild look in her eyes. Well, not a wild look necessarily, but certainly not a together kind of woman.

So much for my intuition. What I got was a beautiful Asian woman, probably in her fifties, wearing a white tennis dress. She smiled as soon as she opened the door. It was clear that she was not a first-generation American. Her accent was pure Mississippi Delta southern belle. I found out later Maggie Wong grew up in Sunflower, Mississippi, and graduated from Delta State, where she met Mack Magee.

"Oh, you must be Miss Faire. I just got home from tennis and was going to change my clothes, but you were a little early," she said, neither apologizing for herself nor reproaching me for my unfortunate habit of being early for everything.

"Being early is a bad habit of mine," I said.

"Oh, sugar, don't think a thing of it. I'm just glad you're here. Come on in," she said, pulling me inside. As we walked toward the sunny kitchen, where she set about making coffee and slicing homemade strawberry bread, she made a confession.

"When I first called you, I thought I was calling a man. Britten Faire sounds like a man's name. I had seen your bylines before, and I always imagined a man writing those stories, an older man in fact, with a wrinkled suit and fedora."

"A lot of readers make that mistake. Britten is my mother's maiden name. She had always planned to name her son Britten, but when she finished up her child-bearing with three daughters, I got the honor. I used to be embarrassed by my name — Britten Faire sounds like a line from a Wordsworth poem — but I got over it, and now it just seems like me."

"Oh, it fits you alright. Faire is a good name for a reporter."

"I've heard that a few times, as well as the opposite."

"I don't understand why they don't run your picture with your column — you're so pretty and you don't wear a fedora."

"I refused to have my picture with my column. I like to be a fly on the wall. I pick up better column ideas by not having a familiar face."

"It's interesting when you write about government and what they're doing or not doing, but I like it best when you write about ordinary people, especially the ones who need help. I need help, Miss Faire. I need to find out who murdered my son and why."

"Why are you so sure he was murdered, Mrs. Magee?"

"A mother knows these things."

"Could it be that a mother never wants to believe that her

son was too hopeless to go on living?" I was testing Maggie Magee. If she got angry or tearful at that harsh statement, I knew I couldn't help her. But she passed the test by pausing to think for a moment before answering without obvious emotion.

"That's a valid point, it really is, and I've thought about that a lot. No mother wants to believe her child could commit suicide, and I'm no different. Still, after a few days of Logan being missing, I began to accept the idea. But the break-in changed my mind," she said as she poured our coffee.

"A break-in here?"

"Logan lived here alone — I moved in after he died. But the break-in happened before I moved in. It was the day of the memorial service."

"It's despicable, but it's not uncommon for thieves to watch the obits and burglarize a house when they know the family will be at the funeral."

"That's what the police told me, but this was different. They didn't steal anything that I could tell. Logan's diamond cufflinks were still on the dresser top and the house is full of TVs, computers, and music stuff that weren't touched. All they had done was turn on his computer and open some desk drawers."

"Are you sure Logan didn't leave the computer on and the drawers open?"

"Well, it would be like him to do that, but in this case he didn't. You see, I had come over here with the police the next morning when they found the car on the bridge. They wanted to look for a suicide note. I walked through every room with them, and all of us would have noticed if the computer had been on and the drawers had been pulled out. But when I came back the night after the memorial service, the back door was open, and I called the police. I made it easy for the criminal — I guess I had forgotten to reset the alarm when the police and I left the day we were looking for the note. I was crying, though, so I wasn't myself."

It was my turn to sit and think for a few moments. Both of us were silent, as we sipped our coffee.

"Mrs. Magee, I'm not convinced your son committed suicide, but neither am I convinced he was murdered. Maybe it was an accident — I'm not sure what to think. But I'd like to look into it a little more."

She became excited, but I stopped her.

"Wait, hear me out. You've got to understand I'm not a detective, I'm a reporter, so don't expect miracles. But reporters do sometimes use some of the same investigative methods that cops use, and I've covered plenty of murders, suicides, and accidents. But if I'm going to do a little checking on this, I have to have one promise from you — I don't expect you to be open minded, but you must promise to cooperate with me in every way, tell me the absolute truth, even if there's something that points to suicide. If I find you've hidden anything from me, I'll drop the investigation on the spot."

"I'm not afraid of the truth, Miss Faire, but I do expect a miracle. In fact, one has already happened — your agreeing to look into Logan's death. You're the first person who's been willing to help me in more than a year."

"What about that psychic you hired?" Another test.

"I paid her, and even though I wanted to believe her, I didn't really, deep in my heart. I guess it was just the last straw of a desperate mother."

"Okay, I need you to stop your investigation — no more psychics, no more calls to Detective Trent, no more conspiracy theories — just let me ask around, see what I can find out. Agreed?"

"Absolutely. In fact, it's a relief. I'm not cut out for detective work — everybody I go to just thinks I'm a crazy old lady."

I ate the last bite of strawberry bread on my plate before she took me on a tour of the house. During the tour, we agreed to call each other by first names. Not only didn't I think Maggie Magee was a loony tune, but I liked her enormously and thought she was a very cool lady.

"Have you changed the house much since you moved in?" I asked as we started up the stairs.

"Oh, no, everything is exactly the same as Logan left it, except for the kitchen and the guest room I turned into a bedroom for myself. Most of my things I put in storage, so I could rent my house, but I had to bring my kitchen stuff. You know bachelors — they never have what you really need to cook."

I smiled, but she saw the look of pity on my face when I realized she had turned the house into a memorial to her dead son.

"Oh, you're thinking I haven't moved anything because I can't face reality, but it's not that. It's just that I want it to be the way Logan left it, in case there's ever a murder investigation."

The master bedroom, Logan's room, was on the front of the second floor, of course, with large windows looking out on the river, and a door out onto the upstairs porch, which was furnished with large, cushiony armchairs and end tables with lamps. I imagined Logan reading the newspaper out here early in the morning and sitting out here enjoying the sunset with Caroline on weekends. The bedroom was attractively masculine in burgundy and navy. Neat, but not too neat. Bed made up, but several articles of clothing thrown over the arm of a chair, and various items scattered around the dresser top. A used bath towel hung on the hook on the back of the bathroom door. Adjacent to the master bedroom was a smaller room, which was probably intended to be a little sitting room, but Logan had used it apparently as a home office. Maggie had left the drawers pulled out as she had found them after the break-in.

"What kind of work did Logan do?"

"Let's sit out here on the porch. He worked for Prentiss-Lamar Investors."

"Was Logan a broker?"

"Not exactly. The company doesn't handle individual investments. It's more like helping companies in America and around the world make deals with each other, mergers and acquisitions, things like that. I never really understood what exactly Logan did."

"That would be good. I'll need phone numbers for Caroline and some others, too, like the friend who made the video. Will you call them and ask them to cooperate with me?"

"Of course."

"But first, Maggie, tell me about the day before the wedding. Did you see Logan that day, other than at the rehearsal dinner?"

"He surprised me that morning by dropping in for breakfast. I cooked him a big old Southern breakfast, all his favorites—grits, eggs, homemade biscuits and sausage. He just ate cereal when it was up to him to fix his own breakfast, but he loved his mom's home-cooked breakfast on special occasions."

"What was his mood like?"

"At first it was great. He was so happy, so excited about the wedding and the honeymoon. While I was making the biscuits, he grabbed me, floury hands and all, and started dancing me around the kitchen, him singing, 'I'm getting married in the morning, so get me to the church on time.' You know, that song from My Fair Lady."

"You said it was great at first — how did his mood change?"

"Well, while we were eating, he was reading the paper. He said his didn't get delivered that day for some reason. He was reading various items out loud to me, like his dad used to do. But one time when he was reading to himself, suddenly he got very intense, and soon after that, he left, said he had a lot to do before the rehearsal dinner."

"Do you have any idea what story he was reading?"

"No, all I remember was that it was on one of the inside pages, because he had it turned back so he could hold it with one hand while he ate."

"Could it have been the business section?"

"Maybe, but I think it was a regular news page."

"How would you describe his mood when he read that story? Angry?"

"No, not exactly. "

"Depressed?"

"No. Maybe agitated."

"Afraid?"

"Not really. Worried might be a better word."

****

When I left Maggie Magee, I drove slowly along the river, which was sparkling in the June sun as if a sea of diamonds were floating down to New Orleans. I wondered how Maggie could stand to live right here on the Mississippi, where she couldn't escape looking at the churning waters of the river that had swallowed up her only child.

CHAPTER SIX

When I got to the paper the next day, I asked Shirley in circulation if she could find me a May 24 paper from a year ago. I could have read it online, but that wouldn't show me which pages would have been folded back to read. Then I went to the business editor's office.

"Hey, Hal, tell me about Prentiss-Lamar Investments."

"What do you want to know?"

"Is it a new company? I've never heard of it. "

"Been around about 15 years. They keep a pretty low profile locally."

"Low-profile? Does that mean they have some shady connections?

Hal looked at me like I had suggested Mother Theresa ran a brothel.

"Prentiss-Lamar is one of the top companies in Memphis. They've been involved in some of the best mergers and acquisitions around the globe. Maybe most people in Memphis have never heard of the company, but anybody on Wall Street would know them. What's this all about?"

"Ever hear of a guy who worked there until a year ago — Logan Magee?"

At first Hal looked like he didn't have a clue, but then it came to him.

"Magee? Wasn't he the one who jumped off the bridge?" I nodded yes.

"Do you remember anything that was said at the time he died? Any speculation in the business community about why he killed himself?"

"When a guy like that kills himself, people always wonder if he got caught with his hand in the till and couldn't stand to face an indictment, but everybody I talked to said he was a real stand-up guy with no hint of scandal."

"Could it be that the stock market took a plunge that day, and he was ruined financially?
Hal smiled at my ignorance. "A guy like Logan Magee would have a diversified portfolio — nothing less than a worldwide financial collapse would ruin him financially on any given day. What's all this about?"

"Just curious. I met his mother the other day, and I was just wondering what happened with her son. Any other scuttlebutt in the business community about why he'd jump off the bridge?"

"He was handsome, rich and was about to marry a drop-dead gorgeous blonde. Does that sound like a guy who would want to die? You'd have to be crazy to leave all that."

"Yeah, well, suicides aren't known for their rational thinking."

•••••••••••••••••••••

By the time I got back to my desk, there was a year-old May 24 paper lying there. For some reason, I felt reluctant to pick it up. Would I open the paper and immediately spot the reason for Logan Magee's suicide and then have to tell Maggie that there was no longer hope that her only child had not died accidentally or at the hands of a criminal, but had taken a coward's leap off a bridge, leaving a heart-broken mother and a devastated fiancée?

But, of course, it wasn't that easy. I went through the newspaper, story by story, and came to no conclusion — I didn't have a clue what could have upset Logan that morning. So I put it aside, wrote my column and took the May 24 newspaper home with me.

At home, at the little oak desk that had been my grandfather's desk at his pharmacy, I opened the paper again and tried to look at each story with fresh eyes. I made a list of all the serious stories in the news and business sections of the paper, even ones that seemed impossibly irrelevant.

• Utility prices expected to soar next fall.

• Another child killed because she was playing too close to a gang shoot-out.

• An anti-government demonstration in London.

• A feature about a man who as a newborn baby had been left to die in a garbage dumpster and was today a college professor in Michigan and was searching for his mother in Memphis.

• A story about the governor of New Jersey resigning.

• A French government official forced to resign because of a wine industry scandal.

• Popular cholesterol-lowering drug taken off the market, because it may cause strokes.

• A South American businessman assassinated.

• Firm accused of selling defective bullet-proof vests.

• Two private plane crashes in different parts of the country.

• Priest in Memphis accused of child sexual abuse.

• Suicide bombing in Russia.

• Trial of Memphis man accused of murdering his wife.

• Historic Memphis home to be converted into a restaurant.

• City Council votes to force certain businesses to pay more taxes instead of getting an exemption.

• Two stories about elections in other countries.

• Various Supreme Court rulings.

There were plenty of depressing, even upsetting, stories in the May 24 newspaper, but was there something that would make Logan Magee want to kill himself or make him fear for his life?

I thought of times when I read the newspaper with someone across the breakfast table. If I read something unusually tragic like the child killed in the gang shoot-out, I would surely comment on it. The same with something that made me angry. This would be especially true of someone like Logan Magee, who obviously enjoyed reading parts of the newspaper to someone else.

What type of story could a person read that would make him feel worried or agitated, but cause him to keep silent and leave his breakfast unfinished? You might keep quiet if you read something that made you feel guilty or if you didn't want to worry the person you were with. You might suspect that an unnamed person in a story was someone you knew, but you want to get more information before mentioning it to anyone else.

I folded the list and put it in my purse. Next time I saw Maggie, I'd ask her if Logan had any connections to any of those news stories. But next I wanted to meet Caroline, to find out what kind of girl Logan Magee would love.

CHAPTER SEVEN

If Maggie Magee was nothing like I expected, Caroline Crawford was everything I expected. Perfect skin, perfect body, blonde hair that might even be natural — Caroline was a cliche — a very lucky cliche. And smart, too — an English degree from Vanderbilt.

She lived in a big house in the suburbs overlooking a golf course with her parents, Dr. Cardiologist and Mrs. Junior League Past President. Caroline was an English teacher at The Hutchison School, an exclusive girls' school.

Worst of all, she had all that and was nice, too.

I'm sure the Crawfords must have a servant or two, but Caroline herself answered the door.

"You must be Britten. Please come in. Let's sit in the sunroom."

"Thanks for letting me come by," I said, pushing my unruly curly brown hair out of my face by shoving my sunglasses onto the top of my head.

"Would you like something to drink — coffee, tea, Coke?"

"No, thanks. I guess Maggie called you and told you I'm here at her request. I'm not writing about it for the newspaper. Just trying to help Maggie get some peace about... well, the situation."

"You can say 'Logan's death.' Those words don't send me into hysterics like they did the first six months. I was so upset at first I had to take a leave of absence from teaching for the fall semester. That's when I moved back in with my parents."

"That's understandable. But you're back teaching now?"

"Yeah, it really helps to have the distraction of going to work every day, and this summer I'm directing a play at Hutchison. That's been fun. I still break down sometimes at the strangest times, like driving down Poplar last week, but the pain isn't constant any more. I feel kind of guilty sometimes, because I'm feeling hopeful again, and I'm trying to go on with my life."

"Have you remained close to Logan's family and friends?"

"Well, when it comes to family, there's only Maggie, and I really haven't talked to her that much in the last year," Caroline said with pain or perhaps guilt in her voice. "My parents thought a clean break from the past might be a good idea. But I love Maggie to death, I really do. Can you believe she wanted me to take Logan's house, instead of her having it? She said it would have been mine in one more day anyhow and that she was sure Logan would want me to have it. "

"It's a beautiful house with a beautiful view," I said, not adding that I never understood why houses overlooking golf courses, like the Crawfords', were supposed to be so desirable.

"Oh, it's a great house, but I just couldn't accept it."

"Too many painful memories?"

"Well, not really. We didn't spend that much time there. But I can't see myself living alone downtown like that. Besides, it would take me 30 minutes to drive to school each way."

Practical, not sentimental. Also not greedy.

"How long have you taught at Hutchison?"

"A year before Logan died and the spring semester this year."

So she's about 10 years younger than Logan. Another cliche.

"How did you and Logan meet?"

"My parents are involved in one of the Cotton Carnival krewes — remember when they called them secret societies back when we were kids?"

She's being polite. She's bound to have guessed that I'm older than she is.

"I always wondered what was secret about them," I said. "The members were always on the newspaper party pages."

"Well, anyhow, I met Logan at one of the parties, and a few days later he called me and after dating three months, we got engaged."

"Was Logan a member of the krewe?"

"No, he was the date of one of the other girls."

He probably never gave that girl another thought after he met Caroline.

"I like to do this with people I interview sometimes — if you had to use only one word to describe Logan, what would it be?"

"Romantic," she said without hesitation.

That's the best you can do to describe someone you were going to marry? Romantic? A bit adolescent.

"Caroline, I'm going to be blunt. Do you think Logan committed suicide?"

"Absolutely not. He would never do a thing like that to me or to his mother."

"Suicide does seem like a selfish act, but sometimes people are just so depressed or hopeless that they just can't face life."

"Logan loved life. When other people would say they hoped they didn't live to be old and senile, Logan would say he wanted to stick around as long as possible, even if he ended up being an old coot driving one of those little scooters around the mall."

"During the time you knew him, did he ever act depressed or extremely worried about anything?"

"Never. I can promise you this, Miss Faire, Logan did not kill himself. I will never believe that."

"Then do you think he was murdered?"

"Of course not. Poor Maggie. It had to be an accident."

"But why would he be on the bridge at 3 or 4 a.m. the night before his wedding?"

"Maybe he had too much to drink at the rehearsal. He loved the river and the bridges — maybe he just wanted to stand on the bridge and feel the wind off the water. Maybe he stumbled and fell over. Those big trucks can nearly knock you over when they pass you going fast."

This was obviously her story, and she was sticking to it.

Caroline had lost patience with me and stood up.

"I'm so sorry, but I have play rehearsal tonight and I have some things to do before."

"Of course, thanks for your help. Can I call you if I think of anything else?"

Her answer was to smile graciously and tell me goodbye as she briskly walked me to the front door.

•••••••••••••••••••••

As I drove back downtown, I thought about what an attractive couple Caroline and Logan were. She with her fair beauty and he with his exotic dark good looks, that I now knew came from being half Asian. Even their names were attractive. I wondered if she kept pictures of him in her room or if her parents thought that too was a bad idea, like staying in touch with poor, lonely Maggie Magee. But who am I to judge any of them? How do I know how I would cope if my fiancé killed himself the night before our wedding?

I still have photos of Drew around my house. I miss him.

You know those corny invitations that were popular a few years ago that said, "On this day, I will marry my best friend"? Well, I wouldn't be caught dead sending out something like that, but in our case, it was really true. I married my best friend, and three weeks later I divorced my best friend, and he divorced me.

I took out my cell phone, dialed Trent's number and asked if he'd like to take me out to dinner — his treat. He said yes.

•••••••••••••••••

Trent was just what I needed. We ate big steaks and fully loaded baked potatoes at Folk's Folly and talked about how much we hate sushi. We don't mind being uncool.

"How's your Logan Magee investigation going?" he asked me between bites of rare steak.

"It's not an investigation. I'm just asking a few questions, trying to find some hope for Mrs. Magee that her son died by accident rather than by suicide. Logan's fiancée, Caroline Crawford, is certainly convinced it was an accident."

"What else would you expect her to believe or try to believe?"

"Good point. Try to get the waitress's attention and get us some more bread, will you? And more butter."

"Did you convince Mrs. Magee to give up her theories on an FBI instigated murder?"

"Trent, you were wrong about Maggie. She's not crazy, just desperate. She admitted to me that she didn't really believe all that, but she does believe it was murder. I think she thought her FBI theory might make a reporter like me more interested in the case. The morning before he died, Logan was at her house for breakfast, all frisky and happy until he saw something in the newspaper, something that made him quit eating and leave in an agitated state."

"That sounds more like an indication of suicide than murder to me."

"Yeah, but try this out — his house was broken into the day of the memorial service and nothing was taken. But they turned on his computer and opened his desk drawers."

"Maybe he was doing something illegal with somebody else and killed himself because he was about to get caught. Maybe his partner in crime came into the house to be sure there was nothing left that would incriminate him."

"Maybe."

"Now, why don't you tell me why you decided after all these years to let me buy you dinner. At what point did I become irresistible?"

I was just about to give him a smart-mouthed reply when over Trent's shoulder I saw Caroline Crawford enter the restaurant. She was holding hands with a guy about my age, who looked familiar. Where had I seen him before?

At first I tried to duck down a little so she wouldn't see me, but then I realized that wasn't necessary. Her companion had her full attention. The look on her face was one I knew well. It was that look of love that Logan gave her on the eve of his death

CHAPTER EIGHT

Am I lucky or what? How many people have a close friend from high school who is a clinical psychologist? Instead of paying some shrink $200 an hour, I just call Nora and ask if I can buy her dinner. She always lets me pay, so that I won't feel guilty about getting free therapy.

I told her about the Logan Magee situation while we were eating our fried chicken, fried okra and corn pudding at The Cupboard.

"If somebody wanted to kill himself, why would he choose jumping off a bridge as the method, do you think?" I asked.

"It could be because he didn't want his family to have to find his body. Or perhaps he didn't have easy access to pills or guns. A bridge would be handy in Memphis if you made a spur of the moment decision to die. No equipment needed, and a sure death, considering the height of these bridges and the swift undercurrent of the river."

"But do people, happy people with a great future, just suddenly decide to commit suicide?"

"Maybe he was a good actor. Maybe he had been depressed or hopeless for a while, but covered it up well."

"But what about those warning signs you see listed during mental health week?"

"Well, most suicidal people do send out warning signals, but there's a percentage of them who give no advance warning, and their suicides take their families and friends totally by surprise."

"Haven't I heard that anti-depressants can make people suicidal?"

"That's usually children or adolescents, but there have been cases where some medication has caused an adult to be suicidal. If the mother really has kept everything the same as it was when he was alive, you can just look in his medicine cabinet."

"I'll go over tonight and check. Nora, have you ever heard of anyone committing suicide on their wedding day or the day before?"

"Not personally, but those things happen. Getting married is a big step for a person. Some times life-changing events, even happy ones, can bring out a person's anxieties. Now, let me ask you a question, Britt. Why are you so obsessed with this guy's death? I hate to put it this way, but since you said you don't plan to write a story about it, what's in it for you?"

"You know I always love a good puzzle to solve — maybe I read too many Nancy Drew and Trixie Belden books when I was a kid."

"Don't give me that. Why can't you admit this has become personal for you?"

"If you could meet Maggie Magee, you'd understand. She's a widow and her only child died a few hours before his wedding. She needs someone to help her get closure on this awful loss. I'd like to prove it's an accident, but at the very least I'd like to find out why Logan killed himself. Maybe that would help Maggie let go. I'm growing very fond of her."

"And?"

"And after watching the video of Logan and Caroline and after meeting Caroline, I just can't buy the suicide idea."

"People are more complex than what appears on a video of a party, Britt."

"I know, but I talked to Caroline a couple of days ago and then that very night, I saw her in a restaurant holding hands with a guy. I know it's stupid, but I felt stung for Logan. It seemed so disloyal. "

"What? You expected her to grieve forever? You thought someone that young would never love again?"

"It's only been a year."

"You're not getting personally involved in this case, huh? Sure you're not."

"You shrinks can be so annoyingly smug sometimes. Do you want dessert?"

•••••••••••••••••

When I left Nora, I called Maggie and asked if I could come over.

We went together to Logan's bathroom and opened the medicine cabinet, where we found the usual stuff, but no prescription drugs. I picked up Logan's aftershave, opened the top and smelled it. The smell was nice, but not familiar. The label was all in French.

"Maggie, had Logan ever been to France?"

"Several times. I think he went there on business a few months before, before the accident. He traveled a lot for his work and for fun, so it's hard to remember exactly where he went when."

We walked back into the bedroom. With Logan's shirt draped across the arm of the chair, it seemed as though he had just changed clothes and gone out and would be back later. I wondered if Maggie found that comforting. We walked out on to the second-floor porch and sat down to enjoy the June night.

"Tell me about Logan as a little boy."

"He was a mischievous little thing, always getting into something. Nothing really bad, but something to get himself into trouble. Getting too close to a wasp's nest and getting stung all over his face — he looked like a monster with all that swelling. And the time he and Ben sneaked into a house they thought was vacant and haunted and nearly got shot by the reclusive owner. They were little rascals, those two boys."

"Who's Ben?"

"Logan's best friend his whole life. They go back to kindergarten. They were inseparable their whole lives until they went to different colleges. But then after college, they both came back to Memphis and took back up where they left off. Ben is executor of Logan's estate, and he takes care of my finances now. He was going to be best man in the wedding."

"I tried to think back to the rehearsal dinner video. I remembered a rather ordinary looking guy proposing a toast, but I couldn't picture him in my mind. Do you have a picture of Ben around here?"

"Oh, sure, Logan had a darling picture of Ben, Caroline, and me that he said was a picture of all those he loved the most. It's framed and on top of the chest of drawers in there."

"I don't remember seeing it when we were going through the room last week."

"It's there. I'll go get it," Maggie said, rising from her chair on the balcony.

She was gone longer than I expected, so I went into the bedroom. There was no picture on the bureau and Maggie stood there looking puzzled.

"I know it was here. Am I losing my mind? Maybe it fell behind the chest."

We pulled the bureau out a little and looked behind it. Nothing but some dust bunnies.

"There's no reason I would have put it away," she said, obviously not completely convinced, because she was searching through the drawers. In the second drawer, she found an empty picture frame under Logan's folded undershirts. She pulled it out with a look of utter bewilderment on her face.

"This is it, but the picture's gone."

"Maggie, does anyone besides you have a key to the house?"

"I'm not sure."

"Think. Think."

"Well, Caroline would probably still have one, and Logan's housekeeper. And, of course, Ben. Ben lives in Harbor Town, too, and whenever Logan was out of town, Ben would collect the mail and newspapers every day. But none of them would come in without telling me. They know it's my house now. I just don't understand."

"When did you last see it?"

"Well, I don't know. I do know it was still there after the accident, because the policeman asked me if the man in the picture was my son. And I'm pretty sure it was there for a while after that. If an empty frame was sitting there, of course, I would have noticed right away, but I guess I just didn't notice when it disappeared."

"Well, in case Logan gave a key to someone else, maybe you should get the locks changed just to be sure. Tomorrow."

"I will, but I still wonder who would want to steal a picture of Ben, Caroline and me."

CHAPTER NINE

That night I dreamed about Drew again. It's funny — when we were together constantly as kids and when we were married, I never dreamed of him. Now I dream of him often, but I never dream of the Drew of now, only the Drew of then.

In this particular dream, Drew and I were about 10 and we were sitting in a treehouse sipping champagne, pink champagne. That was something we really did from time to time, although it wasn't real champagne, of course. It was 7-Up with a drop of red food coloring in it, but we drank it out of real crystal champagne glasses that we smuggled out of my mom's china cabinet. Looking back on it, I'm not sure those glasses really were champagne flutes. More likely they were sherbet glasses. But the effect was achieved.

We sipped our drinks and ate cubes of cheese on toothpicks and sat in the tree house in Drew's backyard pretending it was one of those exotic jungle hotels for big game hunters and other rich people. At that age and for some years to come, Drew and I were obsessed with sophistication, and to us sipping pink champagne was the epitome of sophistication.

I'm sure you're thinking we were kind of weird kids, and we were. Maybe our mutual weirdness is what bonded us. A kinder description of us would be that we both had vivid imaginations and could always make each other laugh.

Actually, we led a bit of a double life. At school we were pretty normal. We were in the same grade, and if we happened to be in the same class some years, we didn't sit together or act friendlier to each other than anybody else. If we were in different classes, we didn't gravitate toward each other on the playground or cafeteria.

But when we were at home, especially during the summer when school was a distant memory for a while, we were inseparable. We lived next door to each other from second grade on, and our parents were friends. We lived in Hernando, a small town just south of Memphis over the Mississippi line. We wandered in and out of each other's houses at will, and we presented a united front against our brothers and sisters, who were all older than us. We ate lunch and dinner at whichever house was having the best offering at that meal.

All through elementary school our favorite game was Pretend, and we were very good at it. We pretended to be soldiers, doctors, astronauts, rock stars — anybody we thought was cool, and then we made up all kinds of dramatic stories about the identity du jour, usually ending with heroic actions on our parts.

Those games would begin something like this:

Drew: "Say you're an astronaut and your capsule is dangling out in space, and I have to come up and rescue you."

Britt: But when you get up there, you get hurt and I'm a doctor and astronaut and I save your life."

By the time we were in junior high, our days often revolved around projects — talking our parents into letting us paint our own bedrooms the color of our choice or rummaging in the attic, looking for something interesting or mysterious, like our parents' old love letters.

And while we did our projects, our imaginations went wild. Sometimes, we came up with elaborate theories about our parents' or grandparents' pasts. Drew was convinced that his mother had a secret marriage before his dad, and that the first husband died in the Vietnam War, leaving her broken-hearted for life. I suspected my dad was in the Witness Protection Program because he claimed his parents died before he was married and that he didn't have any brothers or sisters. I remember so well the day we sat Mom down at the kitchen table, and Drew asked her dead-seriously, "Mrs. Faire, how well do you really know your husband?"

One summer when we were 13 or 14, we made a real find in Drew's basement — his mom's record collection from the sixties, along with an old red and white record player. There was a whole suitcase full of 45s and we listened to every one. Our favorites were *This Old Heart of Mine* by the Isley Brothers and anything by Stevie Wonder and by the Fifth Dimension.

While our friends and siblings were listening to Smashing Pumpkins, we were getting down with Motown. After we listened to *Working on a Groovy Thing* and *A Groovy Kind of Love*, we started using the word "groovy" at every opportunity. His mom might say, "Drew, do you want dessert?" "Groovy," he'd say.

"Britt, how was school today?" My answer would be "Groovy" even if the real answer was "Gruesome." "Groovy" just rolled off the tongue so nicely, we couldn't resist, even though nobody our age, of course, used such outdated slang. We didn't care. We felt like our use of that word made us part of an elite group.

Our very favorite of all the 45s we found in the basement was Stevie Wonder's *I Was Made to Love Her*. It you're not familiar with the lyrics, it's all about a girl and boy who have loved each other since childhood. We listened to it the first time with something akin to reverence and then Drew put it on again. After the second time, he said, "That's our song. That'll always be our song." And it always was. It still is to me.

After that, we started telling each other "I love you" sometimes. But not really in a romantic way. It was more like the way your mother or father tells you they love you, but not exactly, because when Drew said it, it felt different from when my parents said it. I didn't feel he was my boyfriend or anything, but I felt like I was the most special person in his life. He certainly was in mine.

But our best times were spent creating funny characters and pretending they were our relatives. Drew came up with twin cousins whom he named Maybelline and Mascara Motley, who lived at Exxon View Apartments. I argued for them living at Escargot Gardens, but I finally agreed that an apartment overlooking a gas station was funnier.

We created a whole tacky family one summer, and for years afterwards would make reference to them, as if they were real. Like we might drive as teenagers past a house painted a horribly bright color, and one of us would say, "That would be Mascara's dream house."

While we were away at separate colleges — me majoring in journalism, Drew studying to become a special education teacher — we sometimes wrote each other letters or e-mails as if we were writing to that made-up family.

We could always make each other laugh, always. Until we ruined it all by getting married. Now Drew and I only laugh together in my dreams. I wonder if he ever dreams about me.

CHAPTER TEN

A couple of days later, I made an appointment with Ben Spurrier, Logan's best friend. When I arrived at his office, Ben had his back to the door, working at his computer.

"I'll be right with you," he said, finishing the last sentence of an e-mail and pushing the send button. When he turned around, I almost gasped. Logan's best friend, best man, and childhood playmate was also Caroline Crawford's new boyfriend, the man she was holding hands with in the restaurant.

Keep your cool, Britt. Don't let on you know.

He rose and offered me his hand, smiling pleasantly.

"I read your column by the way. I always thought," he paused awkwardly.

"That I was a man?"

"I guess it was a sexist assumption that Britten Faire would be a man. They ought to run your picture with your column, like the other columnists."

"It's more fun this way."

He came around the desk, and motioned for me to sit with

him in the two leather wing-backs by the window.

"Maggie says you're trying to help her deal with Logan's death. I know Logan would appreciate that. It would hurt him to see how much his mom has suffered and how much denial she's in."

"I take it you don't buy her murder theory?"

"Motive is the problem. Who would want Logan Magee dead? He was the most likeable guy imaginable. He was the best. All through school, everybody liked Logan. He was that ideal kid — smart, but not too smart; athletic, but not an obnoxious jock; nice looking, but not a conceited pretty boy. If I had to describe Logan in one word, it would be difficult to do, because "loyal," "courageous" and "likeable" all come to mind."

I hadn't even asked him my trick question. Why was he volunteering his one-word description of Logan?

"So do you vote for accident or suicide?"

"Suicide," he said without hesitation.

"Did Logan have any problems he couldn't face? Anything that might make him want to die?"

"I've asked myself that a million times. You know how some guys only watch sports together or talk about cars? Well, we did those things — I can't go to a football game or a Grizzlies game without missing Logan — but we also talked about real stuff, about our lives. Logan's life had bumps in the road, like anybody's, but nothing that bad."

"You describe him as courageous and say his problems weren't that bad, but you have no trouble believing he would kill himself on the eve of his wedding?"

"What choice do I have? Murder and accident are neither feasible. I have to accept that I didn't know everything about my best friend. There must have been demons inside him he didn't let me see."

"Caroline seems to think maybe Logan got drunk and then went out on the bridge on a lark and accidentally fell off."

"I could believe he was suicidal before I could believe he was stupid."

"Speaking of Caroline, have you stayed in contact with her since Logan died?"

"I call her occasionally to see how she's doing. I think Logan would want me to look out for her."

"I don't know how recently you've spoken with her, but she told me she's trying to go on with her life. She hinted that she's dating somebody. Do you know who?"

"That's news to me, but I'm glad for her. Logan wouldn't want her to give up on life, to live in mourning."

I didn't stay long at Ben's office. No point, I already knew I couldn't believe a word he would say.

CHAPTER ELEVEN

"He's a liar," I said to Jack Trent after I told him about my meeting with Ben Spurrier.

"Okay, he's a liar, but does that make him a murderer?"

"Not necessarily, but don't you think it's odd that Ben not only lied about his relationship with Caroline, but he's also the only person who was close to Logan who thinks he committed suicide. You said yourself that it's natural when you love somebody to not want to believe they would kill themselves, especially when nobody can come up with a reason why a man with a seemingly perfect life would kill himself on his wedding day. But Ben is ready to accept the idea of suicide, no argument. Maybe he and Logan got drunk and went out on the bridge as a lark and maybe Ben confessed to Logan he was in love with Caroline and they struggled and Logan accidentally fell over the side."

"Are you through?"

"For now."

"In the first place, don't you think some passing motorist would have noticed two guys fighting on the bridge and called the cops? In the second place, Logan's been dead for more than a year. Don't you think there's a very good chance this romance didn't start until recently? Think about it, Britt. Who's your best friend?"

I started to say Drew, but said Beth instead.

"Well, let's say that Beth dies and a year later, you start dating Beth's boyfriend. Now you're not doing anything wrong, but is that something you'd be anxious to tell people? Might you feel a little guilty, like you were betraying Beth? Is it possible you might plead ignorance if someone asked you who Beth's boyfriend was dating?"

"Maybe. But what about Ben being so willing to believe Logan would kill himself?"

"That is a little odd, unless Logan confided some things to Ben that nobody else knows and that would make Logan want to kill himself. Maybe Ben is protecting Logan's memory by not revealing those things."

"I guess that's possible."

"But you know, Britt, it's these two break-ins at Mrs. Magee's house that bother me, especially taking the picture out of the frame. And whoever took it used a key, which would indicate somebody close to Mrs. Magee. But the people who were closest to Logan and his mother could just ask her for a copy of the picture — they wouldn't have to sneak in and steal it and hide the frame in the underwear drawer. Make sure she really does get her locks changed and ask her if she kept a spare key under a flower pot or something, like a lot of people do."

•••••••••••

When I left Jack Trent's office in the Criminal Justice Center, commonly known as 201 Poplar or just 201, I walked over to City Hall and took in a couple of hours of the City Council meeting. Then went into the office and wrote my column about how rude the council members treat citizens who come to speak against intrusive development in their neighborhoods. While their nervous constituents stand at the microphone and try to exercise their rights as citizens, most of the Council members chat with each other or take the occasion to get up and get a snack or take a bathroom break, getting back to their seats just in time to vote in favor of the developers. This has been going on for years, but I thought it was time I wrote something about it. The Council being in bed with developers has been a long-standing crusade of mine. This is just the latest installment in my feeble attempt to stand up for the little guy who doesn't want a Jiffy Lube across the street from his house.

I didn't get home until almost ten, and I was sleepier than I was hungry, but by the time I took a hot bath, I wasn't sleepy any more. Aren't hot baths supposed to relax you? Well, I *was* relaxed, but I was also wide awake, so I watched again the video collage of Logan's life that Ben had made for Caroline as a wedding present. It was supposed to be Logan's life from birth until marriage, but it turned out to be his whole life, all 34 years of it.

Ben obviously had plenty of pictures and videos of him and Logan growing up, but he probably had to get other pictures and family home movies from Maggie. He also set the collage to music, using music from various eras. It began with a red-faced ugly, squinting newborn Logan, looking, as most babies do, like Winston Churchill minus the cigar. It was one of those pictures they take in the hospital nursery during your first 24 hours of life. The music with it was "How Much Is That Doggie in the Window?" an old 50s song, I believe.

There was also a photo of Logan, about age 2, wearing a navy and white sailor suit and holding his Easter basket. When you got to the group shots of various elementary school aged birthday parties, the picture of Logan as the well-liked boy Ben spoke of began to emerge.

There were plenty of shots of Logan and Ben in their various Little League uniforms, and an adorable photo of a pre-school Logan wearing nothing but his underwear and a football helmet.

In one home movie segment, Maggie and Mack Magee couldn't seem to get enough hugs and kisses from their beloved only child, who appeared to be about three.

Then there were the gangly junior high pictures of Logan and Ben. Oddly, Ben was better looking at that age than Logan. They were caught in various silly poses.

My favorite still shots were of Logan at three or four, and my second favorites were the pictures from high school. At some point the ugly duckling of junior high had become a handsome, dark-eyed young man with an irresistible smile. His prom date seemed so enamored by Logan that she didn't seem to notice his horrible pastel blue tuxedo.

But my number-one favorite part of the collage was a video of Logan and Ben sailing when they were in their mid 20s I'd guess. They were laughing and the wind was in their hair, their noses sunburned. I wonder who was on the boat with them, shooting the video. It was a perfect picture of the friendships and optimism of early adulthood. It was so poignant to think that just a few years later, Logan would be dead.

At the end of the collage, there was a cute shot of Logan and Caroline together, probably an engagement picture, and the music was the Beatles singing, "Will you still need me? Will you still feed me when I'm 64?"

I put my face in my hands and wept. I wasn't sure if I was crying for Logan and Caroline and what they would never have or for Drew and me and what we had lost.

CHAPTER TWELVE

I spent Monday writing a column about the death of The Cussin' Man.

I live in a part of Memphis called Cooper-Young. It's a Midtown neighborhood of houses built in the 1920s and 30s. Most of the houses are simple wood-frame homes with front porches and railings, but there are a few impressive late Victorian houses, too. The Cussin' Man lived in one of those, an impressive three-story Queen Anne house with turrets and fish-scales and gingerbread. It had been a grand single family home at one time, I'm sure. It was still a beautiful house, but it was divided into 3 or 4 apartments now, one of which was home to The Cussin' Man.

Next door to Cooper-Young is Central Gardens, the rich relation of my neighborhood. Central Gardens houses are usually bigger than Cooper-Young houses and usually made of brick or stone, and it is pretty much all residential.

Even the best houses in Cooper-Young can't come close to the average home in Central Gardens, but I like Cooper-Young better because if feels like a little community with residential streets surrounding restaurants, Burke's Book Store and a cat rescue called House of Mews along Cooper and Young, which intersect. One of the restaurants is The Beauty Shop, where Priscilla Presley used to get her bouffant done. They still have the old dryers and such inside the restaurant.

If you live in Cooper-Young or spend much time there, it would be hard to miss The Cussin' Man, an old man who rode through the neighborhood on an old yellow girl's bicycle, often with his fresh dry cleaning hanging off the handle bars.

He might have been quite unremarkable except that he always, I mean always, was sputtering profanity as he rode. *Loudly* sputtering profanity. Thus the nickname coined by the neighborhood kids, The Cussin' Man.

The first time you encountered The Cussin' Man, you were either shocked, offended, or amused, but after a while he just seemed like a neighborhood fixture worthy neither of scorn nor praise. In the suburbs, they'd probably have him arrested or taken to a mental hospital, but Cooper-Young is a live-and-let-live kind of place.

But when my friend, Beth, who lives near that Queen Anne beauty of a house, told me that she heard that The Cussin' Man had been found dead in his apartment with his cat very much alive, I felt compelled to write about the man, who everybody knew of, but nobody knew.

I found out from the cops that The Cussin' Man's real name was Cornell Whittington and that he was 81 years old when he died. As far as anybody knew, he had no family or friends.

The fact that he had a cat, which the cops said was well-fed and cared for, made me think that maybe he wasn't the miserable, cantankerous old guy he seemed. Maybe he had Tourette's or some other medical condition that causes people to use profanity beyond their control.

So much for that sad, warm and fuzzy story — the misunderstood Cussin' Man. When I talked to people who lived in the house with him and to the clerks at the dry cleaning store, I came away with a picture of someone who really was a miserable, cantankerous old coot.

Still none of these people professed to really know him. They just said their casual contact with him was never pleasant, no matter how they tried to break through the crusty exterior or be kind to him. One neighbor said she felt sorry for him being so alone, so she took him a plate of home-baked Christmas cookies on Christmas Eve one year. He wouldn't answer the door, so she left the plate outside his door. The next morning, she found the plate of cookies in front of *her* front door, not even one cookie eaten.

I hit pay dirt when I ate lunch at Young Avenue Deli and happened to sit near an older man, who kept glancing out the window toward the Queen Anne house.

"Did you know the man who died there yesterday?" I asked.

"Yeah, I knew Cornell. At least I used to know him. He hasn't spoken a civil word to me in 40 years."

"Wow, you've known him 40 years?"

The man, whom I later found out was named Quentin Taylor, took a long swig of his iced tea before he answered.

"A lot longer than that. We went to Ole Miss together and then both served in the Korean War."

"Did the war make him the way he was?"

"Not as how I could tell. I saw him a few times after that year in Korea, and he seemed like the same carefree guy I knew at Ole Miss. A little older and wiser, maybe, but basically the same. He was a Sigma Chi at Ole Miss, a real popular guy, handsome, all the girls he could want. His family was well-off, so he always dressed sharp and had a nice car. I was downright jealous of him, but you couldn't dislike him. He was a real regular fellow, if you know what I mean."

"When did he change, Mr. Taylor?
"Five or six years after Korea, I hear. I wasn't in contact with him by then, but an old fraternity brother of his told me that some girl broke his heart and after that he gradually stayed more and more to himself. He never married. Just worked and played golf and after a

while he just worked and came home every night. I don't know how he got from his family's big house over on Peabody, which I heard he inherited, to living in a boarding house over there," he said nodding toward the house across the street.

"What I wonder is how he got from being a recluse to being The Cussin' Man."

"Is that what they call him?" Mr. Taylor asked. "I don't live around here, just come here to eat sometimes when I'm in the neighborhood. I'd heard he'd gone kinda crazy."

"He rode around the neighborhood on a bicycle cussing out anybody who looked at him or came near, and for some reason he almost always had his dry cleaning on the handlebars. The dry cleaner told me Mr. Whittington had nice clothes and that he had them dry cleaned or laundered even when they looked like they hadn't been worn."

Mr. Taylor shook his head slowly and said, "You can take the boy out of the Sigma Chi house, but you can't take the Sigma Chi out of the ornery old man, I guess."

I love people who give me great quotes — I used that one for the ending of my column.

CHAPTER THIRTEEN

For some reason, I wanted a photo of Caroline and Logan, so I asked Maggie for one. She assumed it had something to do with the investigation, and I guess that's what I thought, too. She gave me the photo without question — the same photo that Ben had placed at the end of the video collage.

A couple of days later, I went out to dinner at Wang's with a group of friends, and as always, we asked for our favorite waiter, John — or at least it sounded like he was saying John when we first asked his name. He seemed satisfied with our pronunciation of his name and very pleased at how impressed we were with his memory. We only ate there every two or three weeks, and yet John always remembered our orders. Two orders of barbecued pork fried rice to share, sweet and sour shrimp for me, chicken with sizzling rice for Bob, sweet and sour chicken for Suzanne and Mandarin Beef for Chris. Two waters and two iced teas, one with extra ice. Fried bananas for dessert.

Sometimes when John walked over to our table for the first time, he'd say he'd turned in our order when he saw us walk in. If any of us ever wanted anything different, we wouldn't dare order it — nobody could bear to embarrass or disappoint John.

There was a time when Drew was part of this happy dinner

group. Now, I suspected that the others alternated between asking me to join them and asking Drew. Divorce doesn't just part a couple — it parts friends, too. In some divorces, the friends take sides; other divorces find friends disappearing from the lives of both ex's, because nobody knows how to handle it; but in our case, our friends loved us both equally I guess and couldn't choose between us. Besides, our marriage was so short, it just seemed like a bad dream to our friends. To Drew and me, the marriage and divorce were all too real, since it ended the dearest friendship either of us had ever had.

This night we were waiting for our entrees when somebody — I think it was Bob — asked how my "bridge jumper investigation" was going.

"If you ever find out how or why he died, are you going to write it for the paper?" Chris asked.

"I keep saying I won't, but I guess if I uncovered something interesting like murder, I would. But if it's just a motive for suicide, I won't subject Maggie or Caroline to public humiliation."

"As if the fiancée hasn't already been humiliated enough," said Suzanne. "How would you like to have everybody in the city know that your fiancée jumped off a bridge a few hours before he was supposed to marry you? Nothing like humiliation piled on top of grief."

There was a shared groan at the thought.

"Would you like to see what they look like?" I asked. They all looked surprised when I was able to produce a photo of Logan and Caroline. Everyone was impressed with what a beautiful couple they were — a study in light and dark.

While they were passing the photo around, John came with our food.

"Caroline! Logan!" he said in his heavy accent, his face lighting up and then falling to a frown. "So sad."

"John, you know the people in the picture?" I asked, utterly astonished.

"Oh, yes, dinner and movie most every week."

"What do you remember most about them?" I asked.

"Most I remember she very pretty and smile big, and he very nice and smile big. Big surprise when he spoke to me in my language one night."

"What is your language, John?" Bob asked.

"Indonesian. I also speak Arabic, but Logan speak to me Indonesian. Speak pretty good, too. Caroline in ladies room, and he start talking just like that to me in my language. When she walk back to table, he went back to English and wink at me, put his finger to his lip not to say anything."

"Did you ever get to ask Logan how he knew Indonesian?"

"Never saw him again. Died two week later. I always wonder. In the four years I live in America, no American ever speak my language before. Very nice man."

CHAPTER FOURTEEN

On Thursday, I got a call from my youngest older sister, Libby, who lives in Nashville, where she's a buyer for a ritzy women's store. When I was visiting her a couple of months ago, Libby took me to the store, Chloe's Closet, because I think she thought I'd be impressed with how upscale and exclusive it was. I was not.

What impressed me was how the clerks fawned over the rich women who shopped there and were barely civil to women who wandered into the store unaware that they were "not our kind of customers." I actually heard one of the clerks say that after two women came in and left hurriedly when they saw the price tags. I guess everybody has to have somebody to look down on, but it still makes me mad.

When I got back to Memphis, I wrote a column about it. I made fun of the fact that the right kind of customers were offered a glass of white wine to sip on while they shopped, and that a simple, sleeveless silk pullover blouse that you could buy at Macy's for $30, had a price tag of $500 at Chloe's Closet.

I swear, it never occurred to me that my sister would find out. She doesn't care enough about my writing to read my column online, and I certainly didn't tell her about the column. But I miscalculated. Somebody from Memphis who knows the owner of the store, whose name is Dora instead of Chloe, as it turns out, e-mailed a link to Dora, who nearly fired my sister, who called my parents and my oldest older sister, Jill, who were all either mad at me or "disappointed" in me, which, of course, is always worse than anger.

First Libby called me and gave me unmitigated hell about it. I apologized and said I didn't think anybody from Nashville, including her, would see the column, and she said, rightfully so, that that really wasn't the point. She said she had to promise to never speak to me again, so that Dora would not fire her.

Just when I thought the fireworks were over, my mother called from Florida, where my parents live now, sniffling and sounding hurt and saying that she didn't raise me to be cruel to my sister or anybody else. And she added, "You're just like your father, anything for a laugh." My dad got on the phone then and said that if Libby got fired, he was going to suggest she come and live with me and let me support her.

That night, Jill, who lives in Jackson, Mississippi, called to tell me I really screwed up. Stop the presses! Jill said it was kind of stupid of me to think Libby nor her boss would find out about the column. Why didn't I just leave out the name of the store, at least, Jill said. Good point, too late.

Jill's criticism really stung, because she's usually my biggest ally in the family. Mom and Dad love me and are proud of me, but they work hard at spreading the love and pride around equally among us three girls, which I guess is a good parent's job. To hear them talk, selling overpriced clothes to rich snobs is just as important as being a pediatrician like Jill.

Jill loves Libby, too, but I'm her baby sister, and she has always been the one to defend me when other people are mad at me. She's also the one who can give me advice without making me defensive.

So when Libby called on this Thursday night and wanted to come for the weekend, I was glad she had forgiven me enough to want to see me again.

Libby made the 3-hour drive from Nashville, which is in the center of the state, to Memphis, which is in the far southwestern corner of Tennessee, on Saturday morning and got here in time for lunch. Normally, I wouldn't drain my bank account to entertain her, but I felt I had some making up to do.

So I took her to a restaurant which is nice and not cheap, but a place where Chloe's customers would go on an ordinary shopping day, not for a special lunch. Libby and I both have always liked the tea-room atmosphere and the yummy homemade soups, chicken salad and basket of little muffins and yeast rolls.

Over lunch, Libby told me about her latest love crisis. I don't even remember the details now — all of her romantic problems seem pretty much the same to me. Libby and a guy fall instantly in love and are meant for each other, and everything is perfect for a while until either she loses interest in him or he stops calling.

Then she needs to talk for hours to me (if somebody more sympathetic isn't available), doing an endless postmortem on the relationship and why the guy wasn't "The One." Often I lose patience with her, but this time, I tried hard to listen and not say anything that would seem insensitive. I imitated Dr. Nora's shrink routine by listening, nodding sympathetically and asking questions like, "How did that make you feel?"

After lunch we went shopping, and I bought Libby a book she wanted in the self-help section of the bookstore. After all, the people who work at Chloe's Closet don't make that much money. The intangible rewards of helping rich women look good is supposed to make up for the low pay, I suppose.

I was going to spring for play tickets that night — *West Side Story* was playing at Theater Memphis — but Libby said that was too sad, that she'd prefer to "have some laughs on Beale Street." That was okay with me, because I like the blues clubs on Beale Street as much as Libby does.

We had dinner at Pearl's Oyster House and then walked over to Beale. As we walked down the street toward B.B. King's, I remembered why I don't like to go places like that with Libby.

If you ask my mom, her daughters are all equally beautiful, smart, and charming. If you ask an objective and diplomatic woman, she'd say that all three of us are attractive in our own way, but that Libby is the only one of us you'd call beautiful. If you ask any man, other than my father, he would say that when Libby is in the room, who cares if she has sisters.

Among our aunts and uncles and grandparents, Jill is called "the smart one," I'm described as "the spunky one" and Libby is "the pretty one." She's the only blonde among us, though not naturally blonde, and she is the only one with dimples when she smiles. She has a great body and dresses well, but most of all, she just oozes charm and sex appeal. In other words, she's a flirt and men always notice her in a crowd, especially if they've been drinking.

Walking down Beale Street with Libby on a Saturday night makes me feel invisible. No, I take that back. Invisible would be better. Instead, I, who normally am a rather self-confident person, feel dowdy and ugly next to my sister. But I survived the evening, and Libby left Sunday morning feeling good about herself again and all indications were that she had forgiven me for my column about Chloe's Closet.

CHAPTER FIFTEEN

I called Maggie to ask if she'd like to meet me for lunch at Paulette's, my favorite expensive lunch place. When I heard how Maggie's voice brightened at hearing mine, I suggested *dinner* at Paulette's instead. When you're lonely, a dinner invitation is better than a lunch date any time.

She ordered the shrimp crepe, and I got my usual crab cakes. While we ate popovers with strawberry butter, I went down the list of newspaper stories from May 24 a year ago, asking her if there was any connection, even the slightest connection, between Logan and these subjects.

Utility prices? MLGW? *No.*

Child killed by gang? *Sad, but no.*

London? *Yes, Logan went there several times on business.*

The Michigan college professor looking for his mother? *Logan cheered for Michigan in football or was it Michigan State?*

Governor of New Jersey? *No.*

French wine scandal? *He liked wine, and he went to France several times on business.*

Cholesterol medicine? *No, he had a physical not long before the wedding and his cholesterol and blood pressure were both good.*

South American businessman assassinated? *He went to Brazil once on vacation. He loved Brazilian music — Antonio Carlos Jobim and some other guy, can't remember his name.*

Bullet proof vests? *No.*

Plane crashes? *No.*

Priest in Memphis accused of abuse? *We're Presbyterians.*

Suicide bombing in Russia? *Don't remember him ever going to Russia on business or vacation.*

Trial of man accused of killing his wife? *Logan liked Court TV.*

Historic Memphis home to be demolished? *Logan loved old buildings and history in general, always got mad when they tore them down.*

City Council? *No, but that lady councilman is sitting behind us.*

I turned around and at the table right behind me was Councilwoman Margaret Carruthers having a very expensive dinner and fine wine with Ray Christie, the city's most notorious developer. When he wasn't doing work on casino additions down in Tunica, Mississippi, Christie was going before the City Council with his many rape-and-plunder building projects, which always seemed to be approved, no matter how much they threatened the integrity of existing neighborhoods or how much virgin woodland would be cut down to build his rows of shoddy houses. Christie is in his 30s or early 40s and attractive, while Councilwoman Carruthers is in her 70s and ugly as a mud fence, as they say in Mississippi. An unlikely couple and yet Christie is paying the check with hundred dollar bills and Mrs. Carruthers is smiling like she's at the prom. Well, I had my next *City Lights* column.

Maggie and I spent the rest of dinner talking about anything but Logan, just two girls chit chatting about everything and nothing. I think our dinner cheered her up a lot. As we were about to leave, I remembered to ask about Logan's connection to Indonesia.

"There isn't any connection, as far as I know."

"Did Logan speak Indonesian?"

"Heavens! Surely not. That doesn't come in handy like Spanish or French, now does it?"

"How many languages does… did Logan know?"

"Oh, sugar, I'm not sure. He just always had a knack for languages. When he was a little boy, he picked up Spanish from Sesame Street and made A's in it in high school. He learned German and Chinese in college. He was an international business major, so being fluent in at least one language was required. I think he picked up French on his own, just from going there on business."

"He sounds brilliant."

"Well, he wouldn't like that word. When somebody was impressed by his foreign languages, he would just say it's nothing to brag about if something comes easy to you. It's the things you struggle to learn that are impressive when you do learn them."

"Can you give me the name of somebody at Prentiss-Lamar who Logan liked and worked closely with?"

"Sure. Just call Barney Foster. He'll tell you anything he knows about Logan. They worked together, but they were friends, too. Logan brought Barney and his wife over to my house for dinner one time."

"Maggie, did Logan ever take you to Wang's Mandarin House out at Park and Ridgeway?"

"Oh, no, honey. I hate Chinese food." She saw the bemused look on my face. "I guess it is kind of funny — a Chinese who doesn't like Chinese food, but you've got to understand, Britt, that my family has been in Mississippi for a hundred years, and that was a time when immigrants wanted to be as American as possible, so I never heard Chinese spoken in our home, and my mother fixed corn bread and turnip greens and black-eyed peas and pork chops like everybody else in Mississippi. I never could understand why anyone would want to eat their meat and vegetables all chopped up in little pieces and mixed together. I wouldn't even know I was Chinese if I didn't look in the mirror."

CHAPTER SIXTEEN

Barney Foster suggested we meet at a coffee shop, instead of my coming to his office. I was hoping to see the place where Logan worked, but it wasn't crucial. I was just curious.

He told me to look for a short, fat, bald man in a dark suit. He exaggerated. He was actually of average height, just a little round in the middle and just starting to lose his hair, but he was right about the suit — it *was* dark. He was sitting at a table in the corner, the furthest away from the rest of the people there and looking ill-at-ease. It seemed amusingly clandestine.

We shook hands, sat down and ordered coffee. This was a place that served coffee, not lattes and frappacinos. He smiled pleasantly. It no longer felt like a B-grade spy movie.

"So what can I help you with? This isn't for the newspaper is it?"

I assured him I was just trying to help Maggie Magee let her son rest in peace. His sad smile made me know he still missed Logan.

"International investments is a pretty intense profession," he said. "You don't make a lot of buddies in this business. Too competitive for real friendship, but Logan was that rare guy who could do his job well, exceptional in fact, and still go to a ballgame with you or stop for a drink after work. Just a very likeable guy and someone with more integrity than killer instinct."

"I've heard nothing but good things about Logan, but surely he wasn't perfect. Didn't he have any faults?"

Barney Foster thought for a minute. "Maybe women."

"He was a womanizer?"

"Oh, hell no. Just the opposite. Have you ever heard that song — Chet Baker sang it and others — *I Fall in Love Too Easily?*"

"I fall in love too easily. I fall in love too fast. I fall in love too terribly hard, for love to ever last."

"You know it. Well, that was Logan. There were other girls before Caroline, and he always fell in love too fast, even with Caroline, and the fall was hard when it didn't work out."

"Why would it not work out?"

"Usually because the kind of women who were attracted to him were attracted to the superficial things — his looks, his money, his charm — and when they got to know him, they were disappointed. They found out he wasn't the driven, ambitious man they were attracted to."

"But Logan was successful."

"Oh, sure, but only because he did a lot of things well, not because he got off on the power. In fact, he talked sometimes about quitting investments and doing something less stressful, something more fun."

"Like what?"

"Maybe getting his Ph.D. and teaching on a college level or teaching tennis at a club. It was when he'd start talking about his dreams that his girlfriends would get disillusioned. They weren't interested in being married to a tennis bum or a student."

"When you said he'd take it hard when a romance broke up,

did you mean he got suicidal?"

"Oh, I know what you're thinking — Caroline called off the wedding and he jumped off the bridge. Maybe, but I don't think so. She wouldn't do that and even if she did, it would be like the others for Logan. He'd mope around for a while, hang out at sports bars and drink too much, not shave on the weekends, swear off women forever, but he'd get over it and move on. He was a very resilient person."

"So, you don't think Logan killed himself."

"No way. Well, I'm pretty sure not. That just doesn't compute. It had to be an accident."

"Or murder?" There was a momentary hesitation before Barney said again that it must have been an accident.

"Barney, did Logan speak Indonesian?"

He looked surprised.

"Nobody was supposed to know. You see, we had three Indonesian businessmen spending some months with us at Prentiss-Lamar. Our boss knew that Logan had picked up Indonesian somewhere along the way. He was a sponge for foreign languages — Logan wasn't fluent really, but he knew enough to get by, and our boss asked Logan not to let on that he spoke the language. It wasn't commonly known that Logan had Indonesian among his talents. He wanted Logan to keep his ears open when the Indonesians were talking to each other or on the phone. People who think nobody knows their language will say things to each other or on the phone that they normally would be too guarded to say."

"Kind of paranoid, isn't it?"

"Well, we had reason to be paranoid. Several years ago, one of our people spent a year with a firm in Japan on a venture that we were supposedly working with them on for mutual benefit. Then one day, one of our people arrived from the states. Nobody knew he was fluent in Japanese, and he overheard things that made him know they were screwing us over."

"So Logan was supposed to spy on the Indonesian businessmen?"

"Well, I wouldn't put it that way. He didn't do anything he wouldn't ordinarily do. It wasn't like he was listening at keyholes or following them or anything like that. He just did his job and listened to things that were said in his presence or nearby."

"And did they say anything in Indonesian that was suspicious?"

"Well, maybe not suspicious, but cryptic. About a month before he died, he told me that he overheard one of the guys, Nat, having a phone conversation that was odd. He didn't know what to make of it."

"What did he hear?"

"He didn't tell me. Said he didn't want to impugn the guys' reputations with so little to go on."

"How long did they stay here?"

"They only stayed at Prentiss-Lamar for a few more weeks, but they are still in Memphis, I hear. They invested in a business here, but I never heard the details."

"Can you give me their names?"

"They have long Indonesian names, so we just called them Nat, Suk and Marty. I guess I could look up their full names in the files, but they won't be able to tell you anything about Logan — they weren't friends with him or anybody else."

"I wasn't planning to contact them. I just wanted their names, so I could do a background check on them. I'm just curious," I said, not sure if I was telling the truth. That creepy B-grade spy-movie feeling had returned.

CHAPTER SEVENTEEN

I was proud of my column that day.

They weren't the typical prom couple out for a fancy dinner before the dance.

He was a 43-year-old white man from New Jersey with the rough hands of someone who does physical labor. She was 71 with delicate, well-manicured hands, a life-long Memphian and an African American. But there was no race barrier here. Her parents might not have approved, but they had passed away years ago. His father and business partner would be thrilled at the pairing.

The happy couple smiled across the table at Paulette's on a Saturday night, she often giggling girlishly at his jokes. He gave her his most charming grin and often touched her hand while making a point in conversation. She looked pleased by his constant attention and smiled graciously as he paid the check with crisp, new hundred dollar bills.

The fairy tale evening had ended, but it wasn't goodbye forever. The couple would see each other the next Tuesday downtown at City Hall.

He would be there with his attorney seeking a zoning variance for his latest building project, despite the busload of concerned citizens who had come to City Hall to protest.

She would cast the deciding vote in favor of the zoning variance, despite her stated opposition to the project just two weeks before.

Like most fairy tales, theirs would end happily. For everyone except the busload of concerned citizens, who will now have 600 cheaply built apartments in their currently single-family neighborhood.

Boy, it really hit the fan. Within hours of my column being published, my spies at City Hall tell me, Councilwoman Curruthers was inundated with angry phone calls and e-mails from Memphians accusing her of taking a bribe, selling out and selling her soul to the devil. Man, I love the power of the press. Of course, the TV stations jumped on it, too, as soon as they read the paper.

That afternoon, Councilwoman Curruthers called a press conference to announce that she had not completely understood all the facts before voting on the zoning variance and that she would be asking The Council to reconsider the matter at the next meeting. Under the rules of the Council, only those on the winning side of any vote can call for a re-vote, and she was exercising that option. When a TV reporter asked her if she was reconsidering because of all the fall-out from Britten Faire's column, the councilwoman said, "Certainly not. I don't even read that scurrilous rag. I'm just trying to do the right thing for the people who elected me, as I always have and shall always do."

Needless to say, it was a very satisfying day for me — the kind of day that reminds you why you chose the profession you did. I went to the bookstore and bought myself a new hard-back novel to celebrate and picked up a barbecue sandwich on the way home. I was too hungry to wait, so I started eating my sandwich while I listened to my phone messages. The first was from a telemarketer offering me a "free" vacation in Florida and the second was my friend, Cindy, calling to say she loved the column and to keep sticking it to The Man. The third was a man's voice I didn't recognize leaving a one-sentence message:

"I hear your favorite phrase is "I'm just curious," but you know what curiosity did to the cat, don't you?"

An occasional threat is part of being a good journalist, a badge of courage, if you will, but this one frightened me a little. I pushed the save button on my answering machine and looked at my caller ID. There was Cindy's number, a number in Fredericksburg, Virginia, and a blocked number. I called Jack Trent and before I could even tell him the whole story, he said he was coming over.

"You don't have to — I'm not afraid."

"I'm coming over, kid. Save your breath."

When he got there, I accepted a hug, although I was determined not to be a wimp.

"It's just some prankster or a bully who's friends with Ray Christie," I said as Trent pushed the play button on my answering machine. "They're just trying to scare me."

He listened to the message twice and saved it again.

"Harassing phone calls usually aren't acted upon, but I always take seriously the ones that say they are going to kill somebody."
"He didn't exactly say he was going to kill me," I protested.

"Curiosity killed the cat? You don't think that's a death threat? Well, it is."

"Trent, do you think Ray Christie might be in the Dixie Mafia?"

"Hell, no, he's in the *real* mafia. No puny Dixie Mafia for Ray Christie and Ray Christie Jr. And they've had a real good thing going around here for a long time. Between the Council members who are actually on the take and those who are just pro-development for tax assessment reasons, the Christies get anything they want. Until you messed things up."

"Now you're scaring me."

"I'm trying to, and I'm staying here tonight."

"You absolutely are not. I appreciate your concern, Jack, but I can't live the rest of my life with police protection. I'll call if anything else happens."

I walked him to the door and then he stopped, as if a new thought had come to him.

"Whoever called you knew your home landline number, even though it's unlisted, and knew that your favorite phrase is "I'm just curious." How would Ray Christie know that? Is it possible that this threatening call didn't have anything to do with The City Council thing. Could it be someone who wants you to stop asking questions about Logan Magee's death?"

That question put a dent in my cavalier attitude. Threats from the disgruntled people you write about are common enough that they don't seem scary, but a threat from a possible murderer was different. I must have looked like a frightened child because he put his arms around me gently and gave me a hug. That was sweet, but I didn't expect what happened next — he kissed me. Well, it was just a kiss on top of my head, but it still *was* a kiss.

He went around the house with me, checking each window and door to be sure everything was locked, and looking in every room and closet. I felt much better when he left, and he called me when he got home to check on me one more time.

"I'm already in bed and feeling safe and sound," I said.

"I wish you had a security alarm or at least a big dog."

"Don't be silly, Mr. Paranoid Detective. Goodnight. I'll talk to you tomorrow."

I slept well until sometime during the early morning hours when I woke up thinking I had heard a sound outside. I listened carefully, my pulse racing in my ears, and finally decided it was my imagination or a dream or the wind or just somebody passing by.

•••••••••••••••••

I woke up feeling pretty good and a little silly. Why did I let that phone call shake me up so bad? I turned on the coffeemaker and put on my pink flannel robe before going out to pick up the blue plastic bag containing the newspaper. As I pulled the newspaper out, something fell on the ground. At first I thought it was an advertising circular, but it was a photo of a cute kitten, torn from the front of a greeting card. Splattered on the kitten's picture was blood, real blood.

CHAPTER EIGHTEEN

The bloody kitten picture didn't shake me up as much as I would have thought, but it made me glad I didn't have any pets they could hurt. Somehow the picture just seemed like the work of a bully rather than a killer, and a bit melodramatic and amateurish. I should have called Trent about it, but I didn't. In the light of day, it seemed silly that I was so frightened last night, scared enough to fall into Trent's arms. I dreaded seeing him. Please don't let him suddenly start acting like he's my boyfriend.

I dressed and went to work. As I drove the short distance from my Midtown house to the paper, I thought about what Trent said about the origin of the threat. My head told me it had to be Ray Christie or some of his cronies, mad about my column yesterday. Nothing else made sense. But my gut wasn't sure.

Why would anyone not want me to ask questions about Logan's death? Unless he was murdered. I probably had used the phrase, "I'm just curious" to Maggie, Ben, Caroline and Barney, and they all had my unlisted home phone number and my cell number, but why would any of them kill Logan? There was one other explanation — none of them killed Logan, but perhaps there was something one of them didn't want to come out in the course of my investigation. But that left Maggie out since she was the one who talked me into investigating his death.

When I got to work, I called Barney Foster at his office and asked him to look up the Indonesian businessmen's names and any other information that might be in their computer database. I promised him again that I wouldn't speak with them directly, but I was beginning to think that was a lie. If only I knew what Logan overheard them say.

•••••••••••••••

I didn't eat out that night, for a change, or even order in. I made a big bowl of Cream of Wheat (one of my comfort foods) and ate it with sugar and butter from the aqua blue Fiesta Ware soup bowl that I snagged from my grandmother's house after she died. That shallow bowl, with its wide, grooved edge, had such happy memories for me. We always had formal breakfast when we visited my grandmother in Alabama, none of that eat-on-the-run or not-at-all of my immediate family. At Meem's house, there was Cream of Wheat or oatmeal, kept warm in the double boiler; scrambled eggs; sausage or bacon; homemade biscuits; and real butter. My parents always bought margarine, which I realized at an early age was virtually tasteless compared to the real thing. I vowed as a kid that when I grew up, even if I was dirt poor, I would always have real butter in my house, and I have, even though it takes me a month to eat one stick, because I cook so little.

So that night, I put on my jammies, made my Cream of Wheat and read my new novel while I ate. I didn't feel afraid and went to bed early, sleeping soundly all night.

The next morning when I went out to get the newspaper, there were no bloody pictures, but there was a note on my car, tucked beneath the windshield wiper. My heart raced a bit as I opened it. It simply said, "Meet me in Tom Lee Park tonight at 8." So I did.

I didn't tell anyone about the note — I just drove downtown that night to one of the parks that overlooks the river and waited on a bench until I heard his voice behind me.

"Britten Faire, intrepid girl reporter, or is it Nancy Drew, girl detective?"

I stood up and turned around and threw my arms around him. I couldn't speak — I could only sob and hold onto him tightly.

"Oh, Drew, I've missed you so much," I finally said. He sat me down on the park bench, the bench where we had spent so many happy hours talking and laughing during high school and later. After I had calmed down, he smiled that tender smile of his and faced me, his hands holding both of mine.

"I've missed you, too, Britt. How did we get in this mess?"

"I don't know," I said, blowing my nose on a tissue I dug out of my pocket. He changed the subject, but I knew we'd return to it eventually.

"I hear from Bob that you've been doing an investigation about a guy who jumped off the bridge."

I told him all about it, and it felt so good to be confiding in him like I did almost all my life until a year ago.

"Well, I just hope Nancy Drew has her flashlight and magnifying glass with her at all times and doesn't hesitate to call her chums when she needs help."

When we were kids, there was one summer that I read every Nancy Drew mystery in the library, and Drew teased me constantly about it. He read just one, "The Secret of the Old Clock," so he could see what was so enthralling to me, but I always suspected his main reason was that he wanted to know enough about Nancy and her life that he could tease me. The Nancy Drew books have been updated and added to many times over the years, but the ones I preferred were the old ones from the 30s and 40s that were full of archaic language like "chums" and "roadsters."

There was so much history between Drew and me. He was my best friend from the moment I met him in second grade on

Phyllis Townsend's front porch. It sounds strange to say seven year olds could have instant chemistry, but we did. We just loved each other almost immediately.

Neither Drew nor I dated much in high school — I think most people assumed we were a couple — but when we went to different colleges, we both dated quite a bit. When it came to the casual relationships in our lives then, Drew and I told all to each other through e-mails or phone calls, but a more serious relationship usually produced periods of silence between us.

I had my share of guys who stopped calling or who I lost interest in, but I only had one big heartbreak while I was at Ole Miss and Drew was at the University of Memphis.

After the breakup, I couldn't get to Drew in Memphis fast enough. I told him everything and cried for days, with him giving me lots of hugs, stroking my hair, wiping away my tears, and most of all listening to me pour out my broken heart.

And now that I was sitting with Drew in Tom Lee Park by the river again, it hurt so much to realize I had lost that kind of friend. But he was here, right? And he seemed as glad to see me as I was to see him, so maybe we could go back to being friends and forget we ever had that stupid three-week marriage.

How did we get into that stupid three-week marriage? Well, after college graduation, he went to work for the Memphis City Schools as a special ed teacher, and I got a job at a small daily newspaper in North Carolina. We stayed in constant touch by phone during those away years, and then I got a job at the Memphis paper covering cops, and we became inseparable again.

After I came back to Memphis, we often talked about our bad luck in love and said we could never find anyone as much fun or as easy to talk to as each other.

It was on this very bench that we proposed to each other and kissed for the first time. Kind of strange for 30-year-olds, huh? We had never kissed before, because you don't kiss friends, except on the cheek. You hug them, you tell them you love them, but you don't kiss them and you certainly don't have sex with them. Maybe some people do, but it really never entered Drew's and my minds before. Maybe we weren't physically attracted to each other, but we definitely loved each other, and we thought love and friendship were the best reasons to get married.

We were so sure we were doing the right thing, so we got married immediately. Our wedding was unconventional and goofy and so like us — the ceremony and reception were at the zoo. Our closest friends gave us away. It was a blast. Then we left on our honeymoon, excited about our trip and smug about our being the only couple who had it all figured out.

When we found ourselves alone in our room at a ski resort in Colorado, we suddenly felt awkward, and we made love like two strangers. We talked about missing our friends and Drew's dog. We skied all day until we were exhausted and found various reasons not to make love. It was horrible.

And it was even worse when we got back home to Memphis, and he and Buster moved into my house. We knew newlyweds were supposed to be going at it like rabbits, and we felt guilty for only occasionally making love.

After three weeks, I had the courage to finally talk honestly about the terrible mistake we had made. He was relieved. We came to the conclusion that when you had sex with someone who had been like a sibling to you for most of your life that it seemed, well, incestuous. He and Buster moved out that same day.

"So how did we get in this mess?" This time I asked it on our park bench.

"I always heard that the best marriages were where each person was the other's best friend, so ours should have been perfect, because our friendship was perfect. Wasn't it?" he asked.

"Yeah, it was the best friendship anyone could imagine. It was magical, mystical, perfect, but..."

"But we found out that unless physical attraction is there,

too, it won't work as a marriage."

"Since our divorce, I've felt so ugly, so undesirable, because I could tell you..."

"Oh, no, Britt, don't ever think there was something wrong with you. You're beautiful — I always thought so, even as early as junior high. In fact, around puberty I felt a strong attraction to you. But when we got to high school and there were other people we both were attracted to, I just went back to thinking of you like a friend, like a guy friend. But I never stopped thinking you were pretty. And when we were married, I liked making love to you, but there was always something missing. That was the first time I realized you can love someone and desire her, but not be *in* love with her. It felt wrong to have sex with you when I wasn't in love with you."

"I know. I felt the same way. It killed me to realize we had ruined a wonderful friendship by getting married." We both laughed sadly. "But, Drew, you're my best friend, and I miss you terribly. Nothing has seemed right since there's been silence between us. Can we go back to the way it was?"

Drew looked out at the river, and I saw tears in his eyes.

"No, Britt, we can't go back to the way it was. I came here tonight to tell you," he paused painfully, "to tell you I'm getting married."

He waited for it to sink in and looked at me to see how much pain he had inflicted. It didn't sink in. It couldn't. It hurt too much. I couldn't speak. Tears poured down my cheeks.

"Who?" is all I could get out.

"Her name is Elizabeth, and she and I work together."

"So you're in love with her, like you weren't with me?"

"Yes," he said softly.

"And you're friends, too?"

"Yes," he said, putting his arms around me and resting his

chin on the top of my head. "Yes, we're in love and we're friends. That's the way it's supposed to be, Britt. That's what I want for you, too. Don't settle for less, promise me you won't."

"But is it a friendship like we had?"

"No, sweetheart, don't worry," he said, stroking my hair while I cried. "There will never be another friendship like yours and mine was for all those years growing up together."

We sat there on that park bench a half hour or so, not talking but lightly touching hands, looking out at the dark river. I almost asked if we could remain friends after he got married, but I knew better. This was our last time to be together, alone.

Finally he said he had to go. Maybe Drew was ready to say goodbye, but I never would be.

CHAPTER NINETEEN

The next morning I woke up with that vague sense of grief where you're not sure for a couple of seconds if someone really did die or if it was just a bad dream. It was real. Drew really was getting married and wisely thought that prevented our being able to go back to being friends.

I called Nora to see if I could buy her lunch or dinner, but she was booked for both, but she gave me a few minutes of phone therapy. I told her about my time with Drew and what he said. She was sympathetic, but agreed with Drew.

"But why? Why can't we go back to being each other's best friend?" I protested with much emotion and little conviction. "If we had never been married to each other and he got married, he wouldn't drop me as his best friend."

"Not at first and maybe never in his heart, but for all practical purposes, he wouldn't stay best friends with you. Britt, surely you can see how uncomfortable it would be for Drew and his wife if he was hanging out with his female buddy and confiding in her instead of his wife. There aren't many people secure enough to not mind their spouse having an opposite-sex best friend. And then in your case, it's even more awkward, because his buddy is also his ex-wife. Come on, Britt, this is real life, not some sitcom."

"Of all the stupid things I've done in my life, marrying Drew was the dumbest. If we hadn't been married, this news that he's getting married wouldn't hurt so much."

"You're kidding yourself, Britt. You would have felt the same sense of loss and betrayal you're feeling now, even if there had never been a moment of romance between you and Drew. Any single person feels loss when a close friend gets married, but it's worse with opposite-sex friendships. I'm sorry, but I've got a patient waiting for me. I've got to go."

I thanked Nora and hung up, not feeling one bit better than I did before I called. I guess even Nora can't help me out of this one.

Late that same morning I dropped by Jack Trent's office. He hadn't even called to check on me since the night of the so-called "death threat."

"So," I said, plopping down into the chair across the desk from him, "Detective Trent didn't even care to check if I was snuffed out by Ray Christie these last two days."

I immediately regretted saying that — it sounded like I was miffed because he didn't call me. But Trent didn't seem to take it that way.

"I guess I did seem to be neglecting my duty to protect Citizen Faire, but I had my ways of knowing you were okay. I drove past your house on my way to work and saw your paper had been picked up, so I knew you had survived the night. And I had the patrolmen in your area do a drive-by several times during the night. I know better than to try to smother Britten Faire with unwanted concern. You do know, don't you, that you are one of the stubbornest people on earth?"

"I prefer the word, 'independent.'"

"Why don't we compromise with "stubbornly independent."

"Well, anyhow I appreciate your keeping an eye on me that first day when even I was a little discombobulated, but I'm fine now and feeling quite safe again."

"So call off my dogs, huh?"

I changed the subject, but he knew my answer was yes.

"Were you able to find out anything about those Indonesian businessmen?" I had called him yesterday as soon as Barney Foster had called me back with the names. Trent hadn't been there, but I had left the names on his voice mail."

"Can't tell you much yet. I've got a call into ICE about them, but all I really know so far is that the three of them have green cards and bought a controlling interest in one of the small independent banks here, and the guys seem to be legit. One odd thing, though, they are all living together in a three-bedroom apartment in Cordova."

"Why would three grown men, obviously wealthy, live together?" I asked.

"Maybe it's some cultural thing we don't understand, or maybe they plan to return to their home country and run the bank from afar."

After I left Trent, I went back to my office and called the three men to ask for an interview. I told the secretary that I was doing a story for the business section on new business executives in Memphis. She said somebody would get back to me.

•••••••••••••••

When I came in from work, there were phone messages from both my sisters. Jill, who is four years older than me and the one I think of as my "Big Sister," called to say she was sorry she couldn't talk to me earlier today when I tried to reach her, but she was up to her neck in kids with strept throat and ear infections and worse, and she didn't get away from the office until the last patient left at 6:30. She said if I didn't reach her before 7:30, we wouldn't be able to talk until she got home from her son's baseball game, which would be over about 8:30, and then she would need to get him to bed.

It was 7:45 when I got the message, so I'd have to move onto Plan B, which was talking to my sister, Libby, who is two years older than me.

Growing up after them was a tough act to follow. Jill was so smart and such a leader in high school, and I always knew the teachers were comparing me to her and wondering what went wrong. Libby wasn't dumb (a solid B student), but nobody would ever say, "Why aren't you as smart as Libby?" But I'm sure they noticed that Jill and I weren't as pretty or as popular as Libby. But who was?

Actually none of us were wall-flowers. We all had plenty of friends, good grades and more than a few accomplishments listed under our names in our senior yearbooks. Jill's said: Senior Class president; Debate Club; Student Council sophomore representative; science club; National Honor Society; Valedictorian.

Under my senior yearbook picture it said: Senior Class Vice President; Most Likely to Succeed — Who's Who; newspaper editor; Girls' State; senior play. Jill and I sound pretty good until you know that Libby's yearbook listing said: Cheerleader, all four years; Homecoming Queen; Cutest Girl — Who's Who; tennis team (state champions). In other words, all the cool stuff.

Libby had called not knowing anything was going on with me. She just wanted to share some good news, the message said, so I called her back, planning to dump my sorrow on her.

Before I could start pouring out my grief over Drew getting married, Libby excitedly told me about her new boyfriend, a wide-receiver on the Tennessee Titans NFL team, which is in Nashville. I was happy for her (sort of), so I listened and oo'ed and ahh'ed when she told me how awesome he was. Then I told her about Drew, and she tried hard to sympathize — she really did — but I could tell she just didn't get it. To her, Drew was our childhood friend, whom I had mistakenly married and now I just needed to move on with my life.

Not long after that call, Jill called.

"What's wrong, sweetie? I could tell you were upset when you called me earlier. I wish I had had time to talk," Jill said.

"It's okay, Jilly," I said and promptly burst into tears. I told her all about Drew's and my conversation on the bench by the river, and she understood totally. I told her Libby's news.

"Great, just what you needed to hear right now with your heart breaking," Jill said.

"To be fair, Libby told me her good news before she knew I was upset."

"But let me guess," Jill said. "When you did tell her, her advice was to find somebody better to replace Drew, right?"

"Something like that. I wish I could be more like Libby — you lose one man, you find another, and you never look back."

"Well, that's not a real healthy approach to relationships, but if it works for her, fine," Jill said. "It *has* been almost a year since your divorce. Is there anybody else in your life that you might want to go out with?"

I told her about Jack and my mixed feelings about him.

"He sounds great. Why are your feelings mixed?"

"Well, part of it is that I don't want to mess up a friendship and a great news source, but mostly it's just that I'm not Libby. I can't unplug one person from my heart and immediately find somebody else to plug in."

"I'm the same way, so I understand. Since Tim's been gone, I haven't had any interest in anybody else. Not that I have time to date anyhow. When it's time to move on, I guess you and I each will know it."

"I love you, Jilly," I said and we said our goodbyes. After I hung up, I cried again, this time because I felt guilty for bothering Jill with my blues over Drew remarrying when she was still grieving for her husband, whom she met while they were both in medical school and who died in an automobile accident when their son, Ryan, was just two. How like Jill not to remind me that her loss had been greater than mine.

CHAPTER TWENTY

It had been two weeks since Councilwoman Carruthers had cast the winning vote for Ray Christie's latest land development scheme, and this afternoon the matter would be put back on the agenda for reconsideration, just as Mrs. Carruthers had promised at her press conference. I didn't want to miss a minute of the meeting.

After the usual chaplain of the day appearance, various resolutions regarding somebody's retirement or death, and a quick approval of the consent agenda, the City Council attacked the regular agenda.

Ray Christie's request for a zoning variance was 43rd on the agenda, so I settled in for a long boring wait. When the comptroller finally called the item, Mrs. Carruthers explained that she had voted at the previous meeting without complete information and upon further study had decided to reverse her stance on the issue. Tearing down four single-family homes in a lovely, older neighborhood to build a high-rise apartment building was not a good idea, she said. The Landmarks Commission and the Land Use Control Board had both voted against the project, and so would she.

I looked over at Ray Christie, who did not look in the least perturbed by the councilwoman's reversal. A few minutes later I learned why.

The Council members who had been vocally opposed to the project before, again spoke of the negative effect the high rise would have on a neighborhood that was making an outstanding comeback after the white flight of the 1960s. Just like last meeting, most of the Council did not enter the discussion, but when the votes were cast, Bill McLemore, who had voted against the project two weeks ago, now cast his vote with Christie.

So the result was the same — Ray Christie would be able to tear down four 80 plus-year-old houses and build a shoddy apartment building with fewer parking spaces than tenants, which meant the neighbors could expect their normally near-empty street to be lined with parked cars and increased traffic. I wondered if McLemore was bought off with dinner at Paulette's or if his vote was more expensive.

I left the meeting and in the lobby of City Hall, I saw Ray Christie walking toward me, a smug smile on his face.

"I always win in the end, Miss Faire. Never forget that."

I should have ignored him, but instead I said, "Mr. Christie, you may discover that the power of the press is even stronger than the power of Ray Christie."

He just smiled and walked away.

•••••••••••

My column the next day wasn't as good as the Margaret Carruthers column, but it wasn't too shabby, either.

Only a few things in life are certain — Memphis summers will be unbearably hot, Memphis barbecue will always be the best in the world and the Memphis City Council will always give real estate developers like Ray Christie exactly what they want.

The column went on and on, skewering the Council for its

devotion to developers and its apparent disregard for quality of life for ordinary Memphians. Of course, I had to stop short of saying Bill McLemore was bought off by Ray Christie. The paper's lawyers would have never let that get by. Still, people could read between the lines, and I gave them ample opportunity to do just that. I ended with these words:

So Memphis City Council members continue to vote in favor of developers, but maybe come August, Memphians will refuse to vote for the Council members. Then Ray Christie can take them all out for dinner and drinks to console the losers.

CHAPTER TWENTY-ONE

The next morning as I drank my coffee at the dining room table, I spread the year-old May 24 newspaper out in front of me. I had gone over my list of stories several times during the last few weeks, but it occurred to me that maybe I needed to go back to the original source, in case I was missing something.

I didn't get past the story about the City Council voting to annex another part of eastern Shelby County. The first time I read the story, I didn't notice that Ray Christie was prominently quoted in the story as a leading proponent of the annexation, which as always was vehemently opposed by the residents of the area, who had moved there in the first place to avoid city taxes and city schools.

Christie was quoted as saying, "This is a rapidly developing area of Shelby County, and it makes sense for the city to benefit from the property taxes of the new businesses and homes in the area. County residents want all the advantages of living in a metro area, but don't want any of the big-city responsibilities that go with it."

Of course, to even the least schooled observer, it was obvious that Ray Christie wasn't concerned with taxes in the least, but in having this vast empty land under the control of the City Council, which he obviously had had more luck influencing than the County Commission, not that they were so pure either.

Finding Ray Christie's name in the newspaper that Logan read the day he died didn't necessarily link Christie to Logan — why would Logan be upset or worried about this. He lived downtown. Still it was something interesting I had overlooked the first time I read the May 24 paper.

There was something else I had overlooked — I had asked Maggie Magee to look at my list of articles, but I had not asked the other people close to Logan. So I called Ben, who said I could come by his office in a couple of hours; I left a message for Caroline; and I talked to Barney Foster, who suggested I fax him the list.

By the time I got to the office, Barney had faxed me back my list with some notations.

• Utility prices expected to soar next fall — *Who isn't concerned about this?*

• Another child killed because she was playing too close to a gang shoot-out — *Logan had a soft heart, but wouldn't over-react to something like this.*

• An anti-government demonstration in London — *We do a lot of business in London. Logan usually went there about once a year, sometimes more.*

• A feature about a man who as a newborn baby had been left to die in a garbage dumpster and was today a college professor in Michigan and had been reunited with his mother in Memphis. — *Logan was a big Michigan football fan. Why, I never knew. He didn't go to school there.*

• A story about the governor of New Jersey resigning. — *Nothing*

• A French government official forced to resign because of a wine industry scandal. — *Logan spoke French well, so he went to Paris a number of times on business.*

• Popular cholesterol-lowering drug taken off the market, because it may cause strokes. — *He never discussed his health with me.*

• A South American businessman assassinated. — *Logan was fluent in*

Spanish, so he did some business in various South American countries for us. Ironically, the only one he ever visited for personal reasons was Brazil, where they speak Portuguese, which as far as I know Logan didn't speak. Seems like he met a girl there.

• Firm accused of selling defective bullet-proof vests. — *Nothing.*

• Two private plane crashes in different parts of the country. — *Even though Logan had to fly all the time on business, he once told me that he had a secret fear of flying, nothing debilitating, but he just felt ill at ease on planes.*

• Priest in Memphis accused of abuse. — *Caroline is a Catholic, I think.*

• Suicide bombing in Russia. — *Russian wasn't one of Logan's languages. As far as I know, he never went there.*

• Trial of Memphis man accused of murdering his wife. — *He followed all the high-profile trials in the papers.*

• Historic Memphis home to be demolished. — *He liked history and old buildings, got mad when they were torn down.*

• City Council votes to annex another part of eastern Shelby County. — *Our company doesn't deal in local real estate or any kind of real estate development.*

• Two stories about elections in other countries. — *Logan wasn't very political, as far as I knew.*

• Various Supreme Court rulings — *He was somewhat interested in Supreme Court cases, like anyone would be, but he much preferred a good murder trial. "Twelve Angry Men" was one of his favorite old movies.*

•••••••••••••••••••••

I went to Ben's office, and he greeted me cordially, if not warmly. He got straight to the point. "What can I do for you, Miss Faire? It's a busy morning. I don't have a lot of time."

"I'll make this quick. Maggie told me that Logan got upset while reading the May 24 newspaper in her kitchen. I've made a list of the stories that were in the sections he was reading that morning. Could you glance over the list and tell me if Logan had any connection to any of these stories or even the city where they happened?"

Ben looked the list over carefully.

"Nothing except London and Paris, which he went to on business a number of times," Ben said.

A co-worker of Logan's, Barney Foster, mentioned a couple of things I wanted to ask you about. He said Logan may have had a girlfriend in Brazil at one time. Did he ever..."

"That's not worth mentioning," he cut me off. "She was just one more of Logan's little love affairs. His friends knew not to take these things too seriously. Who wouldn't fall in love on Ipanema beach?"

"And Barney said Caroline is a Catholic."

"What does that have to do with anything?" He glanced back at the list. "Surely you don't think she was abused by a priest and Logan figured it out by reading the newspaper."

It did sound pretty silly when Ben said it, so I defended myself by saying, "I didn't think that was significant. I was just curious. I have a pretty strong theory about which story upset Logan."

"What?" he demanded with the great urgency I would expect from a best friend. "Which story?"

"I'm not ready to talk about it yet," I said, knowing full well I had no idea which story upset Logan. Ben seemed irritated at my coyness, which was quite understandable.

I thanked him and turned to leave and then had an afterthought.

"Did Logan know the land developer Ray Christie by any chance?"

"He hated Christie's guts."

"He did? Why?"

"He ranted and raved sometimes about how Christie was trying to rape the landscape in Memphis."
"Did he know Christie personally?"

"I got the impression he did, but I can't say for sure. Maybe he just hated him from afar."

• • • • • • • • • • • • • • • • •

I went back to the office and wrote my column and checked to see if Caroline had returned my call after she got out of school for the day. She hadn't. In fact, she never returned my call. But there was a message from the secretary of one of the Indonesian bankers. They had denied the request for an interview.

It was really late when I got home. I thought I had left a lamp on like I usually do when I know I'll be coming in after dark, which is most nights. But apparently I had forgotten.

I picked up the mail, unlocked the door, and turned on a lamp in the living room. I walked into the kitchen, and as I reached for the light switch, a glow in the corner caught my eye. I had left the computer on this morning. Then I realized, no, I hadn't. I didn't even check my e-mail this morning or read out-of-town papers online. I was too anxious to talk to Ben and Barney, so I left home early.

I walked toward the computer, and there on the screen were three short sentences: "Stop asking questions. Matter of life and death. Your friends are in danger."

I ran out the front door and locked myself in my car while I called Trent on my cell phone. He got to my house in less than 15 minutes, followed soon by a crime scene van. While I waited in the car, Trent went through the house, gun drawn, and found nobody. Then while the crime scene officer was dusting for fingerprints on the computer keyboard and on doorknobs, Trent and I went through the house and found nothing missing or out of place. In fact, there was no sign that the intruder had done anything besides leave the message.

"There was no forced entry," Trent said. "Does anybody else have a key to your house?"

"No."

"Most people give a key to a neighbor or a friend, in case they ever get locked out."

"I didn't need to do that, because...." I stopped guiltily.

"No, don't tell me you have a key under the flower pot or under the door mat?"

"I certainly do not," I said defensively. "I'm not that stupid. I keep it in a much better hiding place. It's under a big rock by the back door."

He engaged in much eye-rolling and sighing as I led him to the rock. I picked it up, and of course, there was no key under it."

"Okay, so I *am* that stupid."

"But smart enough to get the locks changed tomorrow and get an alarm installed, right?"

"Definitely. But what about tonight?"

"I know you're too stubbornly independent to want me to stay with you tonight."

"The hell I am. The only thing I'm stubborn about tonight is that there's no way you're leaving me alone. I've got an extra new toothbrush you can use, and you won't need your jammies, because you're sleeping fully clothed in the bed with me with your gun nearby at all times."

•••••••••••••

We lay side by side, not touching, for what seemed like hours, both of us flinching every time the house creaked, as old houses do, or the wind stirred a tree branch near the window. Finally, the tension and fear got to me, and I began trembling uncontrollably.

"Somebody was in my house, Jack," was all I could say.

He pulled me into his arms and held me until I finally fell asleep.

CHAPTER TWENTY-TWO

When I woke up, Trent wasn't in bed. I brushed my teeth and went to the kitchen and found him drinking coffee and thumbing through the Yellow Pages looking for alarm companies and locksmiths. He took his last sip of coffee as he stood up and pointed toward the phone book.

"Gotta go. I've got to go home and shower and change clothes, so I can get to work. Here are some alarm companies you can try. If they can't do it today, do you have a friend or relative you can stay with tonight?"

I nodded yes. "I think my friend Beth could put up with me for a night or two."

"Do you feel safe enough for me to leave you now?"

"Oh, sure. The monsters under the bed don't seem so scary in the light of day."

"You can joke, Britt, but I'm worried. Somebody is trying to intimidate you at best and hurt you at worst. I just wish the perp would make it clear what he's trying to get you to stop asking questions about."

"Maybe he or she thinks it's obvious."

"But it's not. Nosy reporters like you make a lot of people mad. The obvious one is Ray Christie, but then again he got his way with the City Council despite you, so that should be enough revenge. Besides, you really haven't been asking questions about Christie — you've just been writing about him."

"Maybe the threats are vague because the person doesn't want to point the finger too obviously at himself," I said. "Like maybe it *is* Ray Christie, but if he said, "Stay away from City Council," we'd know it was him, and..."

"And the cops would be all over him like white on rice. So he makes it vague, so that you're scared of everybody."

"Trent, I know this is far-fetched, but Logan's friend Ben told me Logan hated Ray Christie, because he's raping the landscape. Ben wasn't sure if Logan knew him personally or just hated him for his actions. What if the threat has to do with Christie *and* Logan? What if Christie had something to do with Logan's death?"

"You're right — that is far-fetched, very far-fetched, almost as far-fetched as Maggie Magee and the psychic's theory that the FBI killed Logan. But I guess we can't afford to overlook anything at this point. Gotta run. I'll call you when I find out anything about the fingerprints."

•••••••••••

"We got a perfect match," Trent said when he called me later that day.

"You did? Whose fingerprints are they?"

"Yours. Every one of the fingerprints are yours."

"But how could they know they are mine? I'm not a criminal in the FBI database."

"I guess you were too upset to remember that Crime Scene took your fingerprints for comparison."

"Oh," I said.

"But there is some good news."

"What?"

"I'm taking you out to dinner tomorrow night. Pick you up at 5:30, dress casually."

"5:30? Where are we going — Piccadilly Cafeteria for the Early Bird Special?"

"Don't ask questions. Just do as you're told, by order of The Memphis Police Department."

"Yes, officer."

•••••••••••••

I was wearing shorts and a T-shirt, the only sensible clothes during a Memphis summer, when Trent came for me the next day. It was a beautiful afternoon, hot, but bearable.

As we drove toward downtown, I gave Trent the run-down on my adventures with the alarm installers and locksmiths. I told him I felt safe and sound again.

"Well, once you get inside the house anyhow. I'd feel better if you had a garage with a door directly into the house."

"I guess I'll just have to take my chances walking from the car to the front door, all 10 feet of the way. I'm just glad I don't have to go inside wondering who's left me a message on my computer screen."

"There's a lot to be said for that."

"Where are we going?" I asked, as we pulled into the Mud

Island parking lot.

"Just get on the monorail and don't ask any questions. Can't you trust me just this oncdfe?"

"I always trust you — I just don't obey you, but maybe just this once."

After he parked his Explorer, Trent pulled a picnic basket from the back seat and insisted I wait for him to come around and open the door for me.

"That picnic basket looks brand new."

"Well, it's not. I've had it for years. I go on lots and lots of picnics."

"Then why is the price tag still hanging off the handle?"

"It is?" he said, jerking his head toward the basket.

"No, but I made you look," I said maturely.

"Great! I'm going on a picnic with a sixth grader," he said, but he was smiling.

We rode the monorail to the public-park end of Mud Island, not the Harbor Town end. I hadn't been out here in years, not since I was a kid and the park was first built with its river museum and exact-to-scale replica of The Mighty Mississippi that runs the length of the park.

I was impressed with all the new landscaping and the addition of tables with chairs and umbrellas. Instead of sitting at one of the tables to eat whatever fast food Trent had put in the picnic basket, he directed me further down the island to a front-porch-style swing on an A-frame facing the Arkansas side of the river. We sat down and put the basket between us, and he began pulling out the goodies, which were goodier than I expected — fried chicken, potato salad, fruit salad, crusty bread with butter and a bottle of red wine. I told him how glad I was he didn't bring bread and cheese or some other pseudo-European meal. The fried chicken looked like KFC or Jack

Pirtle's, but the potato salad looked homemade.

"Who made the potato salad?"

"Who indeed! I indeed."

"You just don't seem like somebody who would know how to make homemade potato salad?"

"That's just your cop bias again. Any time I do anything sophisticated or domestic or kind, you always say you wouldn't expect that from a cop. Why do you hate cops so much?" he said handing me a plate and fork.

"I don't hate cops. I just, well, you aren't like most cops I've known."

"Well, get used to it," he said, plopping a huge spoon of potato salad onto my plate. "White or dark meat?"

After dinner, mindful of the time, since the park closes at 8 p.m., we started talking about the river and movies.

"Did you ever see *An American in Paris?*" he asked.

"Of course. I fell madly in love with Gene Kelly when I saw it on TV when I was in college and was crushed to find out he was already an old man by then."

"My two favorite scenes are 'I've Got Rhythm' that he did with the kids and when he danced on the banks of the Seine with Leslie Caron."

"To *Our Love Is Here to Stay.* I love that scene," I said. "I've always vowed that if I ever got to go to Paris, I would grab some passerby and make him dance with me on the banks of the Seine like Gene and Leslie."

Trent stood up and pulled me to my feet. "You don't have to wait for Paris. We've got a river right here."

We began dancing, ala Kelly and Caron, while Trent sang in an only slightly off-key voice, *Our Love Is Here to Stay*, and then segued into *Moon River*.

"I can't believe you can dance so well," I said, truly impressed.

"Don't tell me, let me guess — cops aren't supposed to be able to dance any way except line dancing."

"I didn't mean to imply..." I was cut off by his kissing me.

"So do I kiss like a cop?"

"I don't know. You're the only cop I've ever kissed."

"Well, that's one bit of good news," he said, as we slumped into the swing.

"Unless you count all the guys down at the West Precinct."

We both laughed.

"When I kissed you just now, I'm surprised you didn't freak out."

"Well, it helped that after you kissed me on top of my head the other night and slept in the bed with me that you didn't suddenly start acting proprietary."

"Well, after waiting years for this first kiss, I'm not about to ruin it by suddenly acting like your boyfriend or something. I know you too well, Britt. Are you skittish with all men or just with me?"

"Just you."

"Why? Because I'm a cop?"

"Maybe. I've never really thought cops were my type."

"Your type? You actually think all cops are of one type?"

"Not fair, is it? But it's not just that — also I didn't want to ruin a great friendship with you by getting romantic."

"Can't two people be friends and romantic?"

"Not in my experience."

We realized it was almost eight, so we packed up our picnic basket and headed back to the monorail.

When we got back to my house, he walked me to the door and kissed me goodnight.

"Let's get one thing straight," I said weakly. "We are definitely not dating. Don't call me when you get home and don't call me in the morning."

He smiled and kissed me again. "Yes, we definitely are not dating."

"Everything is just like it always was," I said firmly and then promptly set off the house alarm that I forgot I had.

The next morning, against my better judgment, I woke up thinking about Jack Trent. Nothing dreamy and love-like — just that happy, high-schooly feeling you have when you suddenly realize you have a crush on the boy who sits next to you in biology.

CHAPTER TWENTY-THREE

My burglar alarm installed and my locks changed, it didn't take me long to start feeling secure again, secure enough that I regularly forgot to turn on the alarm system when I left or went to bed. Life returned to normal — eating out every day, doing things with friends, working long hours, reading out-of-town newspapers online and reading novels that I hold in my hot little hands.

Jack called often enough, but not too much. We had had dinner together once since the Mud Island picnic two weeks before. I had turned him down a couple of times, and he always accused me of not knowing how to relax.

That's so not fair — I know how to chill. What about all the reading I do? Well, Jack's answer is that even when I read, I probably do it with intensity and purpose. I say it depends on how you define intensity and purpose.

And I listen to music a lot and sometimes it's very laid-back music, like Brazilian jazz. Jack's answer to that is that I probably get up and bossa nova with myself while I'm listening. How could he know that? I accused him of being a peeping tom.

I spend some time every morning and sometime in the evening with my laptop reading emails from readers about my columns.

I also do a lot of e-mailing. Sometimes I get a hundred or more e-mails from readers in one day. I get some great e-mails about my column, both positive and negative, and if they're half-way reasonable, I try to write a brief response. If they're wacked out, I always respond, "Thank you for reading my column. I appreciate your feedback." I don't read anything from the online comments section of the paper because they don't identify themselves and therefore are written off by me as cowards.

I was plowing through my column e-mails one Tuesday night when a new one came in. That's unusual, unless it's a personal e-mail, because most business e-mails are sent in the morning right after they read my column. This email address was vague and didn't contain a name.

The e-mail simply said: *"If you are serious about investigating the death of Logan Magee, meet me in San Antonio, Texas, soon. I know everything."*

I read it several times before I hit the reply button.

"Who are you? How do you know everything?"

Almost immediately, I got a response: *"You'll have to trust me, but believe me, I know everything. You won't be sorry you came."*

"Why should I trust you?" I wrote back. *"I don't even know who you are, much less what makes you credible."*

He or she replied: *"Let me know when you decide whether you're coming or not."*

"I'll get back to you," I wrote.

I wanted to talk to somebody about this, but who? Jack would freak big time, trying to make me promise not to even consider meeting some stranger in another city. This person could be a murderer, Jack would say. Maybe he or she knows everything because he or she killed Logan. That's what Jack would say, and he would have a good point. Still.

And Nora and Beth and all my other friends and family would tell me I was crazy to even consider such a thing. I couldn't talk to Maggie about it, because she would be torn between fearing for me and wanting desperately to know what this person knows or claims to know. I couldn't talk to Caroline or Ben, because I don't entirely trust either one of them.

So I talked to myself. A lot. I would be crazy to go, but I would be crazy *not* to go, too. If this person knows something, I could give Maggie some closure about Logan — maybe I could even talk this person into going to the police with the information. I can be pretty persuasive when I put my mind to it.

But I kept coming back to why. Why me, why now, just plain why? And don't forget why not? Well, that was easy. Why not, because I could get myself killed.

An hour later I was back at the computer: *"You won't tell me why I should trust you. At least tell me why you trust me."*

"That's a good question — I would expect no less from a good reporter. I trust you because your column reflects integrity. Most of all, I trust you because Maggie Magee trusts you."

Wow, he or she hooked me with that one, but I didn't reply. I needed to argue with myself more. Who would know Maggie trusted me? I guess a lot of people might. I didn't know how many friends or others she had told about my trying to help her. I never told her to keep it a secret. I picked up the phone and called Maggie. After some small talk I asked her, "By the way, Maggie, did Logan have any friends or associates in San Antonio, Texas? Do you know anybody there?"

No to both questions, she said, but of course, Logan was a grown man who traveled a lot — he could have known people in many places that his mother wouldn't necessarily know about. Good point. Of course, I didn't tell her why I was asking. When she asked why I wanted to know, I said, "Just curious."

And Barney, Logan's work friend, knew she trusted me, as did Caroline and Ben. Ben. Something kept sticking in my mind about Ben. What was it?

I went to bed still trying to decide what to do and trying to remember why Ben came to my mind in all this. What was it I couldn't put my finger on?

The next morning, I called one of the computer guys at the paper and asked if anonymous e-mails could be traced. He said it wouldn't be easy if the person sending the e-mail were clever in signing up for his e-mail address and provider.

"But if some crazy person is threatening you, we could probably get a court order," Lou said.

Not necessary, I told Lou. Just curious.

I was getting dressed for work when the Ben connection popped back into mind. What is it I was trying to remember. Was it something in his office, something he said?

I watched again the video that Ben had made, the Logan retrospective. Toward the end, among the very recent shots, there it was, what I was trying to remember: Logan and Ben at a Redbirds game. Ben was wearing a T-shirt that said: "Don't Mess with Texas."

I know what you're thinking — Texas is the most narcissistic state in the Union. I went to Dallas once and at the hotel dining room, they had waffles shaped like Texas. Most tourists who go to Texas bring back a bumper sticker, T-shirt or something else about Texas, and "Don't Mess with Texas" is a popular one. Still, I wondered about Ben.

I sat down at the computer again and sent this: *"When and where?"*

I got an immediate response — doesn't this person do anything but sit at the computer and wait for my e-mails? *"You say when you can get here, and I'll tell you exactly where and what time."*

••••••••••••••••••

When I got to the office, I went directly into the managing editor's office to ask about using some of my paltry travel budget.

"Otis, you know homeless issues are important to me, and I was thinking about going out to San Antonio to write a series of columns about a homeless shelter there."

"Why San Antonio?"

"Well, I saw a mention in a New York Times Magazine article about a foundation that is doing some innovative things for the homeless, things to get them off the streets permanently whenever possible. Things Memphis could learn from. They're doing it in several cities — New York, Chicago, San Francisco, but I chose San Antonio, because the city is more comparable to Memphis."

I know this sounds like a big, fat lie, but it was mostly true. Homelessness is a big issue for me — I write about it fairly often, and I did read that about a foundation. The lie is that I had chosen San Antonio for the story. Actually, I had planned to go to either Chicago, because I have a journalist friend there I'd like to see, or New York, because I'd like an excuse to go to New York for a few days. So now, I would go to San Antonio, write about the program for the homeless and while I was there, talk to this person who claims to know everything about Logan's death.

Otis trusts me, so it was an easy sell. Against my better judgment, I immediately booked a flight for Friday with return on Monday. I e-mailed this possible ax-murderer that I would be arriving day after tomorrow, and he or she responded immediately telling me a restaurant name and time on Friday.

"How will I know you?" I wrote.

"That late, there won't be many people there, so just sit at the most isolated table available (so we won't be overheard). I'll find you."

He or she will find me — does that mean the person knows

what I look like? How could they know that unless they know me already? My picture doesn't run with my column, and I asked not to have my photo on the paper's website. On the bright side, we'd be meeting in a public place. How dangerous could that be?

But there was still a risk that I was doing something really stupid, so I knew I needed a back-up safety plan. I came up with this: I would confide in one person, maybe Drew, who would tell me this is dangerous, but wouldn't try to stop me — he knows it wouldn't do any good. I'd give him the restaurant name, address and time of the meeting, and tell him that if I don't call him by a certain time, to call the San Antonio cops. Then the cops could search for my body.

•••••••••••••

Thursday night I had trouble sleeping. I was excited but also having second thoughts about the trip. Just how stupid was it to be flying to San Antonio, where I don't know my way around and don't know anybody, to meet a person (I didn't even know if it was a man or woman) who might be a murderer? But then again, how exciting would it be to find somebody who could tell me why Logan died and who murdered him. I might be able to help Maggie and get a great story, too. It's a reporter's dream come true. Then Daniel Pearl came to mind. Look what happened to him when he rendezvoused with a secret source in Pakistan.

I packed a small bag. I'm not one of those women who takes everything she owns for a three-night trip. One pair of black pants and jacket and a reversible silk shell, purple on one side and hot pink on the other, and maybe a no-wrinkle dress. A few toiletries, underwear, a gown and I was set.

There was a little room left in the bag, so I looked around to see if I was forgetting anything. I had a book, but I would carry that on the plane to read during the flight. I spotted the DVDs of Logan and Caroline's rehearsal dinner and the Logan retrospective and the photo of Logan and Caroline, all lying on a table nearby, so I threw them in, too. Maybe the person I was meeting would be in one of them.

I ate a peanut and jelly sandwich with the last of the bread, inspecting it first for mold, and poured myself a big glass of milk, smelling it first to be sure it wasn't sour. Groceries sometimes outlive their shelf life in my house.

Then I waited for Jack to pick me up. I had asked him to give me a ride to the airport. Why? Because I needed not to feel so alone? Or maybe because I wanted to see him one more time before I threw myself into harm's way? Or maybe because being around Jack always makes me feel brave.

He was smiling when I answered the door, but he didn't attempt to kiss me. That's good, right? He took my bag to the car, and we chatted about a murder that had been in the paper that day. The nice thing about knowing a cop is you can always get the inside scoop — who they really suspect and other stuff you don't read in the paper the first day.

As we approached the airport, I was sorry it wasn't later in the day so the lights of the airport would be on. Each terminal of the Memphis airport looks like a tray of martini glasses, especially at night, and I think it is very pretty.

When we got to the Southwest terminal departing level, I hopped out of Trent's car. He calls it a truck, but to me only pick-up trucks and 18-wheelers are trucks. SUVs are cars.

He took my bag out and handed it to me and seemed conflicted about whether to kiss me goodbye.

"Remind me of why we aren't dating?" he asked.

"Because I can't date somebody I call by his last name."

"Then call me by my first name. I don't mind."

I just smiled and walked toward the airport door. As he got back in the car, I shouted my thanks for the lift.

"Bye, Jack," I said then, but he had already driven away.

On the plane, once they said it was okay, I listened to my I-Pod instead of reading. I was listening to Astrud Gilberto's gentle voice to try to relax, but when she did Manha de Carnival, I sighed deeply. She sang it in Portuguese, but when it is recorded in English, it's called "A Day in the Life of a Fool." My theme song today.

CHAPTER TWENTY-FOUR

After I got settled into the hotel, I tried to take a nap, but I was too excited and nervous. The next few hours were endless. About 8:30 I left for the restaurant in a cab. The restaurant was small, but looked fairly respectable. The sign said it was the best Tex-Mex in the city, but I was not hungry.

I sat down in the most secluded part of the dimly lit restaurant and had a Dos Equis while I waited. Nine o'clock, the appointed time came, but nobody came in who seemed interested in me. I called Drew as planned, so he wouldn't call the cops. A few minutes later, a man walked in and looked around, but then went over to a group of men and women on the other side of the restaurant.

At 9:30 I called Drew and then again at 10. At 10:30, I told him I was leaving, but I wanted to talk to him while I waited for a cab, in case the no-show was lying in wait outside for me. Once in the cab, I promised him I would call again when I was safely locked in my hotel room.

After calling Drew from my room, I e-mailed the supposed informant. Maybe he or she looked into the restaurant windows and saw me on the phone and got spooked off. My e-mail asked why he or she didn't show and asked for another chance. For the first time, there was no immediate response. In fact, when I checked my e-mail for the last time at 2 a.m., I still had not heard from the person I had flown 700 miles to meet. A day in the life of a fool ended when I drifted off to sleep a few minutes later.

•••••••••••

I spent all day Saturday at the homeless shelter and interviewing some of the leaders of the program, who took me to talk to some of their success stories — people who were no longer homeless. That evening, the program's director, a really nice guy named Brandon Diaz, and his wife took me to dinner.

Throughout the day and even during dinner, I sneaked off and checked my e-mail. Nothing, not a word. I fell into bed exhausted as soon as I got in from dinner.

On Sunday morning I slept late, and then over brunch alone I had time to think about what an idiot I was. At first, when I realized he or she wasn't going to show up, my first reaction was fear. Was I lured here to be killed? But when Sunday morning came and there had been no attempt on my life, I felt angry that I had been duped.

But why had this person lured me to San Antonio and not shown up. I thought of every possible reason:

• He or she chickened out.

• He or she saw me on the phone and thought I had entrapped them.

• It was some silly act of revenge by somebody like Ray Christie, who wanted me to waste my time and the paper's money and feel like a fool.

Or it could be something more sinister — the person I was to meet was found out and killed before he or she could meet me. Jack would probably tell me I've seen too many gangster movies about stool pigeons getting bumped off. But those things do happen.

I sat around my room all afternoon, trying to work on my column about the homeless shelter, but mostly I just sulked. I considered doing the touristy things like seeing The Alamo, but I wasn't in the mood. I just wanted to go home, but my flight wasn't until the next afternoon.

Then it hit me. I was so busy nursing my hurt pride at being made a fool of that I hadn't thought of another possible reason I had been lured to Texas. What if somebody wanted me out of Memphis for some reason? Maybe they wanted to search my house without fear I'd walk in. Did I turn on the burglar alarm when I left? I wasn't sure.

A worse scenario came to me then and I panicked. I remembered the message left on my computer screen a couple of weeks ago: "Stop asking questions. Matter of life or death. Your friends in danger."

I grabbed the phone and called all my close friends to be sure they were okay. Then I called Jack.

"Jack, I think I forgot to turn on my house alarm. Would you go to my house and check to be sure somebody hasn't broken in?"

"Well, since you called me Jack instead of Trent, I'll be glad to. You sound panicked, Britt."

"I guess these threats have made me a little paranoid, but I'd feel better if you'd check."

"You haven't gotten any more threats have you?"

"No, no, of course not. I just need a little reassurance."

Jack called me half an hour later from my house and said everything looked locked up tight. I thanked him and told him not to worry about picking me up at the airport on Monday. My friend, Nora, who doesn't see patients on Monday, would do it.

Okay, obviously I had come to San Antonio on a wild-goose chase. And I had wasted my travel funds on San Antonio when I could be in New York or Chicago. Well, San Antonio seemed like a nice city — maybe I should try to see a little of it before I left. So I asked the concierge for some suggestions and had a great meal on the picturesque little river that winds through part of the city. Then, like a dutiful tourist, I took a water taxi ride on the river. I was thoroughly enjoying the meandering boat ride when I noticed that one hotel was very close to the river. Many of the windows were well-lit, and it was odd how clearly you could see the people inside some of the hotel rooms.

Suddenly, I sat up straight in my seat. One of the windows revealed a very familiar face. It was Logan. I just knew it. It had to be. I had watched those videos too many times not to recognize him. The man in the window was a little thinner than the Logan of the video and his hair a little longer, but I knew it was Logan. I just knew it. He was talking to someone else in the room, but I couldn't see who. They seemed to be arguing.

Could Logan somehow be alive and living in San Antonio? I watched desperately as the boat moved further and further away from the window. All I had time to do was count the number of floors and the number of windows from the left.

At the boat's next stop, I got off and ran back to the hotel. I looked up and saw the room's lights were off now. I took the elevator to the third floor and counted doors until I knew I had seen Logan in Room 304. I knocked on the door, my heart racing, my eyes blurred with anticipation. Nobody answered, so I went downstairs to the registration desk and asked for Logan Magee and was told there was no such guest there.

"I'm sure he was in Room 304," I said.

The clerk looked at the computer and said another guest was registered in 304.

"Could you tell me the name? Maybe the room is registered in his friend's name."

Of course, the answer was no. Only in the movies can you trick hotel clerks into giving you such top-secret information. I went back to my hotel, which wasn't far away, and got the photo of

Caroline and Logan and took it back to the other hotel. I showed it to the clerk and asked if this was the man staying in 304. He said no, and I believed him. There was no sign of recognition in his face.

I walked back outside and looked up at the third floor, fourth window from the left, which was still dark. I sat in the lobby for a long time, hoping to see Logan or a man who looked like Logan come through the lobby, but that never happened.

I went back to my hotel, doubting my sanity, but still not completely convinced I hadn't seen Logan Magee. I slept fitfully, and I had to get to the airport by 1 p.m., but I took the photo and went back to the other hotel and went to the day desk clerk.

"This is my cousin," I said, showing the photo to the clerk. "He said he would meet me here, but he hasn't shown up. Have you seen a man who looks like this?"

The answer was no, so I went to the third floor and showed the picture to every housekeeper I could find. One spoke English and helped me canvass the others, but nobody thought Logan looked familiar. One housekeeper said, "Man in 304 check out. Not handsome like your friend."

My friend, my imaginary friend is more like it. But I still had the tiniest of hope that Logan was alive. On the flight home, I kept looking at Logan's picture and asking myself if this was really the man I saw in the hotel window. I wasn't sure anymore. All I was sure of was that I wanted him to be alive more than anything.

CHAPTER TWENTY-FIVE

As soon as I got into Nora's car at the Memphis Airport, I blurted it out — I had seen Logan Magee in a hotel window in San Antonio. Nora didn't gasp or act excited, she just listened. When I finished my story, she looked me straight in the eyes and said bluntly, "Britt, you are so wrapped up in this case that you see what you want to see. With all the Hispanic people in Texas, there are thousands of men who from a distance might look like Logan with his half-Asian dark good looks. But that's not the point. The point is that you've become so obsessed with Logan and his mother and his friends and trying to find out who killed him that you've lost your balance."

"What are you saying, that I've imagined the whole thing? Did I imagine the e-mail telling me to come to San Antonio?"

"I don't pretend to know who e-mailed you or why. I'm just saying that once you made that trip to San Antonio and the guy didn't show up, then you were subject to the power of suggestion. You saw Logan in the window, because Logan is all you think about any more."

"So I just imagined the whole thing?" I said again, more indignantly.

"Logan is the perfect man to you, Britt, because you don't really know him, and he can never fall off his pedestal, because he's dead."

"But Logan loved Caroline," I protested.

"It doesn't matter who Logan loved. It's who you love."

"That's ridiculous, Nora. I admit I may be a little overly focused, and I would love to give Maggie back her dead son, but I am not in love with him. I'm not that crazy."

"I never said you were crazy. Just understandably obsessed," Nora said. "Britt, promise me you won't tell Logan's mother or anyone else who loved him that you think he's alive. Promise me, Britt."

"I wouldn't build their hopes up like that. That would be cruel beyond imagining."
"I'm glad we agree. Now, what can you do to regain your balance? How about a vacation or throwing away those videos you've watched way too much?"

"I'll give it some serious consideration," I said, knowing I would make a beeline for Jack Trent to tell him what I saw in San Antonio. Would he think I was crazy, too? Probably, but he had that suspicious cop mind that would at least consider any theory for a minute or two.

After Nora dropped me off at home, I called Trent on his cell phone. He was at his office and said he would be in for a while and was glad I was coming by, because he had something to tell me. That's all he would say.

When I opened his office door half an hour later, Trent looked like he was about to give me bad news.

"What's going on, Jack?" He looked pleased that I had used his first name, but immediately returned to his sober look.

"The Logan Magee case has been solved," he said.

"Somebody confessed?"

"Yes, somebody confessed, but not to murder. A truck driver, who was passing through Memphis a year ago on May 25 about 3 a.m. came in about two hours ago to say that he saw a man fitting Logan's description jump from the bridge into the river. He said there was a dark BMW nearby and nobody else around."

My legs went weak. My throat was dry. I had to sit down.

"Why has it taken him a year to come forward?"

"That was my first question. He said he was using pills to stay awake that night and had been driving longer than he was legally supposed to, so he was afraid to stop or even call the police. He said he was sure somebody else saw the jumper and would call the cops, so he didn't. But on his way back through four days later, he was talking to a guy who works at one of the truck stops in West Memphis, who was talking about a rich guy whose car was found on the bridge on his wedding day, and how they weren't sure what happened to him. The driver went on his way, but his conscience has been bothering him ever since, he said. So he came forward and told the truth today. He said he figured the only thing worse than having somebody you love die would be not knowing how he died."

But I wasn't sure he was right about that. For a year Maggie and Caroline could cling to the belief that Logan didn't intentionally take himself away from them. Now that small comfort would be denied them.

"Have you told Maggie yet?"

"No, I wanted to tell you first and see how you think we should handle it. I'll tell her or you can, whichever you think will be easiest on her."

"I *want* you to do it, Jack, because I'm a terrible coward when it comes to things like this, but I think it would be better for Maggie if I did it. We've become friends these last few weeks, and I think she should hear it from a friend. I think she would be more likely to believe me, too. It's time for denial to end, mine as well as hers."

"Well, one thing we know now — it must have been Ray Christie who was threatening you."

"I guess so, but there's always a possibility that Logan's suicide had darker implications, that he killed himself out of guilt, a guilt that he shared with somebody else, somebody who didn't want the truth to come out from my snooping."

•••••••••••••

Jack wanted to take me out to dinner that night, but I told him I needed some time alone to think about how I was going to break this news to Maggie.

I ate a bowl of cereal for dinner and wandered aimlessly around my house, trying to figure it all out. I knew Nora would strongly disapprove, but I watched the two videos again and felt even sadder knowing Logan had killed himself, than I had felt thinking he had been murdered.

I concluded that Nora must have been right about me imagining Logan in the hotel window, but the e-mail question just wouldn't go away. I read the e-mail again. *"If you are serious about investigating the death of Logan Magee, meet me in San Antonio, Texas, soon. I know everything."*

When I got it, I assumed the person meant he or she knew about Logan's murder, but as I reread the e-mail, I saw that it said death, not murder, so maybe this person knew why Logan killed himself. Could it have been the truck driver who sent the e-mail and then decided to go to the police instead of meeting with me? No chance — some trucker driver passing through wouldn't know I was involved in investigating Logan's death and sure wouldn't have any reason to want me to come to San Antonio.

Maybe instead, it was Logan's partner in guilt who e-mailed

me. Or was it somebody who hated Logan enough to want the world to know why he died?

I left my house about midnight and drove down to the river. I sat for a long time on Drew's and my bench in Tom Lee Park, staring into the water to which Logan had surrendered his life. Memphis sits on a high bluff of the river, so most people never get close to the water itself. From the bluff, you can see the turbulence of the fast-moving water, especially when a tree or something else large is rushing down river, but the river is always silent from the bluffs. I imagined that when Logan jumped from the bridge, there was no sound at all until he hit the water.

I stood up, walked to the edge of the bluff and hurled the two DVD's into the river.

"Goodbye, Logan Magee. Rest in peace."

CHAPTER TWENTY-SIX

The next day when I had gotten over the initial shock that Logan had actually killed himself, I have to admit there was a part of me that was relieved. Looking for Logan's murderer had really taken over my life and my head, and maybe now I would be able to get back to my real life.

But I was heartsick for Maggie. I'm sure an amateur shrink would say I was attached to Maggie because I was seeking a mother figure in my life, but that was baloney. I have a perfectly good mother figure in my life already, thank you very much. The mother figure in my life is supplied by my mother, who I talk to regularly since she moved to Florida after retiring as a high school English teacher.

"Retiring to Florida is such a cliché, Mom," I said when she told me that she and dad were selling the house and taking off.

"So we're supposed to retire to Minnesota, just so we won't be a cliché?"

Mom's a hoot. No, Maggie isn't a mother substitute. I just like her. She's my friend, and I guess I hoped I could help her deal with her son's death by finding out it was an accident or who murdered him.

I called Maggie early the next morning and asked if I could

come over. While driving out to Harbor Town, I wasn't sure what I was going to say, but one conclusion I had come to: People with no problems don't jump off bridges. Maggie, Ben or Caroline had been holding out on me. One or all of them knew something about Logan that they hadn't told me, something important, a reason he would kill himself.

It was a perfect summer morning. I hated to ruin this beautiful day and perhaps all beautiful days to come for Maggie. But she deserved to know the truth, and so did I.

●●●●●●●●●●●●●●

Maggie normally offers me coffee and goodies when I visit her, but not this day. She sensed that this was not a casual social call.

"Something's happened," she said. "Do you know who killed Logan?"

I nodded sadly. "Maggie, a witness has come forward who saw Logan jump from the bridge. He was alone and near the BMW on the bridge."

We both had tears in our eyes. I expected her to argue with me, but she only sat there, silently willing it not to be true. Only when I put my arms around her and pulled her to my chest did she let the sobs rush out. After a very long time, she sat up straight and blew her nose on a paper towel she had in her hand and looked me straight in the face.

"I just didn't want to believe it. Can you blame me?"

"No, Maggie, of course I don't blame you, but the one thing you owe me is the truth. I think either you or Ben or Caroline knows some reason Logan might have wanted to end his life."

"Maybe the test came back positive. Maybe he didn't tell me the truth or maybe he found out the day before the wedding that there had been a mistake, and he had it after all."

"Had what, Maggie?"

"The gene."

"What gene?"

"The gene for Huntington's Chorea." She could tell from my face that I had never heard of Huntington's Chorea, so she explained. "It's a rare hereditary disease. If one of your parents has the gene, you have a 50/50 chance of having it. If you have the gene, you have a 100 percent chance of getting it."

"Is that what your husband died of?"

"My husband isn't dead. He's in a nursing home where he's been since he was 44 years old. His mother had it, but nobody knew back then that it was inherited. Most people don't have symptoms until they're 35 or older, and by that time they've had children and passed on the gene to some or all of them. Mack and one sister both got the gene, but their other three sisters didn't. Mack got the first symptoms when he was in his early 30s when Logan was four, so we decided not to have other children."

"Couldn't you use genetic testing to find out if Logan had the gene?"

"Our doctor advised against it. He said it's usually best not to know."

"But why? Isn't early detection important in treating or curing it?"

"There is no cure, Britt, not even any treatment. It's a death sentence, a horrible, agonizing, lingering death sentence. People with Huntington's usually die from choking or falling or from heart disease. It usually takes 10 to 20 years to kill you, but you and your family will wish you were dead a long time before that. I watched what happened to my mother-in-law and then to Mack, and my greatest fear was that it would happen to Logan, too."

"What does it do to you?"

"It causes all kinds of erratic movements that come on gradually and eventually you become insane. They call it dementia, but when you've got dementia and you're only in your forties, it seems like insanity. My husband's first symptoms were depression and irritability and then he became argumentative and did things very impulsively. Before that he had the sunniest disposition you could imagine. That's why we knew something was terribly wrong. He had to quit work and go on disability by the time he was 40. By 44 he was too violent and uncontrollable, so I had to put him in St. Francis nursing home, so he wouldn't hurt me or Logan."

"But how could you live knowing Logan might have the gene, but not knowing for sure?"

"Think about it, Britt. The only thing worse than the possibility of having the gene is knowing you definitely have it. That's why most doctors advise against genetic testing. If you have it, but you don't know it, you can at least enjoy 35 or 40 good years and have some hope. But if you know you have it, you'll probably commit suicide when you find out. That's the only reason I can think of that Logan would jump off that bridge."

"When was he tested?"

"Well, he never wanted to know, said he wasn't tempted to find out, but when he and Caroline started dating seriously, of course, he told her about his dad and what might happen to him. She played it down, so he took her to see his dad at the nursing home. She was shaken up badly, but later when she calmed down, she said she wanted to marry him without knowing. They would just adopt, instead of having children, and take their chances on Logan. At first he accepted that, since he had lived his whole life that way, but as the wedding approached, he told me that he was going to be secretly tested and if he was positive for the gene he was going to call off the wedding, but he told me the test came back negative. So I don't know if he lied to me or if he found out just before the wedding that there had been a mistake. If he had the gene, he was probably just a few years away from developing symptoms. After watching what it has done to his dad, I can see why he would prefer a quick death."

With that, Maggie collapsed into sobs again, and I held her for a long time before she calmed down.

••••••••••••••

The next day, I made an appointment with Ben, telling him it was very important, that there had been a break in the case.

When I got to his office, I told him right away about the new witness who had come forward. He didn't seem surprised.

"I told you all along, Miss Faire, that I was convinced it was suicide."

"But why?"

"Only God and Logan know."

"I think a third person knows — you."

"You don't know what you're talking about. When are you going to get out of our lives and leave us alone?" It was a far more defensive reaction than I expected.

"Ben, did Logan find out just before the wedding that he had the gene for Huntington's Chorea?" He looked confused and then he answered.

"Yes, Caroline insisted that he find out before the wedding, and the test was positive."

"Why didn't he just call off the wedding?"

"He thought it was better this way. He didn't want to put Caroline in that position of either calling off the wedding and feeling guilty about it or marrying him against her better judgment. So he didn't tell her the bad news."

"I'm sorry," I said and walked out.

•••••••••••

As I drove away, I couldn't understand why Ben and Maggie's stories weren't exactly the same, and I still couldn't understand why the newspaper had upset Logan that day. Was there a story on Huntington's Chorea in the newspaper that day? I had already called the paper and told them I wasn't coming in today, so I went home and got the May 24 newspaper out once again.

I saw a quote in one of the stories on my list that I had never noticed before, and suddenly I felt I knew why Logan Magee had to die.

CHAPTER TWENTY-SEVEN

I knew who killed Logan and why, but I couldn't figure out exactly how. I was reasonably sure they didn't take him to a busy bridge and push him off. The car was probably left on the bridge before or after they killed him so that everyone would assume it was suicide.

Another thing I wasn't sure of was what to do next. Would even Jack Trent believe my unproven and perhaps unprovable theory about who killed Logan Magee and why? I tried to fight my creeping paranoia. Would I be considered one of those whacked out conspiracy buffs, who can never accept reasonable explanations for crimes?

All of this should have had my full attention, and yet I couldn't stop thinking about Logan and Huntington's Chorea and what his life would have been like if he had lived long enough to develop symptoms. I even went to St. Francis nursing home to see Mack Magee — something I never admitted to anyone until now. I didn't get past the open door of the room he shared with another victim of dementia — the difference between them being that the roommate looked to be in his 80s and Mack Magee was clearly middle aged.

Logan's father, whom I had seen in Logan's early childhood

photos in Ben's video collage, was no longer the smiling husband and father of the photos. His dark, wavy hair was now shaven military style, and he was tied into the wheelchair he sat in. And it wasn't the usual restraint across the chest to keep the patient from falling out of the chair — Mack Magee had the chest restraints but he also had his arms and legs tied down. He was one moment limp and listless and the next moment struggling to move, jerking his head about wildly. His eyes were empty and lost. At least he never had to know his son was dead. I left without a word to him or the nurses.

I didn't cry until I was driving down Park a few minutes later, and then huge sobs broke out of me without warning. Drivers next to me in traffic were looking at me, probably trying to decide whether to keep their distance from such an emotionally out-of-control driver.

The purpose of my visit had been to feel better about Logan's murder. I thought if I saw Mack Magee it would make me realize that Logan might have only had a few good years left anyhow and that sudden death, even murder, was better than this kind of suffering. Instead, my visit to the nursing home had the opposite effect — it made Logan's death seem all the more tragic, like a beautiful butterfly captured in a net and killed for some kid's collection during the final hours of its naturally short lifespan. Isn't life more precious when you know it might be short?

I had to shake this melancholy off, so I called Jack Trent, who I wasn't ready to share my revelation with yet, but who I thought could help me with one sticking point. If Logan was murdered by who I thought he was and for the reason I believed to be true, who was this truck driver who claimed to have seen Logan jump off the bridge and why was he lying? And the e-mail still made no sense since nobody met me in San Antonio and nobody tried to kill me. Unless Logan's murderers killed the e-mail informant before he could meet me. But, of course, I couldn't discuss that part with Jack, since I was embarrassed to tell him about my Texas wild-goose chase.

The phone rang only once. "Homicide. Trent."

"Jack, it's Britt."

"Hey, kiddo." It always gave me a little thrill to hear his voice go from gruff, tough homicide detective to teddy bear when he realized it was me.

"I need a favor."

"Don't you always? I've given up on expecting you to call just for the pleasure of talking to me," he said, but there was no real complaint in his voice. "What can I do for you, kid?"

"You know that truck driver who came in and confessed that he witnessed Logan Magee jumping off the bridge? Didn't that seem a little convenient, him showing up just when we were putting together a case for murder?"

"Are you kidding? Of course it did. The only person less trusting than a reporter is a homicide cop. I checked him out. He really is a trucker who travels through Memphis regularly."

"Were there any records to prove he was traveling through here on May 24 or 25 of last year?"

"He's a wild-cat trucker, who works for a couple of dozen small businesses, and he couldn't remember who he was driving for that day."

"Did you ask him for all the company names and then call them to verify?"

"I spot checked a few, and they all confirmed he drives for them sometimes, but nobody had a record on that particular day."

"Why didn't you call them all?"

"Get real, Britt. That would have taken days."

"But isn't that your job?"

"My job is to investigate homicides, and this is a homicide investigation to you, but not to the Memphis Police Department. To MPD, it's a closed suicide case."

"But..."

"But nothing. Britt, I just don't have time for this. I'm working a double homicide in East Memphis. Here's the trucker's name and phone number — check him out yourself, call him if you want to. "

So I did. All I could find out about Russell "Rusty" Martin through public records was that he was from Oklahoma, had been divorced twice and arrested a couple of times for minor offenses — a bar brawl and disorderly conduct at a football game. His driving record was perfect. He didn't answer his phone when I called several times and he never returned my calls.

Rusty Martin seemed legit, but one thing I couldn't accept as a coincidence — he lived in Castroville, Texas, a little town outside of San Antonio.

Was he the one who e-mailed me? I wondered if he had changed his mind about talking to me in San Antonio and decided to go to the Memphis cops. No, that didn't make any sense. Or was it possible he was going to tell me the truth, but instead drove to Memphis and lied to the cops?

CHAPTER TWENTY-EIGHT

I was so sure I was right about Logan's murder, but when I imagined myself telling it to Jack Trent or anybody else, it sounded so far-fetched. I now regretted telling Jack all my earlier half-baked theories about Logan's death. They made the truth seem like just one more figment of my imagination.

And yet I had to tell somebody who could reopen the case and arrest the murderer or murderers. Of course, they'd have to have some pretty good evidence before they could charge anybody with murder, and I had no idea how we would do that?

I made an appointment with Jack, but I was anything but confident as I walked into his office. He was on the phone and as he hung up and looked at me, I thought I saw a look of affection mixed with annoyance.

"Hey, Britt. I can't give you much time, but you said it was important."

"Jack, if I've ever needed you to trust my instincts, it's now. I know who killed Logan Magee and why."

"Spill it. I'm all ears."

So I told him everything, except the real reason I went to San

Antonio, but as I talked, I saw he was being the patient father listening to his child make a heart-felt case for why there really were monsters under the bed.

Hearing myself telling him the story, even I didn't think I made a very convincing case for what I knew to be true.

"Britt, you know how I feel about you — personally and professionally. There's nobody I respect more, but I got to tell you this is a crazy theory. I'm not saying you're wrong, but I can't go out and arrest somebody based on your intuition after reading a year-old newspaper."

"But it makes so much sense — it explains the break-in at Logan's house during the memorial service."

"But it doesn't explain a lot of other things that happened, like the truck driver."

"I'm working on that," I said.

"Britt, listen to yourself. Your theory is interesting, but there's nothing to back it up. There's not even any evidence he was murdered, much less evidence that it happened the way you say."

"I thought if anyone might believe me, it would be you," I said pitifully. Jack sighed.

"Listen, when I get past the worst of this double homicide investigation, you and I'll sit down again and talk it out and see if there's any way to prove your theory. I promise."

He was humoring me, but Jack was my only hope for official help on this. If a guy who has a thing for me doesn't believe me, nobody else in law enforcement was going to give me the time of day. I would keep trying to track down the truck driver, but other than that, I would just have to wait for Jack to help me.

●●●●●●●●●●●●●●●●●

I had trouble sleeping for the next couple of days and when I did sleep, I had terrible nightmares and slept fitfully. I was exhausted. My columns that week were really lame. Finally, I called my doctor and asked him if he would prescribe a sleeping pill for me. He offered an anti-depressant, too, but I declined.

So for the next few days, I slept deep dreamless sleep and felt much better. Jack even called and said things had eased up at work and maybe we could have dinner this weekend and talk about my theory. That night the temperature and humidity were low for July because a cold front was moving in, along with a summer thunderstorm. I turned off the front porch light and did one of my favorite things — I went out in my nightgown and sat on the porch swing and watched the storm come in.

The wind was glorious, and I loved watching the tree branches swaying and the distant lightning, followed several seconds later by the distant rumble of thunder. My dad gave me my love of impending storms. We would sit on the porch and feel the wind and watch the lightning until my mom would finally come to the door and beg us to come inside. When dad and I sat out there and the wind got really strong, I always felt that I could fly if somebody would let me jump off the roof.

Now my mom was in Florida, so couldn't order me inside, but the sound of the thunder became almost simultaneous with the lightning, so I knew I had to get inside since the storm had fully arrived. But I hated so much leaving it and going inside.

I get so tired of air conditioning by mid summer, so I turned off the AC, opened my bedroom window and turned on the attic fan. I took my sleeping pill, even though I didn't think I would really need it as long as I had the sound of the wind and rain to lull me to sleep. It felt so good to have fresh air moving through the house. I'd like to say I forgot to turn the burglar alarm on, but I didn't alarm it intentionally. The alarm I have is way too sensitive, and I knew the branches of the tree just outside my window would bang against the window screen and set the stupid alarm off.

That night I went back to having nightmares. I dreamed somebody was removing the screen in my otherwise open window and coming into the house. My terror woke me with a jolt, and I sat bolt upright in bed, my heart racing. Before my eyes could comprehend what I was seeing, a hand clamped over my mouth. As I started to scream and struggle against the intruder, he spoke urgently.

"Please don't scream, Britt. It's Logan Magee."

CHAPTER TWENTY-NINE

I honestly wasn't sure if this was a dream or if Logan was really in my bedroom. Having chemically induced sleep interrupted can leave you pretty confused.

My first impulse was to throw my arms around him and say, "Thank God, you're not really dead." My second impulse was to just stare at him in disbelief, knowing that I should be terrified of a man who had broken into my bedroom and was restraining me.

I had been wrong about his being murdered — maybe I was also wrong about his being a good guy. All these things were racing through my mind as he loosened his grip on me and gave me a weak, apologetic smile.

"I'm so sorry," he said. "I just had no idea how to do it. Do I walk up to somebody's door and say, 'I'm not dead — can I come in?' and take a chance on somebody who knew me seeing me outside your door. I'd been riding by your house off and on for hours trying to figure out how to do it, but then I saw you on the porch, and the next time I passed by, the lights were out and you were opening your bedroom window, and that's when I decided to just come in the window after you were asleep."

My pulse and breathing returned to something close to normal, and I reached for the bedside lamp.

"Wait," he snapped and then went to the window and closed the blinds. "Okay."

So I turned on the bedside lamp and got my first full in-the-flesh look at Logan Magee. He was as handsome as his pictures, but was thin, disheveled and obviously hadn't shaved for a couple of days. He looked terribly, terribly tired.

"Sit down," I said, and he sat down on the side of my bed like we were two college roommates talking.

"Ben said I couldn't trust you, but I knew I could."

"How could you know that? You don't even know me?"

"He told me my mother trusted you, and she's a better judge of character than Ben, and I knew from reading your column online. I knew I could trust anybody who would stand up to a mobster like Ray Christie."

"Does your mother know...?"

"Oh, no, she can't know until I know it's safe. Not Caroline either."

"But Ben's known all along?"

"Yeah, he was the only one. He and Joe Bedford."

I wanted to ask who Joe Bedford was and bombard Logan with a million other questions, but he looked terrible, his speech was even a little slurred. I prayed it was from lack of sleep and not Huntington's Chorea.

"When did you sleep last?"

"A couple of days ago."

"This is going to kill me, but you've got to sleep before we talk."

I led Logan into my guest bedroom and turned down the covers of the bed. He sat down and took off his shoes.

"When you've had a few hours sleep, we'll talk. You've got some splainin' to do, Lucy." He smiled weakly at my bad attempt at comic relief. "It's hot in here now, but I'll turn the fans off and the AC on, and it'll cool off pretty quick. I don't know exactly what's going on, but I know we don't need to sleep with the windows open. I'll turn the house alarm back on, too. You didn't park in front of my house, did you?"

"I parked around the corner at that small apartment complex."

"Good boy. Go to sleep."

Logan, fully clothed except for his shoes, seemed to be asleep before I had even switched the light off and closed the door. I was sure I wouldn't be able to sleep a wink, but I lay down on my bed after taking care of the air and alarm situation and found that the sleeping pill could still do its job, despite the interruption.

•••••••••••••

When I woke up at about quarter of eight, I was sure it had all been a dream, but I stumbled across the hall to the other bedroom and found Logan Magee, alive, but not yet conscious. All I could think of, as I stared at him, was the indescribable joy his mother would feel when she found her son returned from the dead. But would Caroline feel the same? And Ben had known Logan was alive the whole time and yet had gotten involved romantically with Logan's fiancée. Who was going to break that news to Logan? *Certainly* not me. *Probably* me.

I went into the kitchen and made coffee and looked in my nearly empty refrigerator for something that could become breakfast, something besides cold pizza. I had a few eggs. There was butter, jam and stale bread that could be converted into toast. I guess the smell of coffee woke Logan up, because I heard the shower. I had left a new disposable razor and shampoo out for him.

About the time the eggs were scrambled and the toast made, Logan came into the kitchen, dressed in his same clothes — I had no clean men's clothes to offer him like they always do in the movies. But he was clean and shaven and his hair was wet. He looked wonderful. He smiled shyly.

I wanted to pummel him with questions, but all I said was, "Sit down and eat breakfast. I hope you don't like cream or milk in your coffee, because I don't have any."

"Black's fine. Where do I begin?"

"By eating your breakfast."

"You figured it out, didn't you," he said between bites.

"Well, I figured out who and why, but I thought they had actually killed you because you were on to them. I knew almost from the start that you didn't commit suicide."

"How did you know that?"

"Because you had too much to live for. You had a beautiful fiancée, a loving mother, great friends, money, success, and there was no hint of illegality or debt. Your life reeked of integrity."

"Interesting choice of words."

"And I couldn't find anybody who had anything bad to say about you."

"Either you didn't look very hard, or they didn't want to speak ill of the dead." He smiled sadly.

"And there was the break-in during the memorial service to also make a case against suicide, although my cop friend, Jack Trent, said maybe you were involved in something illegal, something that had caught up with you, and your partners in crime broke in after your suicide to be sure there was nothing on your computer or in your desk to implicate them."

"Lucky for me the cops saw it that way."

"You don't act like a guy who feels lucky."

"It's been a bad year," Logan said, running his fingers through his hair. "At one point I was so depressed and lonely that I asked Ben to steal that picture of him and Caroline and Mom from my bedroom and bring it to me the next time he came to San Antonio. I didn't think Mom would notice it missing. I spent most of last year without so much as a picture of the people I loved. I couldn't take anything with me to San Antonio that a man killing himself wouldn't take with him. I thought I was going away for just a few weeks or a couple of months at most. I thought every day, 'This is the day when I'll be able to go home or maybe tomorrow."

"Were you the one who e-mailed me about coming to Texas?"

"I told Ben I was sure you had figured it all out and that if I didn't talk to you, you'd go to the police or FBI. He didn't agree, but I e-mailed you to meet me, because I felt like if I could sit down with you and tell you everything that you would help me untangle this mess. At first I didn't tell Ben what I had done, but then I got to thinking that Ben had gone this far with me, and I couldn't sneak around behind his back, especially on something this pivotal."

"When did you tell him you had e-mailed me?"

"On Thursday, the day after you had agreed to meet me on Friday."

"How did he take it?"

"Are you kidding? He went ballistic. He hopped on a plane that night and kept me up all night arguing about it. He finally convinced me that I would be endangering Caroline and Mom by confiding in a stranger, a reporter no less. I feel terrible about letting you fly out there and then standing you up. That was lousy. I felt even worse when you kept e-mailing me that you were still in town and begging me to meet you."

"I thought I saw you in a window of a hotel along the San Antonio River on Sunday night."

"We knew you were in town, of course, but Ben and I both freaked when we found out you had seen me. What are the chances of that? It must have been when Ben and I were arguing again in his hotel room. We left and went back to my place for a while, and Ben checked out early the next morning. When he checked out, the clerk told him a woman had been asking questions about his room and showing a picture of some other man. We knew it had to be you asking the questions at the hotel. That's when we really panicked. He was convinced you'd write a story for the newspaper about it and blow everything, but I didn't think you would. Still we couldn't take a chance, so I did a really risky thing.

"My friend, Rusty Martin, the only person I ever let myself get even a little bit close to in San Antonio, was headed toward Memphis anyhow on a trucking job, so when Ben called and told me that you were on to us, I called Rusty on his cell phone, caught him outside Little Rock, and asked him to go to the cops and lie. I didn't tell him why, just that the cops thought I had committed suicide on the bridge and that I needed them to keep thinking that. He probably assumed I was in some kind of trouble and was hiding out from the law, but he agreed without hesitation. I gave him all the details he needed to know and rehearsed him as he drove to Memphis. He came up with the part about him not stopping because he was using pills to stay awake."

"But why would he lie for you, to the cops of all people, and take a chance on getting in trouble himself?"

"He thought I saved his life, so he always vowed that I could ask anything, and he meant anything, of him and he would do it, no questions asked. He's one of those guys that you can't just help. He has to pay you back, and until he does, he's not satisfied."

"How did you save his life?"

"I couldn't work during that year I was in San Antonio, so I did a lot of volunteer work to stay busy. My Spanish came in handy. Never any one place too long. Couldn't take a chance on somebody asking too many questions about me. But anyhow, Rusty was down on his luck, drinking too much, and I stumbled upon him, literally, on the street where he'd passed out. I don't scrape up every bum I pass on the street, but for some reason I helped him up and took him to a rescue mission I had volunteered at. We became friends, and I helped him get back on his feet, get his self-respect back, get back to trucking. I didn't do that much, but he always said I saved his life, so he was glad when I asked a favor of him, even if it meant lying to the cops. He felt like that had evened the score."

"So since it worked, why did you get in your car and drive to Memphis and climb in my window?"

"Because it *didn't* work, at least not with you. Ben and I were feeling like the cops had bought Rusty's story, but then you started calling Rusty and leaving messages, which, of course, he knew not to return, but he told me, and I decided I was going to go to Memphis, lay it all out to you and ask for your help in getting my life back."

"Your instincts were right when you e-mailed me. I would have helped you then, and I will now, if I can."

"Well, if nothing else I've learned that no matter how close a friend is, like Ben, and no matter how much he's helped me, I've still got to trust my own gut, especially when my own life is on the line."

CHAPTER THIRTY

"So Ben doesn't know you're here?" I asked as we moved from the kitchen table to the living room. We sat in big cushiony armchairs opposite each other.

"No. He would have been totally against it. I let him talk me out of meeting you in San Antonio, and you see how that backfired, but I wasn't going to give him a chance to argue with me this time. Ben has been a loyal friend to me — I'll never be able to thank him enough, but I'm the one whose life has been on hold for more than a year, and I had to make the decision, so here I am."

"So how can I help you get your life back?"

"Before we talk about that, can I ask you a few questions?"

"Sure."

"It's obvious you figured this thing out for the most part, but I'd love to know how."

"Well, in trying to figure out if your death was really murder, like I thought it was — that sounds weird doesn't it, discussing someone's death with them. Anyhow, during that process, and by the way, at first I was just helping your mother come to terms with your death. I liked her immediately and felt so sorry for her losing her only son to suicide that I wanted to make a few inquiries thinking that if she knew why you killed yourself, she might be able to accept it and have a little peace at least."

The look on Logan's face was so pained, I immediately regretted talking about his mother's suffering.

"Ben played down all that — I guess he thought I couldn't stand to know just how much I had hurt my mom and Caroline. He made it sound like they were sad, but were going on with their lives very well. Anyhow, go on."

"Oh, by the way, John at Wang's says hi." I said it for shock effect, of course. I got the desired look of utter bewilderment from Logan.

"Well, actually John didn't say to tell you hi, since he thinks you're dead, but it was John who put me on the right trail, even though I didn't know it at the time. I eat there a lot with my friends, and John always waits on us and remembers our orders."

Logan smiled with recognition.

"So one night, my friends were asking me about my little investigation, and I pulled out of my purse a picture of you and Caroline that your mother gave me. John was passing by, and I nearly fell out of my chair when he said, "Logan, Caroline!" Anyhow, he told us ya'll were regular customers of his, and he was very sad when you died. Then he told us about the time you spoke Indonesian to him. So I asked your mother if you spoke Indonesian, and she said no."

"Mom's gotten pretty blasé about my knack for languages. She used to brag about her multi-lingual son to her friends and anyone who would listen, but gradually it just didn't seem like that big a deal to her or me. I picked up Indonesian from my roommate in college my freshman year. I guess mom had forgotten. I'm not fluent, but I understand it pretty well."

"When I found out you spoke Indonesian and your mom didn't know it, I went to talk to Barney Foster. Your mom put me in touch with him. We met at a coffee shop."

"Is Barney still holding out against Starbucks? He's a purist when it comes to coffee, thinks it should come in only two flavors — regular and decaf."

"Still holding out. Anyhow, after we talked for a while and he told me he couldn't possibly believe you would kill yourself, I asked him if you spoke Indonesian. I didn't expect him to look so shocked that I knew, but he told me about the little office plot to spy on the Indonesian businessmen, make sure they weren't stealing company secrets. He told me you overheard them say something cryptic in Indonesian, but he didn't know what it was. That all seemed to me like it might be significant, but it didn't become clear until much later."

"When you talked to Barney did he say if the Indonesians were still at Prentiss-Lamar?"

"They aren't, but they're still in Memphis. Apparently they've bought interest in a small banking firm."

"Of course, gives them a perfect way to bring money into the country legitimately. So, what made you put the pieces together?"

"Well, the first time I talked with Maggie, I asked her for every detail of what happened that morning before your wedding day when you had breakfast with her. She said you were happy and upbeat until you read something in the newspaper that upset you. Of course, I got a copy of that day's paper and went over it with a fine tooth comb, at least I thought I did. I made a list of all the major stories and showed them to everybody who knew you, hoping somebody would know which story had a personal connection to you. The story that upset you was on my list, but I had listed it as 'two stories about elections in other countries.' My list didn't mention Indonesia, so when I looked at the list later, nothing jumped out at me. It was a quote toward the end that was significant, as you know, and I didn't notice it until about a week ago."

I got up and walked over to my desk, where the newspaper was in the top drawer. I turned to the stories about newly elected leaders in two countries, including Indonesia, and read the key paragraphs to Logan.

The new Indonesian president is expected to take a tougher stand against extremist Islamic terror groups such as al-Qaida-linked Jemaah Islamiyah, which has been blamed for several bombings, including the 2002 Bali nightclub bombing and an attack outside the Australian Embassy.

"Jemaah Islamiyah is not just a threat to this part of the world," he said. "The U.S. and other target nations must stop expecting terrorists to all be alienated young Arabs sneaking in with student visas. We must wake up and realize that terrorists can be diplomats and legitimate businessmen as well. This great sickness of terrorism has spread to all levels of society."

"Yep, that's what I read that morning that suddenly made everything clear. What I had overheard Nat saying in Indonesian to one of the other guys was, 'Soon Jemaah Islamiyah will do the work of God here.' I told you I wasn't fluent in the language, so I thought Jemaah Islamiyah was somebody's name. Names in the Muslim world are often variations of Islam or Mohamed or words for God, so I thought it was just a person's name until I read that newspaper article. I knew instantly that I had to do something quick, that I couldn't wait until I got back from my two-week honeymoon."

At that moment, the doorbell rang. I peeped through the curtains and saw that it was Jack Trent. Of all the rotten timing, Jack!

I pushed Logan into the bedroom and took a deep breath, trying to get my composure back before I opened the door to greet Jack.

CHAPTER THIRTY-ONE

"What are you doing here at this time of day?" I asked, trying to cover up my annoyance.

"I was just passing by and noticed that all your blinds and curtains are closed — that's so unlike you, and then I noticed the screen was off your bedroom window and I really got worried."

"No, I'm not being held hostage, but thanks for your concern. Do all Memphians get this kind of police protection?"

Jack ignored the question and looked me over. Here it was almost 11, and I was in sweats and had no make-up on.

"I'm not going in to work today, because I was up all night with a little stomach bug. In fact, I may have to go running for the bathroom any minute."

Now I had to come up with a reason the screen was off. I thought about saying I was washing the windows, but I knew he wouldn't believe that of me.

"About the screen — I locked myself out of the house yesterday, so I turned off the alarm at the keypad, took the screen off the bedroom window and climbed in."

"You shouldn't leave your windows unlocked, even if you do

have a house alarm, Britt. That's just stupid, considering the threats you've had."

I gave Jack a little hug and nudged him toward the door.

"I appreciate your concern, Jack, but I'm headed back to the bathroom now, and that's a moment I'd rather not share with you, so goodbye, and we can talk tomorrow, okay?"

After he left, I retrieved Logan from the bedroom, where he had apparently been listening.

"When he said you'd been threatened, did he mean Ben's message he left you on your computer?"

"Ben did that? How did he learn to burglarize houses?"

"It's not hard when people leave house keys under a big rock by the backdoor. He just went in, turned on the computer and typed that message. Frankly, I couldn't believe he had the guts to do that, but that was when he was getting panicky about your being onto us. When he told me about it, I told him he had wasted his time. You'd never give into that kind of threat."

"You know me that well from reading my column, huh?"

"I guess so."

"Well, it didn't stop me, but I have to admit it scared me to death when I came home and realized somebody had been in my house. That's when I got an alarm. So, did Ben leave the phone message and the bloody cat picture, too?"

Logan looked so appalled that I knew it wasn't Ben.

"Bloody cat picture?"

"Earlier, before Ben's computer stunt, I came home one night and there was a message from a man, whose voice I didn't recognize, saying that I better stop asking so many questions, because curiosity killed the cat. Then the next morning, inside my newspaper was a greeting card of a cute little cat and it was smeared with what appeared to be real blood."

152

"That's sick."

"I was just thankful it wasn't a real dead cat. That would have been sicker and scarier."

"Still, I wonder who would have done that, since Ben didn't."

"Probably Ray Christie. It was a day or two after I wrote the column about him wining and dining the City Councilwoman."

"That was a great column. But it's a little risky to mess with a creep like Ray Christie. I hear he's got organized crime connections."

"That's what Jack said."

"Your cop friend is very protective of you, isn't he?"

"Logan, cops are the most paranoid people on earth. They always expect the worst from humanity."

"What about reporters?"

"We can be jaded at times, but deep down inside we're idealistic and utterly fool-hardy when it comes to ourselves. There have been so many times that I have done really risky things while covering a story and only later realized how dumb it was. For some reason, we feel we're indestructible."

"Do you and your cop date?"

"We've known each other for years because I used to cover the police department for the paper. He used to ask me out and I always said no because it was a conflict of interest and to tell the truth also because cops aren't my type romantically."

"Kind of a broad generalization, isn't it?"

"That's what Jack said, so recently I gave in a little and we've gone out a couple of times. No big deal."

"I think it's a big deal to him. Guys don't worry that much about women they think of as casual friends. Take my word for it."

"Kind of a broad generalization, isn't it?" We both laughed.

Logan walked back into the kitchen to get more coffee, and I remembered how little food was in the house.

"Hey, Logan, after Jack is well out of the neighborhood, I think I'll run over to the grocery store and get a few things. If we're going to figure out how to get you your life back, we'll need food, beer and sugar. Do you have any clothes or anything you want from your car?"

"Yeah, I packed an overnight bag with a few clothes and stuff. Here's my key — the car's an old Ford Taurus, dark blue with Texas plates."

"That's quite a comedown from the BMW they found on the bridge."

"Well, an old car is about all you can afford when you're paying cash with Ben's money, plus it's less obtrusive than a nice car."

"When I get back from the grocery store, I want to hear how you and Ben pulled off the fake suicide."

CHAPTER THIRTY-TWO

When I came back from the grocery store, Logan was sitting at the kitchen table reading the newspaper and drinking more coffee. I put the bags down on the kitchen counter and began unloading them.

"I got ice cream — java chocolate chip and some good pumpernickel and turkey and provolone for sandwiches, chips, of course, cheese dip, milk and cereal, spaghetti with Paul Newman sauce and Sarah Lee coffee cake. I hope you weren't expecting a wonderful home cooked dinner from me, because opening a jar of spaghetti sauce is about as close as I come. You're probably a great cook — that's the modern, sophisticated man way."

"Sorry to disappoint you, but I either eat out every meal or I eat three bowls of cereal for dinner. And there's always canned soup and Spaghetti O's."

"A man after my own heart, but if we're going to be in hiding here for a few days, it would be nice if one of us could cook."

I pried off the top of the ice cream and got out two spoons. Logan and I ate directly from the half-gallon ice-cream tub as we talked at the kitchen table.

"So what did you do after you read the newspaper that

morning?"

"Well, I went straight to the FBI field office. I told the receptionist that I had information about a possible terrorist cell in Memphis, and she took me in to see an agent named Joe Bedford, a real nice guy, very straight laced like you'd expect an FBI agent to be, but easy to talk to. So I laid it all out for him, what little I knew. I felt like a real dunce when he started asking me basic questions like what their full names were. All three guys have long Indonesian names, so everybody called them Nat, Marty and Suk.

"Agent Bedford said the FBI, of course, could subpoena the company records, but that would tip the Indonesians off, so he asked if I could get the information before leaving for my honeymoon and then they could get a court order to set up electronic surveillance. One overheard conversation wasn't enough to charge them with a crime, and besides it would be better if they could cast a wider net and try to figure out what the cell was planning to do and who else was involved. That made sense to me, so I told him I'd go to the office late that night after the rehearsal dinner and get the information he needed, spellings of names, addresses, and some other basic information. I promised him I wouldn't tell anyone, including Caroline."

"Your mom showed me the video that was shot at the rehearsal dinner, and you didn't look worried or stressed."

"I wasn't. The plan at that point was that I would go to the office, get the information, meet Joe Bedford at his office on Saturday morning to deliver the info. and then get married and go to Greece for two weeks. Who me, worry?"

We both smiled.

"What went wrong?"

"Everything. I went into the office — no big deal — the night security guard is used to everybody who works at Prentiss-Lamar coming in at all hours. Everybody who works there is a Type A. But nobody was there that night except me. I guess I left my office door open while I was going into the personnel files on my computer. I had information on Suk on the screen when I heard Nat's voice behind me. It would've scared the hell out of me, even if I hadn't been spying on them. In Indonesian, he said, "I suppose the U.S. government will find this very interesting." I fell into the trap. I answered in English, but it was obvious I had understood what he had said in Indonesian. I stumbled through some excuse why I was looking at their files at 11 o'clock on a Friday night, but there was no use. He knew what was going on. He said when he let it slip to Marty about Jemaah Islamiyah, he thought he saw a strange look on my face, like I understood him, but he wasn't sure until now."

Logan got up and got a glass of water and got me one, too, without asking. I guess ice cream makes everybody thirsty.

"How did he know you'd be at the office?"

"I wondered, too, and at some point in our conversation he told me that when he read the article in that day's newspaper about Jamaah Islamiyah, he figured I might see it, too, and that I might put two and two together, so he started following me to see if I would go to the police or FBI."

"So he knew you went to the FBI?"

"No, thank God. Remember, I read the paper at my mother's house and went straight to the FBI. If I had gone home first, Nat would have followed me and known, but as it was, he didn't pick up my trail until later in the morning when I came back home, so as far as he was concerned, I didn't do anything suspicious until I came to the office after the rehearsal dinner."

"I'm surprised he didn't kill you right then at the office, especially since you had the other guy's personnel file there on the computer screen."

"He couldn't have gotten past the metal detector with a gun, and if he had stabbed me with a letter opener or something like that, everybody would know he did it, because he and I were the only two people signed in with the security guard. And he couldn't have forced me to leave with him, because, of course, I would have dashed for the security guard as we passed, so I guess he had to at least temporarily negotiate with me."

"Did he directly threaten you?"

"Just as calmly as can be, he said, 'If you feel you must share this information with the police or FBI, I'm afraid we must kill your mother and your wife. And if you have us arrested, there are others who will do it for us. But I am willing to deal with you.'"

"So he thought you were getting all this information together *before* you went to the FBI?"

"He said they wouldn't hurt me or my family if I kept this information to myself and that by the time I got back from my honeymoon, he and the other two guys would have returned to Jakarta since I had foiled their plans. They would reorganize in some other part of the world. I played the naive American and agreed, as if I thought they could be trusted. Of course, I knew they had no intentions of really breaking camp while I was gone. Terrorists on a mission don't give up that easily. But we both played the game, hoping the other was buying the lie."

"I guess you were both just buying a few hours."

"Exactly. I told him as long as they didn't hurt any Americans or my family, I didn't care what they did in other parts of the world. We shook hands on the deal, and we both left the building. He wished me well in my marriage and told me Greece was a beautiful country. It unnerved me to know he knew where I was going on my honeymoon."

"Did you think he would kill you and Caroline in Greece?"

"Maybe, although I have a feeling they would have killed me in the next few hours. Just to be sure, I didn't go to the police or FBI. I didn't dare go home, because they were probably waiting for me and would have made it look like I surprised some ordinary criminal during a burglary of my house."

"How did you know they wouldn't be waiting outside the office to kill you then?"

"I figured they couldn't do it anywhere near the office, because that might draw attention to Nat, since he had been there late at night with me. But if I was murdered by burglars I surprised at my house or a traffic accident, they wouldn't be suspects. After all, they were considered legitimate foreign businessmen. Still I couldn't take a chance, so I told Nat we needed to leave separately and when he left, I called Ben and told him to pick me up in the parking garage. I was parked on the street outside the building, so if they were watching, they wouldn't notice Ben driving into the parking garage and out again, still apparently alone. I was on the floor of the backseat with a blanket over me."

"What a horrible dilemma. How did you decide that a fake suicide would solve the problem?"

"Well, I knew I had to take one trusted person into my confidence, one person I could trust with my life, and that was Ben. After he picked me up we went to his house and talked. He suggested I send my mother to stay with some out-of-town relative for a month or so and that Caroline and I could go somewhere other than Greece. But there were all kinds of holes in that plan, like the fact that I would have to bring Caroline and her parents and my mother into the loop and when you start doing that everything falls apart.

"Besides, I was sure that no matter what we did, these guys couldn't be trusted to keep their word. You know, Britt, before 9/11, I wouldn't have believed that those guys would do something so cold-blooded as to kill my family for a political cause, but since 9/11 everything terrible and cruel and far-fetched has seemed possible. The kind of people who would kill thousands of innocent people in the World Trade Center, wouldn't hesitate to kill Caroline and Mom."

"Didn't you think you could trust the FBI to protect you and your family?"

"Do you remember a couple of years ago when that Memphis DMV employee was arrested for selling fake driver's licenses to a group of Middle Easterners?"

"Sure."

"And remember how the DMV employee mysteriously died in a fiery car crash the day before she was supposed to testify before the grand jury? Well, I remembered that when Nat pointedly mentioned that he knew we were going to Greece on our honeymoon. What could the FBI do for us if we had an 'accident' like that in Greece, or in Memphis for that matter?

"Like the FBI or police would assign three full-time bodyguards to Mom and Caroline and me for weeks or months? I hate to sound totally cynical, but once the FBI had the information I gave them, they didn't need me, they could take it from there without me. It's not like I was a material witness or anything. I was just a tipster. Why would they waste resources protecting us night and day?"

"You're probably right," I said as I put the top on the ice cream and returned it to the freezer.

"So Ben and I decided that the only way to protect Mom and Caroline and give the FBI a chance to nail these guys and their co-conspirators was for the Indonesians to believe I was dead. So I went back to the office the same way, on the floor of Ben's car, and quickly printed out the information on the three guys, while Ben kept watch outside. I wrote the FBI letter on Ben's computer, because I was afraid the Indonesians would check my computer hard-drive at home and at work and gave it to him to mail to Agent Bedford. And Ben said there *was* a break-in during the memorial service, so I guess that hunch was right. After I got the information, I went down to my car, because Ben had been circling around and didn't see anybody watching my car or the building. There's almost no traffic or people in that part of downtown in the middle of the night."

"Did you tell the FBI agent in the letter that you were going to fake your suicide?"

"At first I was going to tell Bedford what my plan was, but I was afraid it would somehow backfire, so I told him Nat caught me and that I was going to kill myself to protect my family. Then I wrote a similar letter to Nat, telling him that I was sure he would understand that suicide was an honorable method for protecting what was most important to you — in his case his radical cause, and in my case, protecting the ones I loved. I assured him I had not told Caroline and mom or anybody else about any of this."

"Why did you think he would believe you?"

"I didn't expect him to accept my word on face value, but I knew at least one of them would go to my funeral and when they saw the genuine grief Caroline and mom were experiencing, they'd believe it was real."

"But how could you put your mother and fiancée through all that?"

"I hate to sound sexist, Britt, but you're thinking like a woman. When a man experiences the fight or flight thing, when the people he loves most are in danger, he doesn't think about their emotional needs, as least I didn't that night. A man thinks about physically saving the lives of his loved ones first."

I reached across the table and put my hands on his. I couldn't speak, so he continued.

"Looking back on it, faking my own death was probably stupid, but you've got to remember, I had just a few hours to make a decision and carry it out. It's like knowing someone you love is inside a burning building. You just rush in to try to save them without thinking through the consequences.

"But it wasn't just saving my loved ones and myself. I truly believed, and I guess I still do, that national security rested on my shoulders. I really believed that if I didn't make a personal sacrifice, there could be another 9/11, and this time it could be in Memphis and involve people I knew. I asked myself, 'If on September 10 you had known you could spare the people in the Towers and the Pentagon by giving up a few months of your life, would you have done it?' Was I playing hero? — I don't know. I just know it was all Ben and I could figure out in those few hours."

So I asked how they did it exactly?

"I drove the car to the old bridge, which isn't nearly as well traveled as the I-40 bridge, and it always has some dark spots where lights are burned out. I parked my car in the right lane of the bridge and got out and looked out toward the water until there was a break in the traffic, and Ben came along and picked me up. We drove straight to Little Rock, where Ben gave me one of his credit cards and his driver's license and all the cash he had. He drove straight back to Memphis, and I caught an early morning flight to San Antonio. Ben and I don't look that much alike, but nobody has ever questioned my ID. We both have brown hair, and I guess they just glance at the picture and make sure the name matches the ticket or credit card."

"Why'd you pick San Antonio?"

"Because Ben has business there occasionally and would have an excuse to come to see me while we waited. We agreed that I would buy a disposable cell phone, stay in a hotel for a few days and then rent a room. And we agreed we wouldn't contact each other for a few weeks in case somebody was listening or watching. I had made him executor of my will a couple of years before, and I knew my mother would depend on him for financial things, so it wouldn't be hard for him to slip out a little money for me from time to time. Mom would never notice."

"You figured out a lot in those few hours. How did you think you would know when it was safe to come home?"

"Well, I knew if the cell was broken up, it would make national news, and I would know it was okay to come home. I was so naive. I really thought it would just be a few weeks, a few months at most."

"How could you know? This is not the kind of thing any of us has any prior experience with."

"If I had known it would take away a year of my life, I might have done it differently, but then again maybe not. All I could think about was saving my loved ones and my city. Does that sound corny?"

"Not at all," I said. "Let's make a sandwich."

I thought both of us needed a few minutes' break from all this intensity.

CHAPTER THIRTY-THREE

Logan went to the bedroom to change into some clean clothes that I had picked up from his car when I went to the grocery story, and I made us each a turkey and provolone sandwich. We ate at the kitchen table, where we had spent most of the day.

I asked Logan when it really hit him, the gravity of what he had done.

"During the first few hours, it was all adrenaline — saving the ones I love seemed like it was worth any sacrifice. Then once I got to San Antonio on what was supposed to be my wedding day, I was totally preoccupied with losing Caroline. Every minute in the next couple of days, I was tortured over what was supposed to be happening at that moment. I bought an iPod and downloaded all the songs I associated with Caroline, with us. I wallowed in my loss. My arms, my whole body literally ached for Caroline. I was ripped apart thinking of Greece and how we were supposed to be making love and eating breakfast on the balcony and making love some more — things that should have been."

"I'm sure she was going through the same thing, along with just the raw grief of your death."

He sighed and nodded sadly.

"After a couple of days of feeling sorry for myself, the reality hit me of how much pain I had inflicted on Caroline and my mother, and then I fell into depression over what I had done to them in trying to protect them. And asking myself if I really had the right to manipulate them that way.

"And of course there was the anger and regret — why did I pick up that newspaper that morning? Why did I eavesdrop on the Indonesians' conversation? Why did I have to be a hero and go to the FBI? Why did I go back that night so Nat could catch me getting his information off the computer? Why, why, why?"

Our sandwiches sat half-eaten on our plates.

"Then I went through a period of acceptance where I told myself that the worst of Caroline's and Mom's grief was over, that it was just a matter of a few weeks or months and then I would read about a big arrest of terrorists in Memphis, and I would come home and get my life back and ask for their forgiveness. I watched CNN and MSNBC constantly. It was during that time that I started doing volunteer work to try to stay busy, and that helped for a while. A couple of times the Homeland Security color was changed or there was some report of "terrorist chatter," and I would get excited and think this was it — I would be going home soon.

"Then when months passed, I wasn't just faking being dead — I really was a dead man. I would go days without shaving or showering, I wore the same pair of jeans and T-shirt for days at a time. I drank to numb the pain. I didn't care if I ate or not. I went from not being able to sleep to sleeping all the time. Sometimes I would sit in front of the TV for hours and realize I couldn't remember a single show I had watched. I didn't even watch the news channels any more. I was totally hopeless. Nothing made me laugh or cry. I just felt dead, like my life had never existed. I felt like I was standing over in a corner watching myself go through the motions of daily life. On the rare occasions when I left my room, I felt invisible as I walked down the street.

"Ben came out during that time and was blown away by how low I had sunk. He made me go to a shrink and get anti-depressants. I wasn't sure how doctor/client privilege applies to homeland security, so I didn't tell the shrink all that was going on. I just said I was depressed because my wedding was called off and I lost my job. Since I wasn't being honest with him, the therapy didn't help much, but the anti-depressants helped some, and I started thinking more rationally and realized I couldn't just sit around and wait much longer.

"I had made a terrible mistake, and I had to take some action, but I couldn't figure out what exactly that might be. That's when Ben started telling me about Mom asking for your help and how close you were coming to the truth. He was upset by that — he said after all this sacrifice, we couldn't have you ruin it or it would be all for nothing. We were in too deep now."

"Ben was worried about you exposing us," Logan went on, "but I was relieved. I wanted you to figure it out so the decision would be taken out of my hands, and I could come home. Then I decided I didn't want to just wait for you to maybe figure it out. I wanted your help, even if I had to engineer it, so that's when I e-mailed you."

"So Ben talked you out of it by saying Caroline and your mom would be endangered?"

"That and he promised he'd go see Joe Bedford at the FBI again and ask if I would jeopardize the investigation by suddenly coming back from the dead. He said Bedford was shocked that I was alive and said it was a stupid thing for me to fake my suicide, but since I'd gone this far, I should sit tight a little longer."

"Again? Ben had talked to the FBI before?"

"Once before. About six months into the exile, I got crazy and said I was just going back to Memphis, that I didn't care about the terrorists anymore, so Ben said he'd go to Joe Bedford. He didn't tell him I was alive, but he said he was the best friend of the informant who killed himself and was just wondering if his friend's sacrifice had been worth it — was the investigation panning out? Of course, Bedford wouldn't tell him any details, but he reassured Ben that my sacrifice was worthwhile, that the information I had given them would save a lot of lives. When Ben told me that, I had the courage to go on for a while longer."

"But a few days ago, you decided to confide in me after all?"

"I knew there was a risk, but I thought since you had gotten friendly with my mother and she trusted you, according to Ben, that you would help me rather than expose me."

"I've got some ideas about how we might do that," I said. "And then after we get things squared away with the FBI, we'll have to figure out how to tell Caroline and your mom that you've returned from the dead."

Logan looked so relieved, and he gave me a big bear hug. It was a sisterly hug, but it felt good nonetheless.

CHAPTER THIRTY-FOUR

I could tell our hours of heavy conversation were taking their toll on Logan, who after all had hardly talked to anybody for more than a year. So I suggested he get some exercise on the treadmill collecting dust in my spare bedroom or maybe take a nap. He wisely chose the nap.

While he slept, I tried to think of an idea for my column the next day, but it became increasingly obvious I was going to have to call in sick for a couple of days.

While I was cooking dinner with the help of Paul Newman and a glass of red wine, Logan came in looking sleepy eyed but rested. I poured him a glass of wine, and he peeped into the steaming pots on the stove.

"Anything I can do to help?"

"You could cut us off a few slices of that Italian bread and get the butter out of the frig."

We made small talk about how the cold front had come and gone, leaving us with a typically sticky, steamy July day. As we were serving the plates, I asked him something I had been oddly curious about since this morning.

"Logan, when you went out and bought that iPod when you got to San Antonio, what music did you download?"

"You're going to think this is really cornball, but I downloaded Frank Sinatra. I know people our age aren't supposed to like that kind of stuff."

In answer, I went over to my CD holder in the living room and took out my favorite Sinatra CD.

"There are six more where this came from," I said as I put the CD on. The first cut was "I Only Miss Her When I Think of Her."

"Sweet!" Logan said, smiling. "You like Ole Blue Eyes, too."

"Were those songs special to you and Caroline?"

"No, she was, is nine years younger than me, so she doesn't care for this kind of thing, but still a lot of Sinatra's stuff reminds me of her, the love songs and the torch songs."

"Nobody does a drinking song like Frankie."

"Don't I know."

When we sat down to eat, I asked him how he met Caroline. I had heard her version, but wanted to hear how he would describe it.

"We met at a party. She had a date with an acquaintance of mine, but when I called him a few days later to feel him out, he said it wasn't going anywhere anyhow, so feel free to call her if I wanted to. So I did. Ben actually had introduced us at the party — he had known her casually for a couple of years."

"What was it that attracted you to her?"

"At first it was just her beauty and charm, but after we went out a few times, I was drawn to her down-to-earthness. The night I met her, she was all dressed up and made up, of course, but after that when we did things together she usually wore jeans and had her hair in a ponytail. And I admired the fact that a girl from a well-off family would be happy to be a high school English teacher at a school where the pay isn't that great."

I didn't say that girls from rich families don't need big salaries and that they'd rather make less by teaching at a sanitized suburban girls' school than to deal with inner city public-school kids.

"I was impressed when your mom told me that she had offered to give the house to Caroline, and she turned it down. That was very unmaterialistic of her."

"Maybe, or maybe she just didn't want it. She's a suburban girl through and through — she was never that fond of Harbor Town. She said she'd love the house if it were out East. We made a deal that we'd live in my house for a year, and if she still didn't like downtown living, we'd move to the burbs."

"When I talked to her, I used an old reporter's trick and asked her if she had to describe you in one word what it would be. She said, "romantic.""

"I guess that's a reflection of what a short courtship we had. If we had dated for a year or so, I probably wouldn't have seemed like the ultimate romantic to her."

"I don't know — men who listen to Sinatra torch songs have to be romantics at heart."

We ate in silence for a few minutes and then I said, "I know you can't wait to finally see her again and pick up where you left off."

"It may not be that simple. I still miss her, but it's, well, how do I say this? Because we only knew each other for a relatively short time, sometimes I feel that our relationship never really happened, like it's been a romantic fantasy or a love story I read in a book. Does that sound too weird?"

"Not to me, and knowing each other for a short time isn't necessarily the reason. I was married for just three weeks, but I had known Drew since second grade, and our marriage seems like a movie I saw, not real at all."

The next hour was taken up with my ludicrous love story, but

Logan didn't act incredulous like most people do when they hear it all.

"Yeah, the best marriages are between people who are both friends and lovers, I think. I'm not sure Caroline and I dated long enough to be each other's best friend, but we certainly had sexual attraction. I guess we assumed the friendship would develop after marriage, if we thought about it at all."

"Drew tells me he's found both lover and friend in Elizabeth. They're getting married. He just told me a few weeks ago."

"Sounds like you took it hard."

"The worst part was that he said we couldn't go back to being friends, that his wife wouldn't like him buddying around with his childhood friend."

"Who also happens to be his ex-wife."

"You sound like my shrink."

"Even under the best of circumstances, marriage can affect our friendships," Logan said.

Yeah, if Ben marries Caroline, it's definitely going to affect his friendship with you.

"Do you think your marriage to Caroline would have, will have any affect on your friendship with Ben?"

"Probably not, but there's no guarantee that Caroline will still want to marry me."

"Why do you say that?"

"Well, for one thing she's thought I was dead for the past year and when you think somebody's dead, you try to get over it, you try to go on with your life. Who could blame her?"

"What does Ben say? Does he know if she's dating anybody?"

"I asked him, and he said not that he knows of, but he may

just be trying to spare my feelings. He may figure that I might not be able to take the truth."

"Could you handle it if Caroline had found somebody else?"

It's a cruel question, Logan, but you might as well start preparing yourself for the reality.

"I don't know. I really can't let myself think about it too much until I get the rest of this figured out. But something kind of strange happened when I was going to that psychologist in San Antonio. Of course, I couldn't tell him the whole truth, but I told him I was losing my mind thinking about the girl I had lost, and he took me through a strange little exercise.

"He asked me if there was any hope of our getting back together, and for some reason I said no. I guess that was just a reflection of how hopeless I felt about everything. So he said maybe he could help me let go, that he had a technique that worked for some people and not for others.

"So he told me to imagine that Caroline had been in a terrible accident and was brain dead and on life supports. Then he took me step by step as I went into the hospital room and walked over to her bed. He described each little movement in detail. He had me acknowledging that she *looked* like the person I had loved, but no longer *was* the person I loved, that the person I loved had already left her lifeless body. Then he had me kiss her goodbye and turn off the life supports."

I gasped and Logan looked up at me with tears in his eyes.

"It was horrible. I cried and cried after I imagined turning off the life supports, but the strange thing is that it worked."

"You stopped loving her in an instant?"

"Of course not, but I did sort of let go of my obsession. I didn't feel so crazy after that."

"How on earth are you going to let her and your mother know you're alive?"

"I have no idea, but I do know one thing — my mother won't have mixed feelings about my being alive."

I smiled my assurance that he was absolutely right.

"I think it's in the mothers' rulebook," Logan said, "that they always have to love you and take you back even when you've put them through a year of hell."

CHAPTER THIRTY-FIVE

At breakfast the next day, Logan and I decided that he needed to talk to Agent Joe Bedford himself and in person, but he certainly couldn't ride or drive down the streets of Memphis to the FBI office. As anybody who's lived here for a while knows, Memphis is the smallest big city in the world. It's hard to go anywhere without running into somebody you know. A dead man couldn't take that chance.

So the plan was for me to go to Bedford and set up a meeting at my house. We first thought of Logan calling, but decided an in-person visit by me was better.

"Is the FBI in the federal building?" I asked.

"No, they moved it out East, a new building on Humphreys Blvd. Joe Bedford told me that after the Oklahoma City federal building was bombed, federal offices were spread out around cities, so that there would be no one high-profile target for future domestic terrorists."

"I'm glad I asked. I would have headed downtown."

After I got dressed for work, I went back in the kitchen and Logan looked up from his newspaper and coffee and smiled sweetly.

"Good luck, Britt. I'll be holding my breath while you're gone."

"I'm going to stop in at the paper for a few minutes and arrange to take a few days of vacation and check my snail mail. Then I'll go to the FBI office."

I patted Logan on the head like a dog — I don't know what possessed me to do such a silly thing. Maybe I just wanted to touch him. I left home feeling pleasantly strange at having a handsome man to say goodbye to.

•••••••••••••••••••

After an hour in the office, throwing away most of my mail without opening it (reporters know from the return addresses what is worth the effort of opening) and taking care of a few other things, I checked out for a few days. When I eventually got to break the story on the Memphis terrorist arrests, I would reclaim my vacation days and admit I was working these days secretly.

I thought briefly about stopping off at Ben's office and making a dramatic entrance, telling him, "I know Logan is alive, but I'm not going to write about it until I get the go ahead from the FBI. But I have one question for you, Ben. At what point did you plan to tell your best friend, who has been living a lonely and desperate non-existence for a year, that while he was gone, you stole his girlfriend?"

Then, according to my fantasy, I would turn and leave without giving Ben a chance to answer my stinging accusation. But I knew such a declaration would cause Ben to panic, maybe even fly out to San Antonio, and we didn't need that kind of complication right now.

During the 25-minute drive from the newspaper office to the FBI building, I practiced what I would say to Special Agent Joe Bedford. I'm here not as a reporter, but as Logan Magee's friend. I know you told Ben Spurrier that it was best for Logan to lay low for a while longer, but Logan has reached the breaking point in his patience, and he came back to Memphis secretly and would like to meet with you at my house.

When I entered the FBI office, a friendly, but all-business receptionist asked how she could help me. I asked to see Special Agent Joe Bedford, and she told me there was no agent by that name at the Memphis Field Office. Could somebody else help me?

"But a friend of mine talked to him a few weeks ago. Was he transferred to another city or did he retire?"

"I'm not at liberty to give out that kind of information, ma'am, but somebody else can speak with you if you'll wait for about half an hour. Everyone's in a meeting at the moment."

My heart raced at the thought that the meeting might involve an impending arrest of the Indonesians and their other cell members.

At first I waited, but then my gut told me to get out of there. I felt strongly that we needed to talk to Joe Bedford first, rather than try to explain to somebody chosen at random by the receptionist that I was the friend of a dead man who's not really dead, who faked his own suicide for the sake of his country and family. I told the receptionist I'd come back tomorrow.

Driving back home, I came up with a plan for locating Agent Joe Bedford, wherever he had gone.

•••••••••••••••••

Logan was surprised and disappointed when I told him what had happened.

"Why didn't Bedford tell Ben he was about to retire or be transferred? Those things don't happen suddenly, do they?"

"Unless," I said, "Bedford made somebody important mad and got booted out or he resigned on principle. Remember some of the intelligence community said after 9/11 that they had noticed certain warning signs before hand, but nobody would listen to them? Maybe it was a situation like that. But in this case, you have the power of the press behind you, and if they've written off the Indonesians as no threat, we'll bring it out in the open somehow and make them take action. "

"I hope it doesn't come to that."

"It probably won't," I reassured. "Joe Bedford probably knew he was being transferred, but didn't tell Ben for some good reason. Or he could be on assignment somewhere else temporarily."

"Logan, I'd like your permission to bring my cop friend, Jack Trent, slightly into the loop on this. I won't tell him why I want to know — I'll just say I'm trying to find a long-lost acquaintance, Agent Joe Bedford, and could he ask a few questions for me. I've heard him say before that he's got a friend, a Memphis cop, who's assigned to a joint task force run by the Bureau."

"Sure, whatever you think will work. I do feel strongly about talking to Bedford first, so I don't have to deal with being treated with suspicion and doubt by other people at the FBI before they figure out I'm legit."

So I called Trent, who said he would find out where Bedford went and why, as long as I would agree to have dinner with him tomorrow night. I said yes and then Logan and I made a pact to forget all this for the next few hours and try to act like normal people, who laugh and talk about regular stuff.

I picked up our dinner from The Cupboard and after dinner we played Scrabble. Then we settled in on the sofa to watch "Raising Arizona" and laughed ourselves silly. It was miserably hot outside, so we had the AC on a sub-Arctic setting. When we got cold, instead of turning the thermostat up, we just put a down comforter over us and snuggled.

He willed himself to act like he wasn't in the middle of a terrible mess involving the FBI and foreign terrorists, and I willed myself not to think about the fact that in a few days Logan would be leaving our hiding place and going back to the arms of the woman he loves.

CHAPTER THIRTY-SIX

Trent and I had said we'd meet for dinner at Dino's at six, but he called late in the afternoon and said we needed to eat somewhere where we could talk without being overheard. He suggested his place at seven, and I thought it was just an excuse to be alone with me. Until I got there and saw the expression on his face — romance was the last thing on his mind.

When he told me what he had found out, I lost my appetite and left for home as soon as I could without arousing his suspicions.

I had no idea what I was going to say to Logan, so I just blurted out the truth as soon as I walked into the kitchen, where he was standing, waiting anxiously for me.

"Logan, Joe Bedford is dead."

"How? When?"

"He was taking his morning run, and he just dropped dead of a heart attack at the age of 47."

"In the last few days?"

"No, he died early on the morning of May 25 a year ago."

"My wedding day," Logan said numbly, the full implications

of Bedford's death not sinking in yet. "But Ben said he's talked to him twice since then."

Logan looked confused, like it was impossible that his best friend had lied to him.

"I guess you'll have to ask Ben why he lied, but not until you talk to the FBI tomorrow morning. Two agents from the Joint Terrorist Task Force are coming here first thing."

"So Agent Bedford never knew I didn't show up for the meeting on Saturday morning, and he never got my letter, but obviously somebody did, and they started the investigation."

Logan must have seen the look of pain on my face.

I took his hand and led him into the living room, pulling him onto the sofa beside me.

"Let me tell you everything Jack Trent told me. We won't have the full story until tomorrow. Jack called his friend at the FBI, just as we planned, and said he was looking for an acquaintance, an agent named Joe Bedford. The friend said he thought Jack would have heard, Joe Bedford died a year ago.

"At first Jack didn't think too much of it, until the friend mentioned the date, May 25, and Jack remembered that that was the day Logan Magee committed suicide. Then he remembered me telling him my theory about who murdered you and why. Jack was the only one I told, and he thought it was too far-fetched to be true. But when he heard that an FBI agent I was asking about had died the day you died, it was too much of a coincidence."

"So they all know I'm alive?"

"No, the agents think they are coming to talk to me. I figured it would be better if you explained your actions yourself."

"I guess so. Did your cop friend find out if they're close to an arrest?"

This was the moment I had been dreading most.

"They're not. In fact, there is no investigation. The Indonesians have had a year to work on their plot without so much as surveillance."

Logan slumped forward and put his face in his hands.

"I gave up a year of my life for nothing and put my mother and Caroline through hell, for absolutely nothing," he said, shaking his head slowly. "For nothing. What a fool."

I put my arms around him and my tears seemed to release his. He collapsed into my arms and we both wept, holding each other tight. His face was against my breasts and I rocked him back and forth like a baby until he was quiet, but we didn't let go of each other.

Then he raised his face to mine and kissed me desperately as if everything could be made right by our coming together. I've never wanted anyone so much in my life, but I stopped him.

"No, Logan, I don't want to be a temporary substitute for Caroline."

"I wasn't thinking of her."

"Maybe not now, but afterward you would. Let me ask you this, have you been faithful to Caroline this whole year?"

"Of course."

"Then you've got to return to her the same loving, faithful man you were when you left her. Besides, I'm not planning to exit your life when all this terrorist stuff is resolved. I'm planning on staying friends with your mom and you, and I don't want you to feel guilty every time you look at me."

Just what I need — another male friend who's going to marry somebody else.

Logan and I went to our separate beds earlier than usual — we were physically, emotionally, and mentally exhausted. But about 2 a.m., I woke up to the faint sounds of the TV in the living room. I found Logan sitting on the sofa in his boxers and a T-shirt, shivering and watching a show about World War II on PBS.

I got the down comforter out of the closet and sat down beside him, wrapping the quilt around us both. We sat there cocooned, not talking, not touching, until we both fell asleep, our heads leaned against each other until dawn.

CHAPTER THIRTY-SEVEN

Logan and I waited anxiously for the FBI agents to arrive. We kept peeping through the window blinds until a black Tahoe with tinted windows pulled up in front of my house. We had decided that we wouldn't play games, that we'd both meet them at the door rather than slowly breaking the news that reports of Logan's death had been greatly exaggerated, as somebody, Mark Twain, I think, said.

The doorbell rang, Logan and I took a deep breath, and I opened the door. They didn't know what Logan looked like or even his importance in this whole scheme, so they registered no surprise at seeing him there.

"Miss Faire, I'm Special Agent Jim Alexander and this is Special Agent J.D. Starnes. We're with the FBI, and I think you were expecting us."

"Yes, please come in."

They each handed me a business card after showing me their identification. Logan and I later talked about being surprised to see the agents in jeans instead of suits and ties and handing out business cards like businessmen.

"Is this your husband?"

"No, this is Logan Magee. He's really the one you'll want to talk to. It's a very long story, but everybody in Memphis, except for one of Logan's friends, thinks he's dead. I'll let him tell you everything."

The FBI agents seemed nonplussed, but I'm sure they were anxious to hear Logan's explanation. We all sat down in the living room.

"Do you mind if we record this interview?" Alexander asked, already activating his iPhone's recorder.

"No, of course, not."

"So Mr. Magee, could you tell us why everyone thinks you're dead and why you believe Memphis is a terrorist target."

It was almost an hour later when Logan finished his story. The agents only interrupted him occasionally to clarify certain points.

"So you met with Agent Bedford on Friday, May 24?"

"Yes."

"And that was the only time you spoke with him?"

"Well, we made plans for me to meet him at his office on Saturday morning."

"But you didn't keep that appointment."

"No, by 9 a.m. I was on my way to San Antonio."

"Did Agent Bedford advise you to fake your own death?"

"No, of course not. When I met with him, my plan was to go to the office late that night, get the full names, addresses and such of the Indonesians and bring them to him the next morning and then I was going to get married and go on my honeymoon and leave the rest of the investigation to the pros."

"Did Agent Bedford record the interview with you?"

"No, he said we'd do that on Saturday morning when I had all the information. And then he said he would get a rush job on the transcription and get me to sign it later on Saturday before I left town on my honeymoon."

"So the last Agent Bedford knew, your plan had not been discovered by the Indonesians?"

"That's correct."

"But you said you wrote Agent Bedford a letter and mailed it, and wrote a letter to one of the Indonesians. Did you by any chance make copies of those letters before you sent them?"

"Yes, I make copies of everything before I mail it. In my business, we always have to have a paper trail of everything we do and say."

This was the first I had heard of these copies of the letters.

"Mr. Magee, do you have those copies with you here?"

"Yes, I'll get them from my suitcase."

The agents looked at both letters and asked Logan to read the letters aloud for the benefit of the tape-recorded record of the interview.

"Dear Agent Bedford, by the time you receive this, you'll know from reading the newspaper why I didn't come to your office on Saturday. Late on Friday night, I went to my office to get the information you needed, which I enclose, but one of the men caught me and threatened to kill my family if I turned over the information to the FBI. They didn't know I had already spoken with you, so I lied and said I wouldn't go to the FBI if they would return to Jakarta while I was on my honeymoon. I knew they couldn't be trusted, but I played the naive American, who would take their word for this.

"Later that night I realized that the only way I could be sure that they would not harm my family was if I was dead. Although I won't be here to answer your questions, I have confided in one person, a trusted friend who will not tell anyone about this. His name

185

is Ben Spurrier, and you can contact him to ask questions about what I told him."

Then Logan ended the letter with the names, addresses and phone numbers of Ben and the Indonesians and some other information from personnel files about the Indonesians.

"And now if you would read the letter you wrote to one of the Indonesians."

"Nat, by now you have read the newspaper and know that I am dead. I realized after I left you tonight that the only way I could be absolutely sure that my family would be safe was for me to talk to no one about all this and then jump from the bridge. I knew it was the only way you would know your secret was safe. I'm sure you understand that suicide is justified when the cause is important enough."

"And did you sign your full name on the originals of both letters, Mr. Magee?"

"I signed my full name on the letter to Agent Bedford, but I put only my initials on the letter to Nat. So can you tell me what happened to my letter to Joe Bedford when it arrived on Monday?"

"We don't know at this point," Agent Starnes said. "Your name is in the log the receptionist keeps, for 8:05 a.m. on Friday, May 24, of last year, but that is the only record of your having had any contact with the Bureau. Agent Bedford didn't start a file, and your letter hasn't been found so far. We started investigating internally when a homicide detective with MPD called one of our agents about the situation yesterday."

Then Agent Alexander added, "Everyone at the field office was shocked and upset at the unexpected death of Special Agent Bedford. He was well-liked by his colleagues, and I can only guess that perhaps in the confusion that follows such an unexpected death, your letter never got into the proper hands. Agent Bedford was not part of the Joint Terrorism Task Force, and now that I read your letter, I realize you never mentioned a terrorist plot, so perhaps it was forwarded to the wrong person."

"We don't really know what went wrong," said Starnes, "but it is regrettable not only for you personally, but because if indeed these three men are part of a terrorist cell, we've lost a whole year in the investigation, and they've gained a whole year in planning a possible attack."

"So until you heard about this," I asked, "there was no indication of terrorist activity in the Memphis area, no chatter, as Homeland Security always calls it?"

"We are always investigating suspicious activity," one of the agents said. "Because of the two bridges that cross the Mississippi River at Memphis and the Port of Memphis, which handles 16 million tons of petroleum products and other goods each year, Memphis has been identified as a place of possible interest to terrorist organizations. If somebody takes down the tag number of a tourist photographing one of the bridges, we look into it, so certainly there would have been a great deal of investigative activity if your letter had reached us and gotten into the proper hands."

"Nobody regrets that it didn't get in proper hands more than I do," Logan said.

"Mr. Magee, I'm not trying to pour salt into the wound — I know you didn't have long to make a decision about how to protect your family — but I just want to make sure you realize that the FBI would never encourage a citizen to do what you did. Not only is faking your own death a crime, it is dangerous and foolish."

"I've had more than a year to realize that, Agent Starnes," Logan said bitterly. "I've made quite a mess of all this."

"Don't be too hard on yourself — since 9/11 most Americans have felt that the impossible is possible, including your own family being killed by terrorists."

"So how do I undo the mess?"

"We'll take it from here, but the Bureau may send a special interrogator down in the next few days to talk to you. You say you don't remember anything else suspicious happening or being said, other than the Jamaah Islamiyah remark, but these special interrogators can sometimes help people dig out helpful memories. We all hear things every day that we don't remember because we don't think they are important at the time, but it doesn't mean those things aren't somewhere deep in memory. It's a fancy way of saying jog your memory."

"So when will it be okay for me to go to my family and tell them I'm alive?"

"Well, as I said, we would never have recommended you take this action, but since you did, it would be helpful if you would stay underground a while longer until we find out exactly what we're dealing with.

CHAPTER THIRTY-EIGHT

We spent the rest of the day dissecting the morning spent with the FBI agents and talking about what to do next and what to do eventually.

The what-to-do-eventually part was the hardest — how would we let Caroline and Maggie know that Logan was alive without causing cardiac arrest? We came to no conclusion about the exact way such a revelation should be worded, but Logan felt strongly that Ben should tell Caroline and that I should tell his mother. I said we'd talk more about it later.

The what-to-do-next part was easier. It was time, we both agreed, to bring Ben into the loop on Logan's return to Memphis and to demand some answers from Ben. I called Ben and told him it was absolutely essential that he come to my house sometime the next day or night. No, it couldn't wait until later in the week, I said.

Logan said he wanted me to be part of the discussion, and I correctly predicted that Ben would not like that. I wanted to make sure Ben completely came clean, not just about the lies about calling Joe Bedford, but the secret life he'd been living with Caroline.

Ben came to my house after work, about 6:30, and Logan waited in the bedroom. I greeted Ben at the door in a friendly if not warm way and he greeted me with understandable suspicion. He had good reason to be wary — after all we had lured him into a trap, where he would be called on to answer tough questions with no chance to prepare excuses or apologies. The reporter in me relished it. As Logan's friend, I anticipated it painfully. Logan would find out the whole truth tonight and it would hurt him deeply.

I sat on the sofa and Ben sat in an uncomfortable straight chair near the door. I guess he was sending me a message that he didn't want to be here and didn't plan to stay long.

"Ben, Logan is in the next room. He wants to talk to you."

My bluntness had its desired effect. He jumped to his feet as Logan walked into the room.

"What are you doing here? I thought we agreed..." he said angrily.

"Sit down, Ben. We've got a lot to talk about."

Logan sat on the sofa next to me and leaned forward, his arms resting on his knees.

"Can we talk alone?" Ben asked pointedly.

"No, we can't. Britt is very much involved in all this. If it weren't for her, I'd still be wasting my life in San Antonio. You see, Ben, I found out a couple of days ago that I've thrown away a year of my life for nothing, for absolutely nothing."

"But what about the terrorist investigation?"

"There is no investigation, and you would know that if you had really tried to call Agent Bedford those two times you supposedly talked to him."

"But I did call..."

"Joe Bedford dropped dead of a heart attack on the same day I took off for San Antonio, and my letter to him either was lost in the chaos after his death or somebody read it and discounted it as the ranting of a paranoid patriot. So the bottom line is that I gave up everything for nothing, and Nat and the others have had a whole year to establish their cell and maybe put their plan into effect. Why'd you lie, Ben?"

"I had no idea there was no investigation, I swear, Logan. I would have never let you stay out there, if I'd known. I lied to you the first time because you were so mentally unstable, and I wanted you to have something to cling to so you wouldn't feel hopeless. The second time I was trying to keep you from rushing back and confiding in a reporter who would probably ruin everything."

"I don't buy it," Logan said. "Your excuses have some ring of truth, but there's more you're not telling me."

I spoke for the first time. "It's time to tell the whole truth, Ben."

Ben's eyes looked teary, but he worked them away with the thumb and index finger of one hand, looking down at the floor until he composed his answer.

"I have no idea how to say this, Logan. I didn't mean for it to happen, but Caroline and I, we, I don't know, we just..."

Logan stood, his whole body stiff with anger and disbelief.

"You stole my girl while I was living in hell out there? You son-of-a-bitch, you..."

"No, Logan, you stole *my* girl," Ben said, returning the anger. "I loved Caroline before you even met her, but you never noticed, because you were always too self absorbed in your own little romantic dramas."

"You dated Caroline before I met her?"

"Not really, but I was around her a lot — we were in the same social circle, and I wanted to take her out so much, but I could never get my nerve up — she seemed above me, like somebody who would only want to be friends with somebody like me, not date me."

"Somebody like you? That's ridiculous — what's with this low self-esteem shit?"

"Logan, you've never had an insecure moment in your life — girls always liked you."

"I've had plenty of girls break up with me."

"But you never hesitated to ask women out, and they always said yes. Maybe it didn't always work out, but you never had trouble getting relationships started. Maybe your parents just adored you so much that it never occurred to you to have any self-doubt. And it never occurred to you to notice that your best friend had it bad for Caroline for a long time."

"You never told me, or I wouldn't have put the move on her at that party."

"Actually, I did talk about her to you sometimes, but you always brushed it off with, "Just call her, Ben, don't be such a wuss, just call her."

"I guess I didn't connect those things you said with the girl at the party."

"No, you were a heat-seeking missile as soon as you spotted her," said Ben, his voice rising in anger. "You said, 'Who's that blonde?' and I said, 'That's Caroline Crawford, the one I've told you about,' but you weren't listening, you just insisted I introduce you to her. And before I knew what had hit me, you were engaged to her. You had slugged me in the gut and were too much in love to even notice."

I feel like I'm the one who's been hit in the gut. This Caroline lovefest is getting to be too much for me. I want to leave the room, *so why instead do I listen as Ben goes on?*

"You knew her for three months before you proposed — that is so you, Logan, so damn you," Ben said bitterly.

"What do you mean it's so me? I've never proposed to any other woman."

"I don't mean just that. You're so damn impetuous, so impulsive about everything in your personal life. When we went to

Gulf Shores in high school with my family, he bought a surf board," he said to me, "a surf board when he lived 500 miles from the nearest ocean. He used all his savings and borrowed money from me, and there was no talking him out of such a dumb-ass move."

"I was a kid. Kids do dumb stuff."

"So you think proposing to Caroline when you barely knew her was a rational adult move?"

"Of course it wasn't rational. Love isn't rational."

"No, but it doesn't have to be completely devoid of common sense either. That was too soon. She hadn't even had time to find out that you aren't what you seem on the surface."

"What in the hell is that supposed to mean?"

"I'm talking about truth in advertising. You come off to women as this upwardly mobile, smooth, I-know-what-I-want-in-life kind of guy when actually you're like a kid trying to decide what he wants to be when he grows up. When Caroline and I talk about you, I can tell she fell in love with your image, not with the real you."

Now that was a low blow, Ben. I was starting to sympathize with you, but...

"The hell she did! And I suppose you're quick to tell her all my faults, so she won't want me back when she finds out I'm alive."

"No, I'm quite sure she'll want you back, and she'll hate me for deceiving her for the past year. I knew this would all come to an end, but I wanted my dream to last as long as possible. I love her, Logan, I *really* love her, the real her. I know I can never really have her, but these past six months might be enough happiness to see me through the rest of my life. I'm just sorry I've lost my best friend in the process."

"So did you encourage me to take off for San Antonio, so you could move in on Caroline?"

Come on, Logan, you know how unfair that accusation is.

"That's not fair, damnit," Ben said, echoing my silent assessment. "I did everything in my power to talk you out of it — you know I did, but when you get on an impulsive spree, there's no stopping you."

"I was trying to save the lives of Caroline and my mother, and maybe a few thousand people that the terrorists might be planning to kill."

"I know that, and when you convinced me that might happen, I got behind you, and it wasn't for selfish reasons either. Do you think it's been fun for me this past year living a lie, watching your mom and Caroline grieve, knowing I could stop their suffering if I just told them the truth?"

"I'm sure it was hard, but not as hard as it was for me, a man without a life. So how long after I died, did you start dating Caroline?"

Sarcasm doesn't become you, Logan.

"At first I was just her friend, the best friend of the man she loved, who she could talk to about it all. She was so upset she had to take a leave of absence from work. She didn't teach the fall semester at all. So at first I just listened to her and then I started taking her places sometimes to cheer her up, things she likes like the ballet and plays at the Orpheum. It was like that for six months before it got romantic, and our first kiss was initiated by her, not by me."

I'll never again think that women are the catty sex.

"But you didn't resist," Logan said seething.

"No, Logan, I didn't. I should have, out of loyalty to you, but I didn't. I love you, buddy, but not as much as I love her. That's just the cold, hard truth."

Logan sat silently for several minutes, his head in his hands, staring at the floor.

After a long silence, Logan said, "I need some time to think."

I decided to bring the conversation back to the more immediate issue at hand.

"Ben, two FBI agents were here yesterday talking to Logan. I guess they'll be doing surveillance of the Indonesians, and they said an interrogator from FBI headquarters might be coming in to talk to Logan in the next few days. In the meantime, they want Logan to stay dead."

Ben stood and walked toward the door. He couldn't seem to make eye contact with Logan. To me he said, "Just let me know what I should do and when." He walked out of the house without looking back.

CHAPTER THIRTY-NINE

After Ben left, I asked Logan if he wanted to talk about it, and much to my relief he said no. So we ate scrambled eggs and toast for dinner and went to bed early.

The next morning he slept late — maybe, I thought, he was falling back into his depression — so I left him a note saying I had to go to the office today and wasn't sure when I'd be back.

The truth was that I just needed to get away from the intimate prison we'd shared for almost a week. I had loved every minute of our time together until last night. Now I needed some time alone to think, too.

It's not often that a woman gets the dubious honor of listening to two men bitterly quarrel over which of them loves another woman the most.

As I was driving to work, my mind continued to ponder the question that had kept me awake late last night — what about Caroline Crawford, besides beauty and a certain amount of charm, made her worthy of such adoration by both Ben and Logan?

Logan gave up everything to protect her and had faithfully waited this year to return to her. And Ben, with no hope for long-term happiness, thought six months with Caroline was enough happiness to last him for the next 40 or 50 years.

Okay, I know what you're thinking — I was just jealous.

Damn right I was. I had never had even one man love me that much, much less two. Okay, I'm not blonde, I'm not beautiful, I don't have the perfect body, but I'm not butt-ugly either, and I'm smart and I understand the West Coast Offense better than most men I know. And I'm sure I have many other good qualities as well.

But another thing was eating at me, too. I had disliked Ben Spurrier from the minute I met him, and my bad vibes about him had been confirmed when I found out he had lied to Logan about Joe Bedford and had broken into my house and scared me with that computer threat.

And yet, I found myself sympathizing with Ben, against my will, when he talked about caring for Caroline for a long time before Logan swooped down and claimed her. There was so much genuine agony in his voice and face. I could imagine the frustration and pain he must have felt when he saw his best friend planning a wedding with the girl Ben loved. And then to be asked to be best man when clearly he was not the best man in Caroline's eyes. I hated having to sympathize with somebody I didn't like.

Instead of driving to work, I drove to Harbor Town, hoping I'd find Maggie at home. I had been neglecting her lately.

I knocked on the kitchen door, and she looked so happy to see me as she peeped through the curtains.

"Dear girl, come on in," she said, pulling me inside. "I'm cooking sausage and I've got biscuits in the oven. Logan loved my homemade biscuits and sausage. You'll eat breakfast with me, won't you?"

"Are you kidding? Of course I will. Do you cook a big breakfast like this every day?"

"I don't make biscuits every day, but I do like a big, hearty breakfast. Logan never liked breakfast that much. He was happy with a bowl of cereal, but he did love his mama's big, country breakfasts from time to time."

I had been so pre-occupied with helping Logan this past week and so happy contemplating the good news that Maggie would get soon, that I hadn't felt guilty until now. I had been eating breakfast and talking and watching movies and playing board games with the dearly loved son she still thought was dead. This definitely wasn't fair, but I had to keep quiet a little longer. When and how to tell Maggie that Logan was alive was not my decision to make.

We ate breakfast and visited, and she asked me if I had been on vacation since she hadn't seen my column for a few days. I told her I was just taking off a few days to take care of some personal business.

"Oh, that's too bad, sweetie. I was hoping you were lounging on the beach somewhere or in New York going to plays and museums. You really need a vacation — you work too hard."

"I don't think my editors would agree with you, Maggie, but thanks. Listen, I got to go now, but I did want you to know that just because I'm not still investigating Logan's disappearance, it doesn't mean we won't go on being friends. You're stuck with me, like it or not."

"I like it, sweetie."

I hugged her goodbye and promised to come again soon. She stood in the driveway and waved to me as I drove away.

•••••••••••••••••

I went into work for a while but told my editor I was still on vacation officially and there would be no column the rest of the week.

I drove out of the newspaper parking lot fully intending to pick up some groceries and go home, but instead I got on Sam Cooper and headed East.

I showed up at the Crawfords' door without warning, but the

housekeeper who answered the door summoned Caroline, who looked very surprised to see me, but was nonetheless quite gracious.

She had on shorts that showed off her perfectly shaped tanned legs and a T-shirt from some 5-k charity run. We sat down in the living room.

"It was terribly rude of me just to drop in like this — thanks for not slamming the door in my face." She smiled as if to say that I *was* rude, but she'd forgive me. "Anyhow, Caroline, I just wanted to check on you and see how you're doing. I was visiting with Maggie this morning and it made me think of you and wonder if you were continuing to do well."

"That was sweet of you, but you really didn't have to worry about me. I really am doing well. When Logan died, I thought I'd never have another happy moment, but somewhere along the way, the fog lifted, and I wanted to live again, really live again, not just exist."

"I'm really glad to hear that. You're dating Ben and I think that's just great."

She looked shocked that I knew, but not ashamed.

"How did you know?"

"I saw the two of you in a restaurant holding hands, and it looked like a lot of love was crossing that table. I was really happy for you after all the suffering you've been through."

"Thanks, Britten, that's sweet of you to say that. Neither one of us saw it coming. He was just Logan's best friend, who grieved with me after Logan died. We both loved Logan, so we comforted each other, and it helped a lot. Then we started doing things together and a few months ago we just realized it had gone from friendship to love.

"I felt guilty at first, like it was disloyal to love someone else so soon after Logan died, but now I'm okay with it. I think Ben still feels a little guilty. What do you think?"

"Oh, no, I don't think you should feel guilty. It's only right that you should go on with your life. But isn't it hard not to compare the two men in your mind?"

"I do that some, even though I try not to, but it doesn't make me feel conflicted, like I would have thought. Logan was a wonderful man, and I loved him very much, but I actually have more in common with Ben. Ben actually enjoys a lot of things that Logan just endured for my sake, like the ballet. And we like the same movies and restaurants. It's so funny — he'll say where do you want to eat, and I'll think of a place, but not tell him and then he'll suggest that very restaurant. We're just so on the same wave length about so many things.

"And he's just so sweet and dear and we can talk for hours about anything. It's hard to believe a girl could come upon two such great men in one lifetime."

"I'm glad you're happy, Caroline. Well, I'd better get back to work. Take care of yourself."

"Maybe we can have lunch some time."

"Maybe we can," I said, feeling like a lying dog as I left Caroline Crawford.

As I drove back from the suburbs, I called Ben's cell phone and left a message.

"Ben, this is Britt Faire. I just had a nice little visit with Caroline. I didn't want you to panic when she mentioned that I dropped by her house. I didn't give away anything, I promise. I'm not going to tell Logan about my little visit, by the way. But, for what it's worth, I just wanted to say to you that I think Caroline loves you more than Logan, and I don't think his returning from the dead is going to change that.

•••••••••••••

That night, over a pizza at my kitchen table, I told Logan about my visit to his mother that day, but conveniently omitted mention of the drop-in assault on poor, unsuspecting Caroline. He wanted to hear everything his mother said and every other detail of my visit.

Then as we ate our dessert directly from the cookie-dough ice cream carton, he said, "You seem different tonight."

"Different? How?"

"I can't put my finger on it. Withdrawn maybe or just deep in thought?"

"Last night was very enlightening. Not many women get the chance to see two guys ready to kill each other over a woman they both love."

"A slight exaggeration — I don't think either of us were contemplating murder — aggravated assault maybe, but not murder."

"Well, anyhow, it was interesting, and I've been thinking today..." I paused, not sure how candid I was going to be with Logan on this subject.

"You were thinking..." Logan prodded.

"I was thinking, well, wondering actually, why it is that you never hear of two nice, smart, good-looking men like you and Ben fighting over sweet, wonderful, ugly or fat girls with mousy brown hair, the kind of girls who are crass enough to eat directly out of the ice cream carton?"

"Are you talking about yourself?"

"What are you saying, that I have mousy brown hair?" I said in mock defensiveness.

"Not at all, but that reference to the ice cream made me wonder if you were referring to yourself and if you were, I was going to say you obviously don't have a very accurate self-image."

"What are you saying, that I'm not sweet and wonderful?"

Logan laughed and ruffled my hair with his hand. "You're impossible. I give up."

"Well, it's a good thing, because if you and Ben were thinking of fighting over me next, I was going to tell you to forget it — neither of you is my type."

"Oh, is that right? And what's wrong with Ben and me?"

"Well, Ben has no discernable sense of humor, and I hate ballet. As for you, you're too handsome. I like a man with acne scars and premature balding."

"You are the most ridiculous woman I've ever met, and I don't know how I'm going to live without you as a roommate when I finally come out of hiding and go home."

CHAPTER FORTY

The call came early the next morning. A special investigator, I think they called him, would be coming in from FBI headquarters and wanted to meet with Logan in the afternoon.

Logan and I found this to be exciting news, though we weren't sure the excitement was justified. Maybe the Indonesians checked out completely legit, and this special interrogator was coming to accuse Logan of making the whole thing up. That was one of our theories as we talked during an early lunch of peanut butter and jelly sandwiches.

"Well, if he comes in with a naked light bulb dangling from an electrical cord, I'll know I'm in trouble," Logan said.

"Tell us, Herr Magee," I said in a fake German accent, "exactly what was your motive for misleading the U.S. intelligence community and besmirching the reputations of these three fine international businessmen?"

"Mister Magee," Logan carried on the joke, but without the German accent, "why couldn't you just admit like a real man that you didn't want to get married, instead of fabricating this elaborate hoax to avoid matrimony?"

Our more optimistic theories about this afternoon's impending visit included the possibility that surveillance was picking up something interesting on Nat, Marty and Suk.

"I don't know whether to be excited about that possibility or scared to death," I said.

"Yeah," Logan said, draining the last of his ice cold milk, which we both agreed was the only drink possible with PB & J. "It would be nice to be vindicated, nice to think I didn't give up a year for nothing, but not if we're days or hours away from a terrorist attack, and it's too late to stop it."

"I can't imagine much worse than watching you testify before a Congressional committee on the intelligence failings of another 9/11. And if something like that happened here, it wouldn't be like 9/11 where we grieved for strangers. This time it might be people we know."

"In San Antonio, I met a guy from Oklahoma City once and he told me that after the federal building bombing, you couldn't find anybody who didn't know somebody affected by the bombing in some direct way, even if it was something like my daughter's teacher's husband was injured."

We had lost our joking mood pretty quickly. We straightened up the house after lunch — Logan doing the vacuuming and me cleaning the bathroom. We cleaned the kitchen together, not that we thought the FBI guy would go in there, but it was something to do to pass the time. Then we changed our clothes.

"What does the well-dressed FBI informant wear, do you think?" Logan asked.

"Well, I don't see why we should dress any better than the two agents who came last time, so jeans and polo shirts should be fine. I'm not even going to tuck my shirt-tail in."

When our visitors arrived exactly at three, Special Agent Starnes was wearing dark pants with a dress shirt and tie and his partner wasn't along. In his place was a middle-aged man in jeans and

T-shirt, his hair longish and wind blown in a Kennedys- playing-touch-football-at-Hyannis-Port sort of way. Not at all the formal ex-military look and manner we were expecting. It made me wonder if he was CIA instead of FBI. He smiled warmly and introduced himself as Roy Scott, showing us his ID, which connected him to the Joint Task Force on Terrorism, but not specifically the FBI.

Apparently, my small part in all this had been explained, so Scott didn't ask me to leave before the interrogation began. Agent Starnes began by giving Logan a transcript of his previous interview with him and asking him to read and sign it if it was a correct reflection of his statements and answers a few days ago. We all sat quietly while Logan read, so as not to distract him, but once the document was signed, we made small talk for a few minutes. Then Scott got to the point.

"Mr. Magee — would you mind if I called you Logan?"

"Please do."

"And call me Roy. We'll record this interview, if you don't mind."

I assumed this first name stuff was all part of a put-the-subject-at-ease tactic.

"Logan, I'm not at liberty to divulge any details, but I can tell you that there is some intelligence to back up your suspicions about the three Indonesian businessmen. In fact, there is a sense of urgency in the investigation. I'm sure you both know that national security could depend on your discussing this with no one."

We both nodded yes.

"Our intelligence so far tells us only that an attack may be planned for the Memphis area sometime in the near future, so it is important for us to look at all possibilities. Obviously, security has been stepped up for obvious targets like the bridges, the Port of Memphis, the airport and the Federal Express hub, but the target may be as unconventional as the demographics of the suspects. These three men do not meet the usual profile, so their target may be equally unexpected. Logan, since you were able to understand the suspects' native language, you may have heard something important and may not even know it was important."

"I've gone over and over it in my mind for the past year, trying to remember if they said anything else suspicious, but I never came up with anything."

"But isn't it true that prior to the Jamaah Islamiyah statement, you were only listening for business-related suspicious remarks and may have overlooked something else?"

"It's entirely possible."

"Let's go back to when the Indonesians arrived at Prentiss-Lamar," Scott said, leaning forward, elbows on his knees. "What time of year was that?"

"I know it was in early fall, but I don't remember exactly when."

"What was the attitude of most of your co-workers toward the men?"

"Friendly, typical Southern hospitality. Several people invited them to their homes or out to dinner, but they always declined politely. After a while people stopped trying to entertain them."

"So the three men — I believe you called them Marty, Suk and Nat — showed no interest in seeing the sights of Memphis?"

"No, they were actually very interested in experiencing the city and appreciated it when people offered to take them on a tour. They just didn't seem interested in getting to know any of us personally or visiting our homes or meeting our families."

"It's easier to kill people you don't know. Do you remember any of the places they visited?"

"Let's see — they went to the Civil Rights Museum not long after they arrived."

"Do you remember any comments afterwards?"

"One of them, I think it was Suk, said something about Dr. King giving his life for a cause. He was impressed with how prophetic Dr. King's speech was the night before he died."

"When he talked about Dr. King and The Movement, did he speak with emotion — anger, admiration, inspiration?"

"No, mostly they just seemed to find it interesting in a touristy sort of way."

"Where else did they visit? Were they particularly interested in the river or the bridges?"

"Not at all. I remember thinking that they showed very little interest when I said I lived in the middle of the river on Mud Island. Usually visitors are pretty fascinated with this little community sitting in the middle of the river. And one day, it was a perfect fall day, some of us were going to take our lunches and sit in Tom Lee Park by the river, soak up some rays while we ate. We invited the Indonesians to join us, but they showed no interest."

"What other tourist attractions or local landmarks did they visit?"

"Well, of course, they had to visit Graceland. Nobody comes to Memphis without seeing Elvis' place."

"Did anybody go with them to Graceland?"

"One of my co-workers, Barney Foster, did. He told me all about it when they got back. He said they took a lot of pictures like the other tourists were doing and were impressed with how many people were still interested in Elvis this long after his death. They commented on how many different foreign languages and different regional American accents you heard among the tourists."

"Did your co-worker say if the men showed any disdain of Elvis or Graceland?"

"No more than your average Memphian does. Barney said he told the Indonesians that Memphians dread "Dead Elvis Week" when thousands of tourists show up on the anniversary of Elvis' death. The city is crawling with them."

"It's a running joke to the locals," I interjected, "but the tourists take it very seriously. People come from all over the world, and there's a group of especially loyal fans from around the U.S. who spend their vacations here every August. They book hotel rooms years ahead."

"When in August?" Scott asked.

"Aug. 16," I said.

"That's just six days from now."

The interrogation continued, but Logan and I later agreed that Scott had honed in on the idea that an American pop culture icon like Elvis would be a possible target with a multi-national contingency similar to the people at work in the World Trade Center on Sept. 11, 2001.

CHAPTER FORTY-ONE

There were three voice mail messages from Trent when I got to work on Thursday. One said, "Remember me?" Another said, "I'm sick of being just a sex object to you." And the last one said, "I feel so used."

I was still laughing when I called him at his office.

"You poor neglected homicide detective."

"It's murder trying to be your friend. I guess it's really true — you only call me when you need information."

"Or when I need a picnic on Mud Island or a steak dinner. Yeah, I guess I am using you."

"So when are you going to invite me over to meet the formerly dead Logan Magee?"

"How did you know he's alive? I didn't tell you."

"I know you didn't, and I'm pretty pissed off about that, to tell you the truth."

"I'm sorry, Jack, but I promised Logan I wouldn't tell anybody. But you didn't answer my question, how did you find out?"

"My buddy at the FBI told me."

"Well, so much for Homeland Security and confidentiality and 'Loose Lips Sink Ships,'" I said, genuinely indignant. "I guess Logan was right not to trust the FBI with the fact that he was hiding out in San Antonio."

"Oh, get off your soap box, Miss Self Righteous Reporter. The FBI agent didn't tell just anybody — he told a cop, a trusted friend and colleague and by the way, the person who started the investigation by inquiring about Joe Bedford. Because of that, he just assumed I knew and mentioned casually that they'd interviewed Logan at your house. Imagine my surprise."

"I'm sorry, Jack, you deserved to hear it from me after all the help you've given me. Why don't you come over tonight, and I'll try to scare up some grub."

"Please. Don't punish me with your cooking. Unless Logan's a good cook..."

"Forget it. He's as useless in the kitchen as I am."

"How about I pick up some ribs and beans and onion rings and bring 'em over about seven?"

"If you don't mind being used again, I'm fine with it?"

●●●●●●●●●●●●●●●●●

I got home in time to warn Logan that Jack Trent was coming over and that he had been tipped off by the FBI that Logan was alive and well and living in my house.

Jack arrived a little after seven loaded down with greasy, yummy smelling paper bags full of Memphis' specialty — pork barbecue. We're not talking about what people in other parts of the country call barbecue. No beef brisket doused in barbecue sauce at the last minute like you get in Texas or Kansas City or hamburgers cooked on a grill as Californians mean when they say, "Come over for a barbecue." No, we're talking about pork ribs or shoulder cooked slowly in a pit and basted with sweet, tangy barbecue sauce throughout the long cooking process. And if it's chopped pork shoulder served on a bun, it's also topped with cole slaw unless you ask them to leave it off.

Memphis probably has a hundred barbecue restaurants or joints, and they all do a good business. Everybody has their favorite and will debate the merits of the barbecue variations, which seem slight or nonexistent to the out-of-town uninitiated. They think it all tastes alike and is all good. Recently a group of fashion designers came to town for some charity event, and our fashion editor told me these New Yorkers tasted their first Memphis barbecue for dinner and loved it so much, they got up and had it again for breakfast before catching their flight home.

"Where'd you get it from, Jack?" I said lustfully looking into one of the bags.

"The BBQ Shop. It was on my way here." Actually, there are probably a half dozen barbecue places between downtown and my house in Midtown, so the truth was that Jack just likes BBQ Shop best.

"What's your favorite barbecue?" I asked Logan after introducing the two men.

"I like Germantown Commissary's ribs best, and they've got the best potato salad, but I guess Corky's is my favorite for a barbecue sandwich and onion rings."

"Forget it," Jack said. "They can't do barbecue right in the suburbs."

We were spreading all the goodies out on the kitchen table when Logan stopped and took a deep whiff of the sweet aroma.

"Now I really feel like I'm home. That stuff they call barbecue in Texas isn't worthy of the name."

"That, I think we can all agree on," I said. "Let's eat."

Over the next couple of hours we ate and talked, Logan filling Jack in on the hows and whys of his faked suicide.

"I always thought that nobody could pull off a faked suicide except people in movies, so I got to hand it to you," Jack said.

"Don't give us too much credit — it was luck more than anything. If we hadn't found one of those rare moments when there was a break in the traffic on the old bridge, we never could have pulled it off. Besides, the joke was on me, since Joe Bedford died of a heart attack before he got my letter."

Then we shifted to events of the last week.

"So that day I stopped by because your screen was off your bedroom window, Logan was here and you lied about the stomach virus."

"Sorry, Jack. I really felt bad about lying to you, but Logan had only been here for a few hours at that point, and he wasn't even sure he could trust me, much less my cop friend."

Then we told Jack everything we could remember about both interviews with the FBI.

"What do you make of it, Jack?" Logan asked.

"Well, there's no doubt they're taking this thing seriously. They wouldn't have brought in the big gun from D.C. if they weren't."

"My gut told me he might be CIA instead of FBI, since he seemed less formal in his manner than the G-men," I said.

"That's not far-fetched — it's a joint task force and includes local cops, FBI, CIA and Homeland Security. The CIA types carry a pocketful of cards and use whatever suits their purpose at the time. While FBI SOP is to hand out cards and fully identify yourself and record interviews and get transcriptions signed, the spooks aren't so forthcoming. If Scott is CIA, it definitely tells you they see an immediate threat from these Indonesians. Did this Scott guy really act like he was taking the Graceland idea seriously?"

"That's what Logan and I both took away from it. Scott said these guys aren't the typical profile, so maybe their target isn't either."

"Well, I'm not sure I buy the Elvis plot, but I've been saying since 9/11 that I thought the next major attack or attempted attack would be something in between the coasts and something that would strike at the heart of ordinary Americans."

"If you don't buy Graceland, what do you think could be a target in Memphis, Jack?"

"Well, the river bridges are an obvious choice, but that wouldn't kill many people, and security has been beefed up tremendously around the river, even though it's not obvious to the casual observer. The Coast Guard, you know, is under Homeland Security now, and they're even getting patrol boats here mounted with .50-caliber machine guns. They've been taking river safety real seriously since 9/11, so I don't know how good a target the river and bridges are now."

"FedEx seems like a likely target with all those hundreds of planes out there at the hub every night," Logan said, "but I hear FedEx security is really good, so I don't know."

"Does the Indonesians getting into banking have any significance, do you think?" I asked.

"I doubt it," Logan said. "It's probably just a convenient way to launder money from and to Jamaah Islamiyah."

"I think you're right," Trent said. "Well, if Graceland is the target, we'll know soon, since Dead Elvis Week is the ideal time to kill a lot of people from a lot of places."

"Well, one consolation is that if they blow up Graceland, it won't kill any Memphians, except the poor tour guides," I said and Logan and Jack both laughed.

"So, what do you two do all day and night when you're not busy saving the world in consultation with the FBI and CIA?" Jack asked with what I thought was a bit of an edge, especially the "all night" part.

The edginess was lost on Logan, who answered cheerfully, "It's been like summer camp — fun and games." The way he smiled at me let Jack know that Logan really meant it. In all this chaos and worry and questioning by the FBI, still Logan and I were having fun the rest of the time.

"Although the food could be better," he said. "I would have liked to hide out with somebody who could cook, but I guess you can't have everything."

"Well, I think I make a mean peanut butter and jelly sandwich," I said, smiling at Logan.

"Britt and I have discovered our one area of incompatibility is jelly. I'm a grape jelly man, and she's a strawberry jam person, so we've had to buy separate jars. Fortunately, however, we're in full agreement when it comes to peanut butter — extra crunchy all the way."

Logan and I laughed, and Jack smiled weakly.

"So when you're not eating crunchy peanut butter, what do you do?"

"We play board games and cards and watch TV and rent movies and make a concerted effort to avoid exercise," I said. "The treadmill is still collecting dust like it was before Logan came."

"Well," Jack said, standing up. "I'll leave you two to your fun and games, and I'll go home and get some sleep."

"Nice to meet you, Jack, and thanks for all the help you gave Britt on my behalf," Logan said, shaking Jack's hand.

"I'll walk you out to the car," I said. Even at almost ten o'clock, it was still stiflingly hot and humid outside.

When I commented on the heat, Jack said sarcastically, "Yeah, good weather to stay inside and have fun and games."

"Could you strike that phrase from the record? I would hardly describe hiding out in my house for two weeks as fun and games. We've just made the best of a bad situation. Are you jealous, Jack?"

"Hell, yeah, wouldn't you be jealous if I...don't answer that question. I could be shacking up with the whole wait staff at Hooters, and you wouldn't care."

"Jack, I've never seen you this way before?"

"You know how I feel about you, Britt, and..."

"Actually I don't."

"Well, I'm sure not going to tell you right now. I've got a little bit of self-respect."

"What do you think is going on in there night after night, hours of torrid sex?"

"Probably not, since he's engaged to a beautiful blonde and is probably counting the days until he's back with her."

"Ouch. That was a low blow."

"I didn't mean it that way, Britt. It's just that all night, I felt like you and Logan were a club I didn't belong to. You probably have no idea how many times you two looked at each other and laughed that knowing laugh or went on and on about how much you have in common."

I caught both Jack and myself completely off guard when I leaned forward, took his face in both hands and kissed him.

"That's something I've never done to Logan, so maybe you and I have our own exclusive club."

CHAPTER FORTY-TWO

Don't ask me why I kissed Jack Trent that night. All I know is that I didn't regret it later. At first I was concerned that it might have been a pity kiss, but it's more likely that I was turned on by his vulnerability. It's so uncharacteristic of Jack to play the little boy hurt because he had been left out. It was really very endearing. I hoped that I hadn't kissed Jack because I felt stung by the Caroline Lovefest I had witnessed during the confrontation between Ben and Logan, but I couldn't swear to it.

Not long after I had arrived home with Chinese takeout the next night, Jack stopped by to tell us that there would be a lot of non Elvis fans flocking to Graceland on Aug. 15-16 this year.

"An awful lot of uniforms will be putting in overtime out of uniform this weekend, along with Feds," he said. "Hopefully nobody will notice, but Graceland will be crawling with cops during the Candlelight Vigil and during the tours the next day."

"So they *are* taking the Elvis plot seriously?"

"They really can't afford not to take *everything* seriously right now, what with a year lost in the investigation because of somebody's screw up at the field office when Logan's letter came in," Jack said.

Logan asked if the cops and FBI agents would search the

Elvis fans and question suspicious people.

"There are a lot of strange people who attend an Elvis candlelight prayer vigil, so it'll be tough to profile suspicious people, but they'll be looking for people who might be Indonesian and people with camera bags that look too big — stuff like that," Jack said.

We invited Jack to stay for dinner, but he said he had to go. Unlike last night, he didn't act threatened by leaving Logan and me alone, and he left with a smile and a wave.

●●●●●●●●●●●●

After dinner, Logan and I watched an ESPN preview special on the upcoming college football season. My mind wandered back to my impulsive kiss the night before, and that got me to thinking about Ben's accusation that Logan has lived his life impetuously.

After the TV show was over, I muted the sound and asked him if he was really as impulsive as Ben had said.

"I've thought about it a lot since Ben said that, and I guess in some ways he's right. I'm certainly not that way professionally, but in my love life, I do tend to act in haste, regret at leisure. Who else but an impulsive person would have done what I did the night before my wedding?"

"What in your personality makes you that way, do you think? Except for marrying Drew, I rarely do anything impulsive. If anything, I overthink most decisions in my personal life. I'm probably too cautious."

"I don't think I have an inborn impulsive streak — I think it's my family history. I was mischievous when I was a kid, but I don't remember being really impulsive and reckless until after my dad got sick. At first my mother and father didn't tell me what was happening, but by the time I was about 11, they had to tell me, because my dad had to quit work at the age of 40."

I just listened, afraid of what I would hear from Logan about his own prognosis.

"I found out much later, when I was a teenager, that Dad's first symptoms had appeared when I was four or five. He developed sporadic depression and irritability. By that time they had figured out why my grandmother had died and that it was hereditary. Have you ever heard of Huntington's Chorea?

"Yes, it's a rare disease," I said, failing to mention that I learned about it from his mother.

"It's not rare in *my* family. My father, who's been in a nursing home since he was 44, has it. My Aunt Mae, my dad's sister, died of it when she was 51, and my grandmother, who everybody just thought went insane and then accidentally choked to death, turns out to have had it. Huntington's is a death's head that hangs over the Magee family and always will unless those of us with the gene stop having children. That's the only way to stop it."

My heart was racing — I could hardly catch my breath. Did he say, "those of us with the gene"? Before I could get up my courage to ask if he had it, he went on.

"If one of your parents has the gene, you have a 50/50 chance of getting Huntington's and there's no cure, not even any treatment. It's a death sentence and a guarantee of spending the last 10 or 20 years of your life acting like a lunatic. So naturally they didn't tell me at first why my dad was acting different. Mom just said things like, "Dad's having a bad day." or "Dad doesn't feel well today."

"But when I was 11, he got so bad that he had to quit work, and Mom finally told me about the disease, but she didn't tell me I had a 50/50 chance of developing it myself. Four or five years later when he had started to get terribly argumentative and even violent sometimes and he was about to go into the nursing home, Mom told me the whole truth. She didn't tell me about genetic testing, because their doctor had advised against it. But she always stayed upbeat and said I seemed to have more of her genes than dad's, so I probably would never get it. I tried not to think about it too much, but one effect it had on me was that it made me obsess about how uncertain life is, and I developed something of an "eat, drink and be merry, for tomorrow we die" attitude."

"Was that good or bad?"

"Both, really. The bad was that it caused me to do things impulsively and risky sometimes, as if I had to make the most of life in case mine was short. I guess another effect was that I could never be completely satisfied with my job. I kept thinking that life is too short to do nothing more than make money. I really would like to be a teacher like my dad or a tennis pro at a club.

"But then there was a good side to all this, too, in that I savored life each day. I've never taken life and good health for granted. That's why it hit me extra hard when I realized I had thrown away one precious year of my life in Texas for nothing, though maybe I did protect Mom and Caroline by doing that. I guess we'll never know for sure."

"When your truck driver friend showed up at MPD and said he saw you jump off the bridge, I was suspicious, but when I told your mother, for the first time she seems to accept the idea that you had killed yourself. She said you must have had the gene after all and didn't want to have to face a life of suffering, so you just ended it quickly."

Tears came to Logan's eyes. "Poor, sweet mom. So much loss for one person."

I took both Logan's hands in mine and asked the question I dreaded the answer to. "Logan, do you have the Huntington's gene?"

"No, I had the genetic testing a month before the wedding. I never had wanted to know, but I couldn't get married not knowing. It wasn't fair to Caroline."

"Ben said Caroline insisted on the testing, but your mom said Caroline didn't want to know, that she just wanted to get married and adopt children."

"Caroline did insist, but I don't blame her. Who wants to

219

marry somebody who may be an invalid in a few years. I guess Mom told you a little fib, so you wouldn't think less of Caroline. But I don't understand why Mom thought I had it — I told her how the test turned out and she cried with relief, so why would she think it was a motive for suicide?"

"She said that if you did indeed kill yourself, the only explanation she could think of was that you found out there was a mistake in the test results and that you really did have the gene. After seeing what the disease had done to your father, I guess she could understand that one reason for your suicide."

"Did that explanation make her feel better about my death?"

"I think it did, but it didn't make me feel better about it?"

"Why did you care, Britt?"

"I don't know, I just did, and finding out about the Huntington's made your murder or suicide seem even sadder to me, because, like you said, when this terrible disease haunts a family — every day, every minute seems precious. And it made me sad and angry that someone deprived you of some of those precious days."

Logan picked up the remote and turned off the TV. Then he turned on the CD player, and as Frank Sinatra sang, "Love is the saddest thing when it goes away," Logan took my hand and held it tight.

CHAPTER FORTY-THREE

Friday, Aug. 15, was my day to be lost in thought and be utterly worthless at work. I should have my column for Tuesday either written or at least planned, but no ideas came to me. I kept staring out the window and thinking of many things except work.

The first mind monopolizer was Huntington's Chorea. Maggie's description of it a few weeks ago really deeply affected me. It was depressing to learn that there was a disease so terrible that it wrecked families by separating them into the haves and the have nots, the doomed and the blessed. What must that be like, wondering which group you fell into and knowing that you could only stop the disease's spread by not having children, by terminating the family line?

Now after hearing how Huntington's had affected Logan's life, I was even more shaken. How could Maggie endure watching her husband and sister-in-law and mother-in-law evolve from life into mere existence, knowing that her only child might be next? And Logan's gradual realization that his father was slipping away and that his own life might be essentially over in his thirties. I imagined all the details of Logan's teen years and life in his twenties, him alternating between denial and a desperate need to live life at top speed, since the road might be short.

After lunch my mind switched over to Dead Elvis Week. Never before had this commemoration had any significance to me. But if the FBI was right, tonight — the eve of Elvis' death when the faithful line up to carry candles and pass reverently by Presley family graves at Graceland — could be the culmination of the terrorist cell's year of planning. I doubted anyone I knew would be hurt or killed, unless maybe it was whichever reporter was assigned to cover the vigil. I couldn't bear to ask who had the assignment. But even if the victims were all tourists, what a horrific thing to happen to Memphis, to happen to the nation and world.

And there was one more thing that would happen if the plot was carried out or squelched — not a tragic thing, but a sad thing — Logan would leave my house and probably never again share that space with me. Never again play Scrabble and Sequence and Trivial Pursuit with me. Never again share take-out meals and crunchy peanut butter and eat ice cream straight from the carton. Never again repair everything he could get his hands on, just to stay busy. Never again cuddle with me under the down comforter and listen to Sinatra.

I came home that night with a 1,000-piece jigsaw puzzle and hamburger meat and buns. We were both nervous about what might happen that night, but we didn't talk about it at first.

He told me about the latest thing he had repaired at my house — Britt's personal handyman had become his job during his Memphis captivity — and I was happy that this time it was something I really did want fixed. A few days before he had proudly announced that he had fixed the squeak of my rocking chair, and I told him I liked that squeak, because it reminded me of my grandmother, so I'd appreciate it if he'd find a way to put the squeak back. He apologized and said he'd try to remember to check with me next time before repairing something. He didn't, but it was okay this time, because I was glad to find the garbage disposal fixed.

I had offered several times to go to the library or bookstore for Logan, but he seemed content reading his way through my bookshelves. He said it was fun to read a book, knowing you had a friend who had also read it and could talk about it with you.

I told him about something that had happened in the grocery

store a few minutes before.

"I got my column idea for Tuesday in the produce department. There's a homeless man I see on Union a lot. He's a burly black man with matted dread locks and a beard, pretty scary looking, but mild mannered. I've never seen him ask for money or bother anyone. He was going in the store at the same time as me — he was counting his money, I guess to see what he could afford. We both ended up in the produce section, and suddenly he seemed to go into a kind of trance. He held up his hand and just stood still, staring straight ahead. Most people around him moved away from him or acted like they didn't notice, but one woman, a middle-aged white woman, said to him, "Baby, are you okay?" and there was genuine concern in her voice. He came out of the trance and said softly, "I'm okay," and she said, "Well, I just wanted to be sure.""

"In other words," Logan said, "she treated him with respect and concern, like everybody ought to be treated."

"Exactly. And that was when it hit me that I should write a column about how it must be so hard to be homeless, dirty, poorly dressed and have to endure the further indignity of people being afraid of you or at least afraid if they're nice to you, you'll ask for something. People in the South smile at most strangers and exchange small talk with everybody they come in contact with, but not with homeless people. We look past them, reluctant to even make eye contact, much less smile and exchange small talk. I'm just as guilty as anybody else most of the time, but I remember one time exchanging small talk with a homeless man, and as I walked away he said, 'Thanks, ma'am, for being so nice to me.' It broke my heart."

"When I was volunteering at a homeless shelter in San Antonio, several people told me that they feel invisible most of the time, like people are afraid to look at them. That's a great idea for a column, Britt."

"Can I use that invisible quote in my column? Anonymous source, of course." We both laughed.

"I bought this jigsaw puzzle, since we can only watch local TV tonight, you know in case something happens out at Graceland

and they break in with a news bulletin. It's a Parisian street scene."

"Oh, yeah, good idea. Why don't you ask Jack to join us?"

"I already did. He'll be here about 6:30."

●●●●●●●●●●●●●●●●●

By the time Jack got there, Logan had cooked the hamburgers and I had set up the card table in front of the sofa. I figured we could eat there and then later set up the jigsaw puzzle on the table.

"I thought about bringing beer," Jack said, "but I didn't. I thought maybe we might need all our faculties at some point tonight."

For all our joking about strange Elvis fans a few days before, now none of us was in a joking mood. The thought of FBI agents and undercover cops infiltrating the tourists at Graceland didn't seem funny at all any more. And the possibility of a terrorist attack was extremely sobering.

We ate our hamburgers and made a half-hearted effort at the jigsaw puzzle throughout the evening, but all that happened was a promo of the ten o'clock newscast that for an instant startled us with a mention of Graceland. But we immediately realized it was the annual feature on the candlelight vigil and nothing more.

"What would you do if there was a news bulletin about a terrorist attack tonight or some other time?" I asked Jack.

"I'd call in to see if I was needed or maybe I would just get in my car and get down there. And you, I'm assuming, would high-tail it to the paper, since you know the background on all this that no other reporter would know."

"I guess I would, but we'd have to make sure Caroline and Maggie found out about Logan before the paper came out. That would be a terrible way to get such good, but shocking news."

"And what would *you* do if that kind of news came on TV?" Jack asked Logan in a kind voice.

"I guess I would sit here and wonder what would have been different if Joe Bedford hadn't died and if my letter had gotten to the right people."

Jack left about ten, and Logan and I turned in early. I lay in bed and thanked God that nobody was hurt at Graceland and that I had Logan sleeping in my house at least one more night.

CHAPTER FORTY-FOUR

Logan had read four of the books on my shelves, had researched the country of Botswana on the Internet just out of curiosity, had fixed my dripping kitchen faucet and my defective toilet and together we had finished the Parisian street scene puzzle, and we still hadn't heard from the FBI again.

I know informants don't have any right to be kept informed, but we felt awfully left out. We were dying to know what they were finding out, and Jack wasn't much help — his FBI information pipeline had dried up. He said that either meant they weren't getting anywhere or it meant they were close, that the investigation was getting red hot.

Then Agent Starnes called and said Roy Scott was coming back to Memphis and needed to meet with Logan ASAP. Starnes, who had always been the model of FBI cool, this time sounded a bit strained. They would be at my house at two, so I didn't go into work.

●●●●●●●●●●●●●●●

Roy Scott sat in an armchair perpendicular to the sofa where

Logan and I sat anxiously. Starnes was in the straight chair near the door. Scott's manner was as casual and confident as before, but he didn't waste time getting to the point.

"There have been some new developments, Logan, that make it urgent for you to try again to tax your memory," Scott said.

"What kind of new developments?" Logan asked.

Scott glanced at Starnes and paused as if trying to decide how much to tell us.

"Two days ago, the three Indonesian businessmen left their apartment at the usual time to drive to work. They weren't carrying anything other than the usual brief cases, and they drove to the bank by the usual route, only stopping for gas. They parked in the parking garage and went into the office. At some point during the day, they were able to leave the bank without being noticed by our surveillance and haven't been seen since. They haven't been home for two nights and didn't go to work yesterday or today. Their car is still in the parking garage."

"How could they disappear without your knowing it?" I asked.

"They could only do it by leaving the office silently and going to the parking garage, where I assume a van or something like that was waiting for them. If they had spoken even a word, our electronic surveillance would have picked them up. Since they left in total silence, we can only assume they knew they were being tracked and found a way to elude us."

"What does this mean?" Logan asked.

"We don't know, but it's disturbing in light of another development — the latest intelligence indicates a terrorist attack is planned for this Saturday, four days from now."

I gasped. Logan sat in stunned silence.

"Will the attack be in Memphis?"

"It wasn't specified. It could be somewhere else in the area —
Nashville, Jackson, Miss., maybe even further away, but we don't
think so. Memphis has long been identified by Homeland Security as
a possible terrorist target, more so than those other places. Logan,
relax and think back to the year you worked with the suspects. Did
they travel to other cities or even mention them?"

"Not that I remember."

"Did you ever hear them ask questions or make comments
about other cities in the area or perhaps do some research in an Atlas
or on the Internet?"

"I don't remember anything like that."

"Switching gears here for a minute, did they ever talk about
Memphis being in the Bible Belt or discuss the fact that there are so
many churches here?"

"I do remember a conversation where somebody at work was
telling them right after they arrived about Memphis and mentioned
that there are more churches in the city than gas stations. They didn't
seem to take any particular interest in that fact, though."

"The country's biggest Southern Baptist Church is in
Memphis," I said. "That could be a target, but then if it's planned for
Saturday, that wouldn't make sense."

"Saturday is the Jewish Sabbath," Scott said, "but I'm told
Memphis doesn't have that large a Jewish community, so it doesn't
make sense to come to Memphis if you wanted to blow up a
synagogue. Besides, I doubt if someone from Indonesia could walk
into a synagogue unnoticed."

"Do we know the plan calls for suicide bombing?" I asked.

"No, we're considering all possibilities, but individuals with
explosives strapped to their bodies is a method whose time may have
come in the U.S. And it would be easier to pull off than hijacking a
plane or loading a rental truck with explosives or blowing up a
bridge. There will be extra security this weekend on the river and at
the airport and FedEx has been put on high alert, but my gut tells me

that the target is going to be something hard to predict, something that hits at the heart of average Americans, a target that would make everyone in America feel vulnerable."

"I don't think there are any large festivals planned for this weekend," I said.

"We've already checked on that. No, there aren't."

"What about shopping malls?" I asked.

"Security will be beefed up at the major ones in the city this weekend," Scott said. "Still, Memphis seems an odd choice for a mall bombing. There are much bigger, higher profile malls in the country, like that one in Minnesota. What do you think of when you think of something distinctly Memphis?"

"Rock 'n roll, blues, Elvis," Logan said.

"The river and barbecue, but the barbecue cooking contest down on the river is always in May," I added.

"Agent Scott, I don't want to give you any false hope, but there's something eating at me that I can't put my finger on, something one of the Indonesians said, I think. Something you said triggered it."

"Logan, let me urge you to try a little mind game that sometimes works in situations like this — try to let go of it mentally until later when you're more relaxed. Take a long bath or lie in bed and just let your mind wander back to the time you worked with the suspects. Don't strain to remember, just let your mind wander back to that time. Let yourself remember all kinds of mundane things that were said and done at work, even things that don't concern the Indonesians. Would you try this later today and call me if you think of anything? Here's my card with my cell phone number on it. Don't hesitate to call, no matter what time of day or night."

CHAPTER FORTY-FIVE

After work, I headed east to my favorite bookstore, a regular hang-out of mine before Logan climbed through my window and changed my life temporarily and then permanently.

Before Logan, it was my favorite entertainment spot. You can browse for books and have lunch or dinner (an avocado BLT is my favorite). What more can you ask for in an entertainment venue?

Normally I would go there, pick out several promising books and road test them in one of the comfy armchairs arranged in the middle of the store. I give new (to me) authors one chapter to win me over. If they do, I buy the book, which means I often leave the store with three or four books.

But this night, I was having an early dinner with two girlfriends who were getting either suspicious or concerned because I seemed to have become a hermit in the past month. Pam says I've got a new boyfriend that I'm keeping a secret for some reason, but Trish is concerned that I'm depressed about Drew getting married and that I might be at home moping. I had to agree to meet them for dinner to disprove both theories.

I ended up telling them that I've been swamped at work and that's why I've been staying home so much. They weren't sure whether to buy it or not, but they both by the end of dinner seemed to feel reassured that I was neither depressed nor a slave to love.

It was a fun dinner and my mood got even better on the way home as I passed the Fairgrounds — the collective term for the property at Central and East Parkway that used to house the Mid South Fair in late September (I never missed it); and still is the location of the Liberty Bowl, the city's football stadium. I live just a couple of blocks from the Fairgrounds and have always enjoyed hearing its sounds from my front porch — like the cannon that goes off when the home team makes a touchdown.

When I arrived home, Logan was working the New York Times crossword puzzle at the kitchen table and eating a peanut butter and grape jelly sandwich. Whenever I broke out of our cloistered routine, I felt guilty, since I was his only source of company, but he never acted deprived.

He'd always say, when you spend a year in a strange city and go weeks without a real conversation, you'll never again complain about eating dinner alone occasionally.

"What's a two-letter word for 'printers' measurement'?" he asked as I sat down at the table with him.

"Either 'em' or 'en'," I said. "But with digital layout, nobody uses those terms any more."

"Why are you so upbeat, Britt?"

"I was just thinking that it's football season and that always gets me excited."

"Is it football season? It's just the end of August."

"Haven't you been reading about the big season opener this weekend between the University of Tennessee and the University of Memphis? It's already sold out, and would you believe that some of the fraternities were already staking out party places near the stadium with their tents when I passed by? More than 24 hours before the game."

"Wish I could take you to the game — you're the only

woman I..."

Suddenly the blood drained from Logan's face as he stopped mid sentence. It was the old "you look like you just saw a ghost" cliché.

"That's it. Oh, dear God, that's it, Britt. The Indonesians are going to do something at that game or some game."

He was frantically pulling everything out of his wallet, looking for the card with Roy Scott's cell phone number. When he found it, he ran for his phone and dialed it with fumbling fingers.

"Why didn't I see it before? I remember now."

"Remember what?" Scott answered on the first ring.

"This is Logan Magee. I remembered. I remembered what they said. Oh, okay." Then Logan hung up. "He told me he'd call me back on a secure line." The phone rang and Logan picked it up mid ring.

"When the Indonesians first got to Memphis, somebody took them to a college football game," he told Scott, "and one of them commented the next Monday that the security guards seemed more concerned about searching for smuggled alcohol than for weapons. It makes perfect sense — weak security and a hard to manage crowd of 60,000."

Scott apparently added something to that list.

"Yeah, that makes it even more ideal for them," Logan said. "The game is tomorrow night. How can we stop them? Is it too late?"

Logan listened a few more minutes and then hung up.

"What did he say?"

"He agreed with me that it makes perfect sense. Not only is security weak and that's an awful lot of people in one place, but he said it was symbolic, which terrorists love."

"You mean like an all-American sport being played at a place called the Liberty Bowl?"

"Exactly. And he didn't mention this, but remember how they started flying dozens of American flags along that street leading into the fairgrounds after 9/11? And of course, every game begins with the National Anthem. And it's on national TV, so they get maximum exposure."

"What did he say when you asked if they could stop the terrorists?"

"He said the problem is all the ways it could be done — a plane crashing into the stadium or a truck filled with explosives, both of which might be preventable by a high alert at all area airports and searching all vehicles entering the stadium area. But his greatest fear, considering what happened in London, is individual suicide bombers with explosives strapped to their chests scattering throughout the stadium. "

"The fans who weren't killed by the bombs would be trampled during the ensuing panic. Couldn't they just call off the game?"

"That's an option they'll consider," he said.

Logan and I just stood in the middle of the floor, too numb and frightened to move. Then we fell into each other's arms and held on for dear life.

CHAPTER FORTY-SIX

After the phone call to Roy Scott, I had called Jack, who promised to come over as soon as he had found out anything. That turned out to be the next morning, and Logan and I both mobbed Jack as soon as he walked through the door. We shouted questions at him, presidential press-conference style, and he waved us to stop.

"I'll tell you as much as I know, if you'll both just cool it for a minute."

We became silent like contrite children.

"There was a meeting this morning of all homicide detectives after an earlier meeting for the top brass, many of whom had been routed out of bed at 4 a.m. by the FBI. They wanted us all to volunteer to be part of the security forces at the game tonight."

"Did you volunteer, Jack?" I asked.

"Of course I did. Do you think I would miss this? Anyhow, unlike the Graceland hunch, they think this is the real thing, and they want as many experienced officers as possible, along with hundreds of FBI being flown in today from around the country."

"Why not just go for warm bodies, the more the better?" Logan asked.

"Because once these suicide bombers are identified in the crowd, it's a very delicate matter to subdue them before they can detonate their explosives. You can't just walk up to them and arrest them. You have to grab them from behind when they least expect it and get their hands hand-cuffed before they can do anything. You wouldn't want to trust that to a uniform unless he had a lot of experience in a tough neighborhood."

"Why don't they just beef up security at the gate when the fans enter the stadium?"

"For the same reason. The first sign that somebody was onto them or that everybody was being searched, they'd go ahead and detonate. I'm sure the ideal would be to detonate once inside the stadium, but worst case scenario they would figure several hundred at each gate is better than nothing. You know how people crowd as they funnel into the ticket turnstiles when it's a really big game like this?"

"But Jack, why don't they just call off the game instead of endangering all those people?"

"That same question was asked at the meeting. It seems that the FBI and local police brass initially wanted to do that, but there were several factors that led them to drop the idea.

"For one thing, how do you get the word out this close to the game? There are thousands of fans driving in from all over the Midsouth, who wouldn't necessarily hear a local radio newscast, so you'd still have thousands of people showing up at the game."

"Another factor is that once the terrorists realized we were on to them, they'd either reschedule for another game and what are you going to do, cancel the whole football season? Or they'd simply go to the most crowded places they could find on a Saturday night and detonate there. I'm sure they have a plan B."

"Not to mention that I'm sure both schools are opposed to

canceling the game because of economic loss from tickets, concessions and TV rights," I said cynically.

"You're exactly right, Britt. Both schools *are* opposed to it. They've convinced themselves it's a hoax or false alarm.

"And then one last obstacle to canceling the game, the most important one, is the Homeland Security system. Nowadays, they can't even get the color on the alert system changed without agreement from a panel of big wigs in Washington, including the President and Secretaries of Defense, State and Homeland Security, not to mention the heads of the FBI and CIA. I guess that false alarm with Graceland made the boys and girls in Washington think we're a little paranoid down here. They say there's no evidence that the attack will happen at the game, except one sentence remembered by one co-worker of the suspects. They're afraid they'll put the city and probably the whole country in a panic if they cancel the game and then look foolish when it doesn't happen."

"What about the panic when Liberty Bowl stadium explodes killing 60,000 people?" I asked.

"Good question, but ours not to reason why at this late date. Gotta go. At 1 p.m. the FBI and CIA are doing a training session on subduing suicide bombers. All the volunteers from homicide, Metro Gang Unit and narcotics will be there. Federal agents from any field office within a few hours' flight from here should be arriving in the early afternoon if they're not already here."

As Jack started for the door, Logan shook his hand and with emotion wished him luck and thanked him for his willingness to do this. I walked Jack to the car while Logan stayed inside.

There was no big passionate going-off-to-war scene at the car. We didn't kiss, but we hugged and clung together for several minutes. I sensed that the last thing Jack needed was for me to act like I thought he was about to die, so I just smiled and said I'd see him tomorrow.

"I think we can pull this thing off," he said, "unless..."

"Unless?"

"Unless the suicide bombs are detonated by remote control. All it takes is a rigged cell phone. If that happens, we're all dead."

CHAPTER FORTY-SEVEN

Logan and I spent the afternoon making a list of our nearest and dearest who might possibly be planning to attend the football game. I called them, one by one, and found that only one had tickets. It was my friend, John, an ardent UT fan.

"John, I can't tell you why I know what I know, but I beg of you, don't go to the game tonight," I said. "Trust me, please trust me. Your life could depend on it. I know that sounds melodramatic, but it's no exaggeration."

After quite a bit of argument, he agreed not to go, but said my reasons better be good when he finally got to hear them.

Then I called the paper and talked to the assistant metro editor, a good buddy of mine.

"Tom, you need at least four reporters, news people, in addition to the sports guys at that game tonight. There may be a major news story developing there. I got it from a confidential source. Just trust me."

I was tired of asking people to trust me and wondered what I would say to them the next day if nothing happened.

About an hour before the game was to start, Logan and I

went out onto the porch for the first time since his arrival. Somehow it didn't seem important any more to so closely guard his existence. We both felt that one way or the other, it would all be over tonight.

Being outside for the first time in two months should have felt wonderful to Logan, but he said it wasn't as good as he'd imagined it would be.

Neither of us had any appetite, so we hadn't bothered with even the simplest dinner. Glasses of iced tea and the television were all we brought outside with us. A long extension cord snaked from the porch through the front door to the electrical outlet. Watching on the laptop just didn't seem to be enough.

"I remember my dad telling me about the summer of 1969, the summer of the first moon landing," I said. "He was on vacation at Gulf Shores, and the rustic little beach house they always rented didn't have a TV or phone. They normally liked it that way, because it was a real getaway from civilization, but they had to see the landing, so they brought a portable TV with them. They sat out on the deck, salt air blowing in their hair, and watched the landing on TV, constantly glancing up at the moon above them. He said it was surreal."

"This evening may turn out to be surreal, too, but I hope not," Logan said.

"I'm not sure exactly what to hope except that no innocent people will get hurt."

"If you were planning a terrorist attack tonight, when would you do it — during the Star Spangled Banner?" Logan asked.

"That would be symbolic, but then again you might not have live TV coverage during the National Anthem. Maybe they'd wait until the stadium was full and the game was going on."

"Probably."

We watched the pre-game show in tense silence. It wasn't dark yet, but the stadium lights were on and plainly visible from my front porch two blocks away. We could hear the faint sounds of the

PA system, but couldn't understand anything that was being said. So far, so good.

The ESPN announcer was talking about how these two teams rarely played each other and had never before played the first game of the season. Even though the University of Tennessee is a national football power and the University of Memphis is not, an intense in-state rivalry had led to a sell-out crowd of 62,476, one of the play-by-play announcers said. And with the Memphis team improving a lot during the last couple of years, U of M fans would be right to think it was very possible to pull off an upset.

Memphis won the toss and elected to receive. They went three and out. During its first possession, UT made two yards on a running play. The quarterback was dropping back to pass when we heard the explosion to the east and then after a couple of second's delay, we also heard it on television. Then we heard the most chilling sound on earth. At first it sounded simply like a crowd cheering at a football game, and then we realized it was the terrified screams of 60,000 people rising up from the stadium.

Logan and I both jumped to our feet and instinctively started running toward the sound, running with all our might two blocks, having no idea what we would do when we got there. At East Parkway, a short distance from the stadium, we stopped, suddenly realizing we could do nothing to help by going further and might in fact do harm by getting in the way.

Two police cars, sirens blaring, sped past us, closely followed by an ambulance and a few seconds later by a fire department pumper. More police cars, more paramedics — red and blue lights reflected in our faces as we stood there in stunned horror. People had come out of the houses on East Parkway and nearby streets. Many stood in their yards crying. Others just stared in disbelief. Others were too afraid to come out of their houses.

Then we saw them, a couple in their teens or early 20s, running toward us, so hysterical they were nearly hit by a car on East Parkway as they ran away from the stadium. The girl collapsed on the sidewalk near us — the boy tried to pull her to her feet.

Logan and I helped the girl up, and we yelled above the sirens that if they could walk a little further to my house, we could help them get away, to get home. They were crying too hard to speak as we all stumbled toward my house. When they collapsed in exhaustion on my porch, they finally calmed down enough to try to call home.

"Call your family now, tell them you're okay, then give the phone back to me." I ordered.

The girl was too shaky to dial the number, so she dictated it to me. A very frightened sounding man answered the phone.

"Daddy," the girl said before she dissolved into sobs. I took the phone from her.

"Amy, baby, are you okay?" her frantic father shouted into the phone.

"Is your name Amy?" I asked the girl, and she nodded through her tears.

"Sir, your daughter's fine. She's not hurt and neither is the boy with her. Yes, yes, they're fine. She's safe at my house."

I could hear a woman's voice screaming in the background, "Is she okay? Is she hurt?"

I gave him the address and suggested he circle around on I-240 to avoid the emergency traffic snarls. Then the boy, Taylor, called his mother, who had not heard about the attack yet, but who began crying so loud on the phone we could hear her across the room.

While we waited for Amy's parents, and Logan got everyone water to drink and cool wash clothes for their faces, I called my own parents, who I knew would be hysterical in Florida, knowing how much I like football and how likely I was to be at the game.

"You know as much as I do, Mom. Just keep watching TV. I wasn't there. I'm at home. I'm fine. Talk to you later."

I hung up and turned to Amy and Taylor, who had at last

regained a little composure.

"We were late," the boy said. "We had just walked through the gate when we heard the explosion. We turned around and ran as fast as we could away from the stadium."

We all turned toward the TV, which we had switched from ESPN to one of the local news stations, which showed footage of thousands of panicky people running in every direction away from the stadium

We began to piece together the story. A number of suspected international terrorists had been arrested entering the stadium and had been subdued before they could detonate explosive devices strapped to their chests. A lone suicide bomber made it into the stadium and blew himself up, killing or injuring at least 30 people. We didn't find out until the next day that the terrorist who was killed was Suk, one of the other Indonesian businessmen that Logan worked with. At first I was sorry that it wasn't Nat, but Logan pointed out that being arrested denied Nat the martyrdom he wanted so bad, and now he'd either be executed or have the rest of his life to sit in prison, knowing he had failed. I liked the second scenario better.

The next day we also found out that in addition to the 30 people killed or injured by the explosion, there were 11 people seriously injured during the panic-stricken stampede from the stadium.

But while we were still watching the spot coverage of the terrorist attack right after it happened, a frightening news bulletin came on TV.

"This report just in from the Memphis Police Department. At least two dozen people have been reported killed, including a Memphis police officer."

I grabbed Logan's arm. All I could say was, "Jack, not Jack."

"It's probably not him," Logan reassured, but it was just words.

Then there was an official statement from an FBI spokesman

telling us what we already knew, that the attack was believed to have been planned and carried out by a group of Indonesians affiliated with the Al-Qaida-related terrorist group, Jamaah Islamiyah. That while the loss of life was tragic, thousands of deaths had been avoided because of quick work by FBI agents and Memphis police officers.

"Logan, wait here with them until their parents get here," I said as I ran out the door.

"Where are you going?" he shouted at my back.

"I don't know, but I've got to do something. I can't just sit here."

I ran back to East Parkway and by that time hundreds of people were running away from the stadium in our direction. None of them seemed to be injured and few seemed to be running *somewhere* — mostly they were just running away, running *anywhere*. Some were screaming for help, while others were silent, their eyes wild with fear and confusion.

One young mother ran toward me, her little girl in a blue and white cheerleader outfit in tow. Both were crying.

"My husband," the young woman said to me, gasping for breath. "He's got our baby. We got separated."

"Just sit down here," I told her firmly. "Give him time to catch up with you. "

She sat down on the curb and held her little girl to comfort her. Someone from a nearby house was bringing bottles of water to some of the stadium refugees, many of whom had run in the opposite direction of their cars.

"We're parked near the stadium," one middle-aged man said, holding his chest as he tried to catch his breath. "When I heard the explosion, all I could think about was running away, far away."

"That was smart," I said.

I looked around and hundreds of people who had been in the stadium were lying on the grass or sitting on curbs or porches. It reminded me of the scene in "Gone With the Wind" when all the injured soldiers are laid out waiting for the troop train. These people weren't physically injured, but their hearts were bleeding. Most of them were asking what happened, and those of us who had been watching TV told them. We in turn asked them what it was like inside the stadium.

"We were just enjoying the game and cheering," one man said between gulps of water, "and then all of a sudden we heard the explosion across the stadium on about the 40 yard line. For a second, there was stunned silence and then somebody near me yelled, "It must be terrorists!" and everybody panicked. Everybody started running for the exits, but they were so narrow and everybody was pushing and shoving and trying to get out. I could hardly breath. But we kept pushing, because we thought any minute another bomb would go off, maybe near us."

The most common comment from everybody gathered on East Parkway was, "I didn't think it could happen here."

People began passing cell phones around to those who had dropped theirs. The little cheerleader's dad and baby brother finally arrived, and the young family fell into each other's arms, crying.

Eventually I went back home, where Logan was waiting alone on the porch. He said Amy's tearful parents had just taken the teenagers away. He and I moved the TV inside and switched back and forth between the local channels and CNN and MSNBC until the call finally came about 4 a.m.

Jack's voice sounded so beautiful.

"Hey, kiddo. Were you worried about me, or am I flattering myself?"

"Jack, thank God you're okay. I've been terrified that cop who was killed was you." My voice broke mid-sentence.

"It was a guy from the Metro Gang Unit, who volunteered.

Witnesses said he grabbed the suicide bomber, but the guy got an arm loose and blew himself up and at least a dozen people around him. Bastard. Got to go, kid. Just wanted you to know I'm okay."

"Thank God you called. I wouldn't have had a moment's peace until you did."

Jack started to say goodbye and then remembered one more thing.

"Britt, tell Logan not to beat himself up over the people who died. If he hadn't remembered that comment about football yesterday, we could be dealing with thousands of casualties. There were 12 suicide bombers, all going in different gates, and they were wearing a very sophisticated type of explosive that we've never seen before. It would have been a massacre. Tell him he did good."

There was no convincing Logan he did well, but he was relieved Jack had survived, and Jack's words gave him some comfort. I made him promise to put off the what-ifs until tomorrow, just as I was putting off my version of this story until Monday's paper. I knew the reporters there would get the breaking news for Sunday's paper.

As morning began to lighten the sky, Logan and I fell into my bed together, not even taking off our shoes, and slept for the next four hours in each other's arms. We knew, but didn't say, that this would be our last night together.

CHAPTER FORTY-EIGHT

The minute my eyes opened the next morning, I eased out of bed so I wouldn't wake up Logan. If Logan expected me to linger in bed with him on our last morning together, he was wrong. That would have been too heartbreaking, and one thing I am not is masochistic.

By the time he came into the kitchen looking sleepy and numb, I was in journalistic overdrive. My Rice Krispies were getting soggy in the bowl next to my laptop, and I had made a good start on my story for Monday's paper.

"How are you able to function after last night?" he asked. "The whole country is probably in shock, and I've never seen you so alive and focused."

"Funny observation from a man who's only known me for two months. You've just never seen me in my reporter's mode. When a big story happens, reporters are personally affected like everybody else, but that lasts for about a minute and then your adrenaline takes over and all you can think about is getting the story. Then later when deadline is past, you go back to being a vulnerable human being. I can't tell you how many times I've been super reporter sending in my story dispassionately from the scene of a crime or some other disaster, and then after the story was done, crying as I drove back to the paper. I'm glad I didn't go into work last night and write this. It will be much better as a second-day story. How does this lead sound?

Logan Magee has had a knack for languages since he was a little boy learning Spanish from Sesame Street, but he never dreamed that picking up Indonesian from a college roommate would lead to his overhearing a terrorist plot in Memphis a year ago.

Even more unimaginable was the fact that he would end up faking his suicide on the eve of his wedding and giving up a year of his life in order to save the lives of his mother and fiancée and many of his fellow Americans. Without Logan Magee's sacrifice, Saturday's terrorist attack at Liberty Bowl Stadium would have been far more deadly.

"Oh, please, spare me the hero talk," he said bitterly. "I screwed up my life for a year and now 30 people are dead and a hundred more injured. Am I supposed to feel good about that?"

"Yes, you are, as a matter of fact. You didn't screw up. You did the best you could with limited information and limited time. It wasn't your fault that Joe Bedford died and the FBI misfiled your letter. You *are* a hero, Logan, and you might as well accept it. Either I'm going to tell your story correctly and with sensitivity or the TV guys are going to half-ass tell it with more dramatic schlock than you can possibly imagine. Take your pick."

He just grumbled and went to the refrigerator. I kept writing and when he came back with his cereal, he said, "I thought we could spend some time together this morning before all hell breaks loose."

"No time for that," I said without looking up from my laptop. "We've got a big day ahead. I've got to turn in my story. And then we've got to figure out how to tell your mom and Caroline you're alive before the rest of the world hears it. Why are you looking so glum? You should be excited. *They* sure will be."

"I *am* glad — it's just that this isn't going to be easy. I want to see Mom and Caroline, but the weird thing is that I've wanted nothing for a year except to get my old life back, and now some aspects of it — I don't know if I want back or not. I just feel confused."

"Your old life is like riding a bicycle — it'll come back to you immediately. You're just scared because you're out of practice."

I know you're thinking that I was sounding a lot more upbeat than I was feeling, but what was I supposed to do, tell him I'd miss him terribly and that I would be crying more than most at his wedding to Caroline? Besides, I *was* happy in a way. I was happy for Maggie, because her dream was about to come true — her son, her baby boy, was coming back from the dead. I wasn't sure whether to be happy for Caroline or not. She had a terrible decision ahead of her — Ben or Logan?

Before I could find out exactly what Logan meant by "confused," the doorbell rang. Still being in journalistic mode, my first thought was that those weasels at the TV stations had heard about Logan from somebody at the FBI and that I would get scooped on my own exclusive story. Caroline gets Logan — the least I can get is a Pulitzer (yeah, sure) or at least a Tennessee Press Association Award.

There's something about a terrorist attack in your own country and especially in your own city that softens your attitude toward almost everybody, even Ben the Liar. When I saw his sad-sack face at the door, I smiled warmly and motioned for him to come in.

"Hey, Ben, you okay?"

Logan heard me and came into the living room. He and Ben embraced like the best friends they had always been.

"One of the guys from my office was injured in the attack last night. Remember Matt Lawrence, Logan?"

"Of course. Is he going to be okay?"

"He'll live, but he's going to have to have some facial reconstructive surgery. I went over to the hospital this morning and talked to his wife. I wanted to get over here sooner, but..."

"We were up all night anyhow watching the coverage. I haven't been up long," Logan said.

"Let's sit down and come up with a plan," I said. "Logan, you tell Ben and me what you want us to do."

"I wish I knew. All I know for sure is that I still want Ben to tell Caroline and you, Britt, to tell Mom."

"I get the fun job, and Ben gets the hard job. Sounds good to me. How are you going to tell her, Ben?"

"I guess I'll just go over there, if that works for you, Logan, and ease into it. I don't think Caroline is the kind who needs bluntness at a time like this. I'll say that what happened last night at the football game was connected to Logan's disappearance and that he was a hero in the deal, and the good news is that he's alive, but couldn't tell her or his mom, because their lives were in danger. Then the hard part — I'll have to admit I've been living a lie and have been involved with her romantically, knowing full well that Logan was alive and would be coming back eventually. Logan, I swear I'll tell the whole truth this time. I won't say anything to minimize my culpability. I know she'll hate me for it, but it's no more than I deserve."

"Then what?" Logan asked.

"That'll be up to Caroline, I guess. She may need a few hours to deal with it before she sees you or she may want to see you right away, so I think you should be on the ready. I'll call you when I know something."

Logan looked at me for my reaction.

"That sounds like a good plan to me."

Ben picked up his cell phone and dialed Caroline.

"Hey, can I come over right now? Couldn't you go to a later mass? This is important."

Ben hung up and said in an upbeat tone that thinly veiled his pain, "You better hit the shower, son, so you'll be ready to see Caroline. With God as my witness, buddy, I won't let you down this time."

They embraced briefly again and Ben left. I was hurting too much for Ben and myself to say anything sensitive, so I just echoed Ben.

"You heard him, son, hit the shower. You've got a big date."

To hide my insincerity, I turned immediately back to the laptop and started writing again. I could tell that Logan hadn't moved, that he was staring at my back, but then without a word, he went to take a shower. I ordered my tears to stay inside and kept writing.

About 45 minutes later, Logan came out dressed in khakis and a polo shirt, hair still damp from the shower and smelling of something sexy. It hurt so bad I could hardly stand it, but I just gave him a throwaway smile and went back to writing. He turned on the TV to see the latest developments in the attack, and I had nearly two more hours to write and had almost finished my story before Ben came back. Logan and I both saw in his face that things hadn't gone well.

"How bad was it?" Logan asked.

"Bad. Like I predicted, she's furious with me for keeping the truth from her and letting her suffer unnecessarily. I expected and deserved that, but I didn't expect that she'd be furious with you, too, Logan. When I first told her you were alive, she was shocked, of course, and cried with happiness, but after she heard the whole story, she said we both betrayed her. She said you should have trusted her with your secret, instead of me. She said what kind of marriage would it have been if you didn't even trust her more than anybody else."

"What did you say to that?" Logan asked.

"I went on and on about how you were doing it all for her and your mother, to protect them and because you loved them more than anything in the world. I said everything I could to persuade her, Logan, I swear I did. But she said she needed you to trust her more than to protect her."

"So she doesn't want to see me?"

"Not yet. I know Caroline will never forgive me, but I think she *will* forgive you, Logan, when she's had time to think about it. When she reads Britt's story tomorrow it may put things into perspective."

"Speaking of that, I've got to go into the paper for a while to talk to my editors. I'll be back in an hour or so, and we can talk about how to tell Maggie. Did you caution Caroline not to tell anybody about Logan being alive until we had a chance to tell Maggie?"

"Yeah, I made her promise."

"I can't wait to see my mom," Logan said.

CHAPTER FORTY-NINE

Of course the newsroom was crazy that Sunday. When a really big story breaks, almost everyone is doing something on it. Those who aren't, feel really left out, but you can't fill every inch of the newspaper with variations of one story.

Naturally my editors were thrilled about my part in all this and scheduled my first-person story for top of page one. My story was 3,000 words long, but they weren't complaining. They wanted to get a picture taken of Logan, but I told them that wasn't possible. Instead I gave them the picture I had of Caroline and Logan and insisted they crop Caroline out.

After I left work, I went home and found Logan alone, sitting on the sofa, not reading, not doing a puzzle, not even watching TV. Just thinking, I guess. I sat down beside him and patted his hand.

"Rough day," I said. "I honestly believe Caroline will come around, Logan. She'll probably be ready to see you by tomorrow. Try to think how great your reunion will be with your mother."

"I hope *she's* not mad at me, too."

"I would bet the family farm on this — your mother is going to be the happiest person on the planet tonight. Since we're not parents, I'm not sure you and I can fully understand this, but Maggie has suffered the worst thing a mother could ever endure, and now we'll get to snatch away all that pain and replace it with the greatest gift a mother could receive."

Logan smiled. "Then let's get to it, if you're ready."

"You'd better go pack up your things, because you'll be sleeping in your own bed tonight."

"I already packed."

Why did it hurt me that he had already packed and was anxious to go? Did I expect a man who'd been in prison to be reluctant to leave?

"So, shall I call your mom now?" He nodded yes.

"Maggie, hey, this is Britt. Are you shaken up like everybody else by what happened last night? Listen, could I come over this afternoon. That would be great. See you then."

When I hung up, I told Logan that his mom was cooking dinner for him, even though she thought she was cooking for me. We decided that I would drop him at Ben's, which is also in Harbor Town, and then Ben would bring him by after I had had about 30 minutes to talk to Maggie.

When I walked into Logan's house, I was hit by delicious smells from Maggie's kitchen. I guessed that even when she moved out and Logan began living alone again, that the kitchen would always be hers.

We talked about the terrorist attack while she finished cooking supper. Then I asked her to turn off the stove and sit down for a minute.

"You know, Maggie, I really didn't want to get involved in all this about Logan when you first called me. It's not that I didn't care, it's just that I'm a reporter, not a detective, and I didn't think I could help you. But it touched me deeply when you talked about the pain of losing a child, especially your only child, and if he was murdered I wanted at least to bring somebody to justice, but..."

"But he wasn't murdered," she said resigned.

"No, he wasn't, Maggie." Just then my cell phone rang. It was Logan saying he was outside waiting.

I went to her and engulfed her in a huge hug, and then pulled back so I could see her face.

"Maggie, this is the happiest moment of my life."

She looked puzzled.

"It's a very long story that you can hear later," I said as I walked toward the front door. "It's the happiest moment of my life, because I can give you your son back."

She looked at me like I was making a cruel joke, but then I opened the door, so that she saw Logan standing there smiling, tears rolling down his face. She let out a little scream of joy, and they ran toward each other and hugged so tight I thought they'd both stop breathing. I have never heard laughter and sobs come together that way. For the first time in my life I understood pure, unmitigated joy. A Bible verse I'd learned as a kid in Sunday School came suddenly to mind: "This son of mine was dead and is alive again, was lost and now is found."

I walked out quietly, leaving Maggie and Logan to their private joy. They didn't notice me leave.

CHAPTER FIFTY

I learned about the stages of grief when I attended a 10-week divorce recovery workshop after Drew and I ended our short marriage.

It's funny, but Logan and I lived together longer than Drew and I were married, and in some ways I suffered more from the end of the so-called relationship with Logan.

I guess it was because the time Drew and I shared in this house was utterly miserable, since we were both painfully aware that we had screwed up by getting married and were constantly trying to figure out individually how we could undo the mess.

In contrast, living with Logan was like summer camp with sexual tension. Even a terrorist attack, as horrible as it was, couldn't ruin the memory of those two months we shared.

One of the psychologists who spoke at the divorce workshop said divorce grief is very similar to grief that follows a death, and the end of my time with Logan was a lot like a death in that we were so happy and then suddenly he was gone. So when Logan left to return to his old life, I started through the stages of grief, a process which usually takes months or years, but in my case lasted about 8 hours.

Denial didn't last long, because it was clear he was gone for good. Since he was a virtual prisoner in my house, I never spent a moment there without him during those two months. Therefore when he left, I couldn't kid myself that he had just gone out for doughnuts and would be right back.

Stage 3, which is bargaining, was short, too. I really wasn't in any position to even kid myself that I could make a deal to get him back.

Stages 2 and 4, anger and depression, were several hours each. Depression is just another word for missing Logan terribly and not much liking my life without him. And anger was only anger at myself, not at Logan or fate or God. After all, I was never misled — I knew from the beginning the arrangement was only temporary.

Then by about 2 a.m., I had arrived at the final stage of grief — acceptance. That was the easiest really, because Logan had never really been mine — he was always Caroline's. I was just borrowing him for a couple of months.

During the depression stage, Ben came by unexpectedly. I think he was in the depression stage, too, from the looks of him. He looked drained emotionally and was carrying a plastic grocery sack.

He was ostensibly there to find out how things had gone with Logan and Maggie's reunion, but I think he was just lonely and depressed. I told him all I knew about Logan and Maggie, which wasn't much since I had slipped out quickly. Ben said he expected them to be up until all hours catching up, and I said Maggie would probably sit up and watch Logan sleep, just to convince herself it was real.

"The whole time Logan was gone," Ben said, "my greatest fear was that Maggie would die suddenly, never having known that Logan was okay."

"Have you talked to Caroline again since this morning?"

"Yeah, she called me about an hour ago. She wants to see Logan tomorrow night, so I called him and set it up."

"Was he happy that Caroline wanted to see him?"

"Sure. Who wouldn't be?" Ben said and then in an unexpected burst of sensitivity added, "Sorry, Britt."

We had been talking standing up in the living room, because I thought this would be a hit-and-run visit. But this last bit of news sent me to the sofa. Ben dropped onto the sofa beside me. He opened the plastic grocery bag.

"I brought potato chips and M & M's," he said in a flat voice.

"Good." We weren't looking at each other. We stared instead at the blackened TV screen. Ben picked up the remote control and turned the set on.

"Sports Center okay?" he said, popping open the potato chip bag.

"Sure," I said, opening the M & M's.

We watched TV in silence for the next two hours. Ben and I just didn't have the kind of relationship that would allow us to talk out our sadness and loss, but having someone to share junk food and TV with was enough for the moment.

Ben left about midnight, presumably still in the depression stage of grief. By bedtime I was unhappily settled in the final stage — acceptance. I ate the last few M & M's and went to bed.

CHAPTER FIFTY-ONE

Poor Logan and Maggie. The minute my story came out, the local and national TV news people were all over them. I expected it and warned them, but I'm not sure they fully understood what was going to happen.

I didn't talk to them that day, but I saw on TV that they had Ben read a statement from the family:

Along with the rest of the nation, we mourn the loss of life and injury caused by this terrorist attack. In addition, the past year has been a stressful one for Logan Magee, his family and friends. They are not ready yet to deal with the media and ask that you respect their privacy.

But, of course, that didn't stop the TV satellite trucks, both local and national, from camping outside Logan's house. When they got tired of waiting for him to come outside and talk to them, some of them would pursue me as I came and went from work and home. I had one line that I used over and over with a pleasant manner: "This is Logan Magee's story, and I will leave it up to him to decide when and if he will discuss it."

I totally ignored the barrage of questions that would follow. But I didn't hide or try to avoid the TV people. I just went about my business and used that line over and over until they gave up on me.

On Wednesday morning, I got a call from Maggie inviting me to dinner that night, which I gladly accepted. I felt like I hadn't seen or talked to Logan in weeks. I never had minded living alone, in fact I preferred it, until Logan climbed into my window and took up residence. Then I had started enjoying coming home to someone special, someone I could tell about my day, discuss the news or books with, play board games with, watch TV with, eat with, say goodnight and good morning to, laugh with and solve problems with. Now that Logan's big problem had been solved, it was just me and the house and an occasional TV reporter banging on the door.

•••••••••••••

I pushed through the reporters in front of Logan's house, using my same line. Logan met me at the door and pulled me inside before even saying hello or giving me a hug. He had become keenly aware that his every movement or facial expression would be videotaped or photographed with who knows what interpretation.

When we were safely inside, curtains all closed tightly, Logan smiled that wonderful smile and hugged me warmly, but in a sisterly way. What did I expect? Maggie came in from the kitchen, wiping her hands on her apron and smiling.

"You made it through the media circus," she said, hugging me like a daughter. "It's so good to see you, sweetie pie. Dinner's ready."

We sat down to a scrumptious meal of chicken and dumplings, fresh turnip greens, fruit salad and corn bread.

"I know you're glad to be home," I said to Logan, after the first bite. "You sure didn't eat like this at my house."

"Well, staying at your house had lots of other advantages," he said and touched my hand briefly.

"So how are you two coping with the media onslaught? Are you ever going to give in and let somebody besides me interview you?"

Before he could answer, Maggie said, "I told him I thought it would be disloyal to you to let any other reporter interview him."

"Oh, no, Maggie, don't worry about me. I got to break the story. Now it's everybody's story. If y'all don't talk to the media, it should be for your own reasons. Don't give me a second thought in that decision. I mean it."

"I'm not tempted to talk to most reporters," Logan said, "but Rachel Maddow called today."

"Really? Rachel herself called, not a producer?"

"Yeah, that surprised me, too. I'm tempted to talk to her. I've always liked her low-key kind of interviews. What do you think, Britt?"

"I think I'd go for it. I mean somebody is probably going to eventually talk you into an interview, it might as well be Rachel Maddow. I like her style, too."

"I told her I'd think about it and call her producer tomorrow with my decision. I'll probably say yes. Have you been inundated with TV people, too?"

I told him the details of my media adventures of the last two days and made him and Maggie laugh.

"But you know the one person who could get me to say yes is Lester Holt from NBC," I said. "I hung on his every word during the Iraq coverage. Besides, I have a huge crush on him."

Maggie and Logan both laughed.

●●●●●●●●●●

After dinner, Maggie insisted on doing the dishes alone and sent us out onto the upstairs porch overlooking the river. As we passed through his bedroom, I remembered the last time I was in this room, when I thought Logan was dead.

On the porch, we were aware that we were being watched from across the street by the TV cameras, but we ignored them.

"I've missed this view," Logan said. "That thing they call a river in San Antonio is quaint, but can't compare to the Mighty Mississippi."

"The first time I came out here to talk to your mother, after I left, I sat on a bench over there and looked at the river and the bridges, and I wondered how your mother could stand to look at that river, knowing it had swallowed you up."

"Mom's more pragmatic than that. She wouldn't blame the river for what I or some murderer did. You've got a tough exterior, Britt, and underneath you *are* a strong woman, which I admire, but you're a lot more sentimental than you let on. I like all of that about you — your strength and your softness. If you hadn't been so tender-hearted toward my mother, you would have never gotten involved in all this. And I would have never known you."

"But you wouldn't have known what you were missing, so it wouldn't have mattered."

"Do you really believe that — that if we don't know what we've missed out on, our lives don't contain a void?"

"I never really thought about it. But I guess that indefinable longing that some people feel could be for things they don't even know they're missing out on."

"I think so," Logan said.

"So have you seen Caroline yet? Ben told me that she had

changed her mind."

"When did you talk to Ben?"

"He came by Sunday night, and we shared a bag of potato chips and a bag of M n' M's."

"I thought ya'll didn't like each other?"

"We don't, but he was just lonely and depressed, I think, and his best friend wasn't available at the moment, so I think I was the consolation prize."

"Once I got over the mads, I felt bad about dating Caroline when Ben had a thing for her, but what am I supposed to do now? I mean Caroline and I were engaged, I guess we still are."

"Does she consider herself still engaged to you?"

"I didn't ask the question directly, but I think she does."

"How did it go when you saw each other?"

"Tense, really tense. She doesn't know whether to love me or hate me. The jury's still out. I wonder how much her feelings for Ben are a factor?"

"Ask her."

"I don't have the nerve yet to broach that subject. Our first time together was mostly devoted to her telling me how much I had hurt her and me apologizing and trying to explain."

"How did you leave it?"

"That we'd keep talking and try to work it out."

"That sounds positive. It's just a matter of time, I'm sure, before y'all set a new wedding date. Well, I've got to get going. Let me know which night I should watch the Rachel Maddow Show."

CHAPTER FIFTY-TWO

Jack asked if he could take me to dinner on Saturday night. It was the one-week anniversary of "Attack on the American Heartland," as the national media had begun calling it, and we both needed to talk. It was a mild night for late August, so we ate on the patio of the Mexican restaurant.

"Just how scared were you last Saturday?" I asked Jack.

"I couldn't let myself think about that. I had to stay focused. When you know you may have to try to subdue a suicide bomber and you know you might not succeed, it could make you crazy if you think about it, so you don't. As we were entering the stadium, an FBI agent and I both spotted one of the terrorists about the same time. Not only was he Indonesian, but he was wearing a windbreaker, which nobody in his right mind would do in Memphis in August."

"Was the windbreaker bulging with the explosives?"

"Not really. When the bomb squad removed the explosives, they were amazed at how lightweight and cutting-edge this stuff was. I'll tell you, these guys were well financed and had the latest technology."

"Go ahead, what happened next?"

"The agent and I both began working our way through the

crowd behind him, trying not to rush him, but also determined not to lose him in the crowd. The agent got to him first, and as he grabbed him from behind and immobilized the suspect's arms, I had to get to him quick and help him secure the guy. It wasn't until hours later that it really hit me how close we came to being blown to bits, and that shook me up pretty good."

"I guess so. I died a thousand deaths until I found out the dead cop wasn't you."

"So I haven't completely lost out?"

"What in the world are you talking about?"

"Logan. Do I have any chance against Logan?"

"Don't be ridiculous, Jack, there's no competition. Logan and Caroline are back together. As you pointed out a few weeks ago, why wouldn't he want to get back with somebody as beautiful as Caroline."

"So their wedding is back on?"

"Not exactly. There are some trust issues there on her part, but they're working it out."

"I'm not really talking about physical competition between Logan and me — I'm talking about your feelings. I know something special developed between you and Logan during the last two months."

"It was foxhole camaraderie," I said dismissively.

"That's BS and you know it, but what I'm wondering is if you've completely written me off."

"Jack, don't ask me how I feel about you and certainly don't ask me how I feel about Logan, because I'm not exactly sure about either one of you. And don't give me that wounded puppy look — I'm just trying to be straight with you. But one thing I've learned since you and I went out the first time — either you're not a typical cop or cops *are* my type after all."

"I hope all cops aren't your type."

"It's probably that you're special. But don't rush me, Jack. Give me time to figure things out."

"It's the least I can do. Anyhow, with the hours I've been working lately, I don't have time to overwhelm you with my spectacular courtship methods anyhow."

"Well, you could impress me right now by getting the waitress's attention and getting us some more chips and queso dip."

CHAPTER FIFTY-THREE

About a week later, I hadn't been home from work long and was trying to decide whether to have Cream of Wheat for supper or a peanut butter and jelly sandwich. Go with the Cream of Wheat, I decided — it sounds silly, but there were too many memories connected to PB & J these days.

I hadn't heard a car pulling up out front, but the doorbell rang. When I opened the door, Logan was standing there holding a square box and smiling.

"I bought this great new board game at the bookstore, and I thought we could order a pizza," he said as he walked in.

"Kind of presumptuous, isn't it? How did you know I didn't have a date or dinner guests?" I said, but he could tell from my tone of voice that I was only slightly offended. He stepped back outside the doorway.

"Let me start over," he said. "Hey, Britt, sorry for dropping in like this without calling, but I was in the neighborhood and had just bought this great new board game and I was hoping we could play it and order a pizza, but you've probably already got plans for tonight."

"Come in, smart ass," I said, pulling him into the living room.

"I was planning to eat Cream of Wheat for dinner, but I'll settle for pizza as long as it hasn't got any vegetables on it."

"I know your motto, 'If it isn't greasy, it doesn't belong on a pizza.' Did you think I would forget that quickly?"

"Well, you've been busy — what with flying off to be on the Rachel Maddow Show and doing interviews with the local TV people. Sit down, Your Highness. I thought maybe you had forgotten about us little people you stepped over on your way to international fame."

"No, I'm making a point to go around to all those little people I stepped on going up the ladder and share a pizza and a board game with each of them, so they'll know I haven't forgotten their contributions, no matter how insignificant."

I threw a sofa pillow at him, and we both laughed.

"Seriously, you were great on Maddow. I thought you did a really good job of explaining it all."

"In other words, I covered up my impulsiveness and stupidity well?"

"Very well. So what Rachel as nice as she seems?"

"She was great, but insisted on calling me Mr. Magee, instead of Logan."

He took out his phone and ordered a pepperoni pizza, thin crust with extra cheese and then came back to the sofa.

"What made you decide to go ahead and let the local TV people interview you?"

"Because I figured they would never go away if I didn't and that if I talked to all of them, they'd move on to somebody else. And it worked. I can actually leave my house without cameras now."

"So life has returned to normal for you?"

"Sort of. Mom wanted to move out right away and go back to her house, which she's been renting out the past year, but I talked her into staying a couple more weeks. I could use some home cooking, I told her, and that's true, but also I think she needs a while longer to soak up the sights and sounds of her returned-from-the-dead son."

"I'm sure you're right. That was very considerate of you to figure that out. Maybe you're not as insensitive as Ben portrayed you."

"Have you and Ben been sharing more M & M's?"

"No, I think it was just a temporary bonding between two shell-shocked people. I haven't heard from him since that night. How about you and Ben — is the friendship on the mend?"

"It is on my part, but he may be too love sick to think about our friendship right now."

"Poor Ben," I said and meant it.

"So speaking of love sick, have you seen Jack Trent lately?"

"I don't know if you think Jack is love sick or me, but yes, I have seen Jack lately. We ate Mex together Saturday night. It was harrowing hearing his description of sneaking up on the terrorist and subduing him before he could blow everybody around him up."

"I admire Jack. He's a good guy."

"Yes, he is. So what else have you done to readjust to the land of the living now that the TV people aren't hounding you?"

"Let's see. I went to the bookstore, since I don't have your literary collection at my disposal any more. I've gotten back to playing tennis. I'm pretty rusty, but I'm gradually getting my game back. Let's see what else I've been doing besides quitting my job and signing up for classes at the University of Memphis?"

"What? Did you really quit your job? And you're already in grad school?"

"Yes, I did quit my job without a second thought, but I have to apply for the grad program before I can be accepted and officially start working on my PhD. But you can take a couple of grad classes while all that's pending. I'm only a week late starting classes, but it shouldn't be a problem."

"Logan, that's wonderful. I'm so proud of you," I said, giving him a quick sisterly hug. "But how will you support yourself without a job?"

"I've socked away quite a bit during the last few years, and I've invested well, so I can go to school without worrying about money. In fact, I can even afford to keep my house, if I want to. Haven't decided about that yet. I might get a little student apartment."

"But it wouldn't have a view of the river, would it?"

"That *is* a drawback to a little student apartment. I won't rush into that."

"So what does Caroline think of your decision?"

"She says I should do whatever makes me happy, but she thinks it was a bit impulsive of me to quit my job."

"She's probably right. So tell me about this new game you bought."

"Well, it's a combination of knowledge questions about psychology and intuitive questions."

"What do you mean by intuitive?"

"Well, they give you a situation and you try to guess how the other players would react to that situation. Let me give you an example. Let's say the card says something like this, 'Caroline tells Logan that she may be in love with Ben and she wants to put our wedding off indefinitely,' and you have to guess how the other player — in this case that would be me — would respond."

He waited for me to give my answer.

"Well, I would guess that you would be devastated and beg her to reconsider marrying you."

"I'm sorry, but you don't get the point and your turn is over. The correct answer is that Logan has never been so relieved in his entire life and will gladly be best man at Ben and Caroline's wedding. Now that I've given you an example, are you ready to play the game?"

ABOUT THE AUTHOR

Candy Justice is a former newspaper reporter and columnist who now is an award-winning journalism professor at the University of Memphis.

Made in the USA
Coppell, TX
01 November 2019